WILD EXCITEMENT

"I don't care about you," she said hoarsely. "Not anymore. And you don't care about me. It's over," she whispered, mesmerized by his face . . . by his wide, provocative mouth and the rugged angle of his jaw . . . the strands of blond hair that had fallen forward, begging her fingers to stroke them back from his cheek.

"It's over," he agreed, his voice husky.

Why couldn't he disagree with her, rile her into an argument—anything that would break this dangerous spell?

She swallowed, repeated, "It's over. And we can't—"

"No, we can't," he agreed again, and yet his face was closer, his lips closer, so close that she could almost . . .

With a groan, Marco bent his head and his mouth lowered over hers.

His lips were pure heat, pressing, alive, daring, delving. She was engulfed by a wave of desire that swept her back through time so that she could do nothing but open her lips, nothing but moan deep in her throat and press herself against him, excited by how much he wanted her . . .

Fabio

W·I·L·D

in collaboration with
Wendy Corsi Staub

P

Pinnacle Books
Kensington Publishing Corp.
http://www.pinnaclebooks.com

This book would not be possible without the tremendous talents and energy of Wendy Corsi Staub. Thank you for your dedication and efforts.

Special thanks to my Kensington family: Walter and Steve Zacharius, Paul Dinas, Lynn Brown, Eileen Bertelli, and Ernie Petrillo for helping to make this venture work so smoothly and efficiently.

As usual, thanks to my friend and manager, Eric Ashenberg, for all of your hard work on my behalf. I am eternally grateful for having a friend like you.

Thanks to my brother, Walter, and sister, Christina, for always being there for me.

Once again, my heartfelt thanks to Bonnie Kuhlman, President of the Fabio International Fan Club, P.O. Box 827, Dubois, WY 82513, for her nonstop efforts and dedication in helping me maintain communication and interaction with my fans on a continual basis.

Thanks to my business associates, Stanley Ralph Ross and Milton Miller, for their assistance in allowing me to challenge myself by undertaking new creative endeavors in the entertainment industry.

Most importantly, thanks to all my fans for their continued loyalty, support, and friendship. You are the basis for my success, and I am forever in your debt.

*Between the light and the dark
lies a path
that is as wide as an ocean
and as narrow as a hair.*

*This book is dedicated to all
those who choose
caring over conceit,
faith over fear,
and love over all else.*

Prologue

Run!

The word screeched through A.J. Sutton's muddled mind as she fought to shut out the inconceivable image before her eyes.

The man she loved, hiding in the shadows, gun poised against his cheek. The moment he spotted her, his jaw fell, his blue eyes widened, and he made a move to grab her.

Run!

Her feet began to move, carrying her away from him.

She heard his footsteps pounding after her on the terra cotta tile floor, heard him calling her name, heard him telling her to stop.

No, she realized as she picked up speed, approaching the massive double doors of the mansion's main entrance. He wasn't telling her to stop.

Nor was he pleading with her.

He was *commanding* her.

Bitter fury and resentment rose in her throat to mingle with shock and fear.

No one ever told A.J. Sutton what to do.

How dare he try?

Did he think she was a fool?

That she would blindly obey anyone, least of all a man who was not the person she had believed him to be?

Without hesitation, she shoved the doors open and burst out into the muggy tropical night.

In the distance, she could hear the shouts of armed guards along the waterfront, and splashing, and barking dogs. And, just behind her, footsteps.

She kept moving toward the distant gate, wildly eyeing the dense undergrowth along the perimeter of the grounds. It beckoned, seeming to offer a haven.

But that would be only temporary, she knew.

Soon he would be upon her, accompanied by the cold-blooded guards who would shoot her on sight . . .

If he didn't pull his own trigger first.

But that's impossible!

He wouldn't shoot me . . .

He loves me . . .

No . . .

No.

She *was* a fool.

He didn't love her.

He didn't even exist.

Her dream man was a figment of her imagination, conjured from her desperate desire to love—to *be* loved.

Reality was the man who chased her through the steamy Florida night.

The man who—only moments ago, before she had stumbled upon him in the shadows—had been her whole world.

How could they have been thrust into such an unthinkable nightmare?

How could her beloved partner have been instantaneously transformed into her darkest enemy?

It didn't make sense.

Nothing was clear.

Nothing but that she had to keep running . . .

Because A.J. sensed, deep in her heart, where her hopes for the future had just withered and died, that her very life depended on escaping.

Chapter One

"So tell me about yourself."

The question was such a cliché that at another time, under other circumstances, Lia Haskin might have laughed at it.

But now, she fought the urge to cringe and forced herself to keep her gaze carefully focused out the car window at the bumper-to-bumper traffic on the Mass Pike.

She'd known this was coming from the moment Tony Lanzone had picked her up at her apartment.

In the half hour it had taken his Honda to creep the ten or so miles from her house, she had done an excellent job of postponing the inevitable; she'd asked him a thousand questions about himself and his work and the condo he'd just bought in the Back Bay.

When he'd mentioned something about rowing in the upcoming Head of the Charles regatta, she'd exhausted the topic, asking him all about the legendary Boston event, then about his own athletic background.

Nothing he had said had sunk in; her mind was whirling as she tried to think of a way to flee.

What was she doing out on a date? She had no business pretending she was a normal twenty-five-year-old woman with a normal social life dating normal men like the affable accountant sitting in the driver's seat.

"Lia?" Tony nudged.

"Yes?" She looked up at him, but refused to make eye contact.

"I, uh, asked you to tell me about yourself. I mean, I don't know anything other than the fact that you live next door to my sister, you work for a credit card collection bureau, and you like burned hot dogs."

She had to smile fleetingly at that.

"Actually," she said, hoping to divert his attention from the original question, "I really don't like burned hot dogs. I was just being polite."

"Well, that was noble of you," he said with a grin. "I knew there had to be some reason."

She smiled back, wishing she could relax.

"Hey, when you smile like that, do you know who you look like?"

Her heart slammed into her rib cage, and her voice seemed to stick in her throat.

"Who?" she finally managed to ask faintly, trying not to show that she was holding her breath as she waited for his reply.

"Demi Moore," he told her. "You look a lot like her. Has anyone ever told you that before?"

The breath escaped her in a sigh of relief.

"Um, yes," she said. "A few people have said that."

It was true; she had been told that she resembled the movie star. Especially in the past year, with her hair dyed brown like Demi's.

But no one had ever told her she looked like that other person . . .

So far, not a soul had recognized her; no one had ever made a connection between the bespectacled brunette from Boston and the deeply tanned blond beach bunny who had been entangled in the Miami murder that had gotten so much publicity last year.

But that didn't mean that someday, maybe soon, she wouldn't be caught off guard by someone saying, "Hey, aren't you . . . ?"

She could feel her hands sweating, clasped tightly on her lap beneath her brown leather handbag, and her jaw was clenched so hard it hurt.

If only she'd never agreed to have dinner at Jaime and Billy MacGregor's last Saturday. She should have suspected it was a setup. Ever since she'd moved in next door and discovered Lia was single, Jaime had wanted to fix Lia up with her brother, and Lia had come up with every excuse under the sun except the real reason she couldn't go out with Tony—with anyone, for that matter.

Though she'd known Jaime was the persistent type, she had never considered that she'd find herself thrown together with Tony at what was supposed to be a casual backyard barbecue with the MacGregors. In fact, she normally wouldn't even have agreed to dine at the neighbors—she liked Jaime, but found her far too nosy for comfort.

Still, the first weekend in October had been glorious, with temperatures in the upper seventies and sparkling sunshine that set the New England foliage aglow, and Lia, caught up in the exhilarating weather, had spontaneously said yes to Jaime's invitation.

Only when it was too late did she discover that she wasn't the only guest.

"Why didn't you tell me your brother would be here?" she'd whispered fiercely to Jaime in the kitchen as the two men worked on starting the grill on the outside patio.

"Because I knew you wouldn't come. Don't you get it, Lia? My mission in life is to see that everyone is paired off as happily as Billy and I are," Jaime said with a blissful newlywed sigh and a swing of her high blond ponytail.

"But I don't *want* to be paired off," Lia protested, hoping Jaime didn't sense that she wasn't just reluctant, she was terrified. "I'm perfectly happy just the way I—"

"Oh, come on. You wouldn't want to be married? Maybe have a couple of kids?"

Lia shoved away the reminder of a dream that belonged to another lifetime, another person. "No, I wouldn't," she'd told Jaime firmly, but she was staring absently out the window as she spoke, seeing not the small suburban backyard with its dandelion-infested lawn and a few scraggly elm trees; but white sand and sweeping palm fronds and the aqua waters of the Atlantic Ocean in South Florida.

"I can tell by the look on your face that you're lying," Jaime decided, drawing Lia back from memories that would be better off buried.

"Of course I'm not ly—"

"It won't hurt you to just talk to Tony. He's a great guy . . . after all, he's *my* brother. And he'll be hurt if you leave, so don't get any ideas about running scared."

So Lia had stayed, and though she'd been filled with trepidation, she'd done her best to make it appear as though she had relaxed and was having a good time.

She'd forced herself to laugh at Billy's jokes and she'd helped Jaime husk the corn and she'd eaten two hot dogs at the good-natured urging of Tony, who was manning the grill and had charred them beyond recognition.

And when Tony had asked her—at the end of the evening, just before she made her escape through the hedge—what she was doing the following Friday night, Jaime had answered for her before she could drum up a lie.

"She's free," she'd told her brother blithely, a mischievous twinkle in her round blue eyes.

"I am not," Lia had protested, trying not to sound panicky.

"Really? You have plans? What are you doing?" Jaime demanded. Her tone was teasing; the expression on her pretty face wasn't.

Lia was so rattled she just couldn't think quickly enough to come up with an excuse. When she finally started to stammer something—anything—Jaime cut her off.

"Lia, come on. We've lived next door to you for almost six months, and you're home every single Friday night. Go out for a change. With Tony."

Flabbergasted, Lia had looked from Jaime to her brother, who looked amused. Obviously, he, like Billy, was used to his sister's manipulative tactics and didn't let it throw him.

All he'd said to Lia was, "You may be free, but do you *want* to go out with me?"

What could she say to that? *No, Tony, I don't want to go out with you, and stay out of my life because I never want to see you, or any other single, eligible man, ever again.*

And so here she was, sitting in the ubiquitous snarl of Mass Pike traffic with a man who had nice brown eyes and a handsome, clean-cut appearance; a man who had just asked her again, politely, to tell him about her past.

Her past.

Something she didn't let herself think about, let alone discuss.

"There's not much to tell," she said at last with a shrug.

"Well, where are you from? You have a trace of a southern accent," he commented.

Her heart tripped. "Do I? Well, I spent some time living in Virginia, so . . ."

"Virginia?" He perked up at that. "Where in Virginia? I went to George Mason University, and lived in Fairfax for four years, so . . ."

"Oh," she said quickly. "It wasn't very long . . . that I lived there, I mean. Just a few months, really."

He raised an eyebrow, and she realized he might be thinking that it would be hard to pick up a permanent drawl in that brief amount of time.

But he didn't comment, just repeated, "Where in Virginia were you?"

"In, um, Richmond," she improvised, then added hastily, "Look out!"

He jumped and his head snapped to look out the windshield. "What?"

"Sorry, I just thought that truck was going to hit you."

"What truck?"

"That one—he's trying to change lanes," she said, pointing to the vehicle next to them.

The vehicle that was sitting still, just as they were.

Tony Lanzone gave her an odd look.

"I'm sorry," she said.

He was silent for a moment.

Then he asked casually, "Uh, Lia, have you ever been in a car accident?"

"A car accident? Why?"

"I don't know—I thought maybe that would be why you're so nervous."

"Me? Nervous? I'm not nervous."

"You really seem like you are."

"That's just because . . . I don't know, I guess maybe it's the traffic."

"But we're sitting still. It's not like it's dangerous, with cars whizzing along, cutting us off, that kind of thing."

She wanted to scream, *Just drop it! I'm not nervous!*

Instead she managed another shrug and told him, "I guess I'm claustrophobic."

"About being in the car?"

She nodded. "And stuck in all this traffic. I mean, we couldn't escape if we needed to."

"Escape?"

It had just popped out. She wished she could take it back, but it was too late.

"Escape from what?" he was asking.

"I don't know . . . nothing. I'm not really *that* claustrophobic. Forget it."

That only made Tony appear more perplexed, and Lia knew he wouldn't be asking her out again. He thought she was crazy.

Thank God.

Her life was difficult enough without worrying about getting involved with someone. It was all she could do to drag herself out of bed every morning and remember who she was supposed to be . . .

Lia Haskin.

Yes, that was who she was now.

If only she could simply forget who she had once been, and the life she had left behind . . .

"Oh, geez, you call that a swing?" Marco moaned and shook his head at the TV. "My freakin' grandmother could've hit that lousy pitch."

A.J. smiled. "Your grandmother plays baseball?"

"Yeah, she's a right fielder for the Angels."

"The California Angels?"

He looked at her, startled. "A.J., I'm kidding."

"Marco, I know," she said, punching his arm lightly.

He laughed, looking relieved. "For a minute there, I was worried."

"You thought I was just another blond bimbo hanging on your every word, huh?"

"Bimbo? You? Never."

"Oh, come on. You're a bimbo magnet," she teased him. "I'll bet I'm the first brainy woman you've ever dated."

"Brainy?" he echoed dubiously.

She shrugged. "Is 'intelligent' a better word?"

"Much. When I hear 'brainy,' I think of one of those boring New England prep school types, with the horn-rimmed glasses, all buttoned up to there, you know? Not some wild Latin-blooded seductress."

"Seductress? Me?" She lifted her hand and was about to stroke his chest when he jerked forward, toward the television set, and shouted, "That's not a strike, you bastard! What game are you umping?"

Sighing, A.J. reached for the bowl of popcorn on the coffee table instead.

It was empty, except for a few unpopped kernels and grains of salt.

"Sorry," Marco said nonchalantly, his eyes focused on the game. "I polished it off while you were on the phone earlier."

"You didn't even save me any of those half-popped crunchy pieces!" she said in mock dismay, plunking the bowl back on the table. "You know I love those."

He shrugged. "I was starving."

She nodded. He always had a ravenous appetite . . .

For food.

For her.

She slid closer to him, so that the length of bare,

tanned skin exposed by her tank top and shorts was pressed against his hot, muscular flesh. He wore only a pair of swim trunks, still damp from the swim they'd taken hours earlier, in the condo pool. She could smell the faint scent of chlorine in his long blond hair, and in her own.

"Come on, Rivera, *swing!*" he called to the poised Yankee batter on the televised baseball game. "All you need is one run to tie it up."

"Tie me up? Sure, we can do that if you want to," she purred, reaching up to stroke his cheek with a seductive fingertip. "Or I can tie *you* up . . ."

He blinked, then looked down at her, a sly smile sliding over his lips. "You don't want me to watch the rest of this game, do you?"

"What gave you that idea?" she asked coyly, moving her fingertip down, over his bulging pecs, toward another bulge below the waistband of his swimsuit.

With a groan, he dragged her into his arms and she could feel his heart pounding beneath his rugged chest.

"Forget the game," he growled.

"But you love the Yankees."

"There are other things I love more."

Things, she thought with a slight pang of disappointment.

Like sex.

He loved sex . . .

And all right, so did she.

But he had never said, or even hinted, that he loved *her.*

Oh, well, she thought, closing her eyes and throwing her head back as his hot mouth made contact with the tender skin at the base of her throat.

Why rush things?

In time, he would fall for her as soundly as she'd fallen for him.

He would tell her he loved her, ask her to marry him . . .

She sighed blissfully and let his mouth and fingers carry her to a place where all her dreams and desires were fulfilled.

"He's *out!*" Tony shouted, leaping out of his seat, along with every other spectator in Fenway Park.

Everyone except Lia.

"What? What the hell! Did you see that?" Tony bellowed, turning to her, throwing his hands up in disgust. "The Yankee bastard was out. How could they call that safe?"

She made a feeble attempt to look outraged.

"Is that ump blind? Did *you* think he was safe?" Tony asked.

"No, I thought he was out," she offered as he plunked back into his seat and picked up his box of Cracker Jack again.

She hadn't seen the play, though she'd been staring blankly at the field, pretending to be engrossed.

"That's what everyone thought," he grumbled. "He was out."

A rotund man in front of them, who had a hot dog in one hand and a tub of popcorn in the other, turned and said, "This is just like what happened back in '95. The boys get this far, and they blow it."

"They're not going to blow it," Tony insisted grimly. "I know they're not."

"How do you know?"

"I just know."

"Yeah? What're you, a professional psychic?"

"Not exactly."

"Sports analyst then?"

"I'm an accountant."

The guy shrugged. "Twenty-five bucks says the Sox lose this game."

"What kind of fan are you?"

The man straightened the Red Sox cap on his head and replied, "A realistic one. No one wants to see the Sox in the Series more than me. But I'm tellin' you, they ain't gonna make it. You up for a bet, or not?"

"I'm up for it," Tony said.

"Okay, fifty bucks."

"Fifty? I thought you said twenty-five."

"So? I changed my mind. Let's up the stakes. You must not be so sure they're going to win if you don't want to risk a fifty."

"They're going to win. Fifty bucks says so."

"Good." The fat man balanced his popcorn in the crook of his arm, against his fleshy chest, freeing a hand to shake Tony's.

Then they turned their attention back to the game.

Lia tried to do the same.

She was, in some remote corner of her mind, aware that it was a perfect night for baseball; warm for October, with a soft, salt-scented breeze blowing off the nearby Atlantic.

She was aware of the enthusiasm around her, of the swarm of people crammed into the charming old ballpark. They ate hot pretzels and Cracker Jack and wore Red Sox gear. And they were all, every one of them, fixated by the action down below, on the brightly lit field.

Lia did her best to fit in, to appear to be one of them, lest she somehow call attention to herself.

"Oh, great. O'Neal's up."

She nodded blankly as Tony grumbled beside her.

How could she concentrate on baseball when she was fearing for her life?

Okay, maybe that was extreme . . .

But maybe it wasn't.

How could she not have asked, earlier, in the car, where Tony was taking her?

How could she have simply assumed they would be going out to dinner, hopefully at some out-of-the-way restaurant?

How could Tony not have mentioned that he was bringing her to the game until he pulled into the parking garage off nearby Kenmore Square?

Only then had she thought to ask, "Where are we going?"

Only then had he proudly produced two tickets from his shirt pocket and announced, "Surprise! We're going to Fenway, to watch the Red Sox kick the Yankees' ass in the playoffs . . ."

To *Fenway?*

The stadium would be swarming with strangers, and . . .

". . . on national television."

National television?

Lia had felt faint, so weak-kneed she hadn't been able to get out of the car for a few moments, even though Tony was standing impatiently with her door open, saying, "C'mon, we're late. The game's about to start."

"Did you say the game's on *national* television?" she'd asked, trying unsuccessfully to keep her trepidation from paralyzing her. She had to move, but she couldn't seem to get herself out of the car.

Tony nodded, looking puzzled, and said, almost impatiently, "Of course it's on national TV. It's the playoffs. Do you know what I had to do to get these tickets for us? I mean—you're a big Sox fan, too, right? My sister said you were."

She had almost protested that she wasn't, that Jaime must have been mistaken, that she'd just as soon skip the game . . .

Then she remembered that she'd used the Red Sox as an excuse more than once over the summer, begging off whenever Jaime had asked her to go shopping or to a movie. Knowing the Sox were on television just about every night of the week, she'd claimed she was a diehard fan, that she couldn't miss a game.

Here was her payback for those lies.

Now as she stared unseeingly at the field below, where a Yankee batter was stepping up to the plate, she felt utterly sick inside.

How many times had she taken painstaking care to avoid crowds in the past year? She had isolated herself from the world just outside her tiny suburban town, never venturing into the city, or riding the T, or even going to a shopping mall.

She'd done her best to steer clear of public places that might draw tourists; to stay away from throngs of people. She always bought her groceries late at night at the twenty-four-hour Stop and Shop; she hadn't been to a doctor or dentist in ages; she didn't have a library card or even a membership at Blockbuster Video.

She was probably being unduly cautious; yet there was always a chance that somewhere, somehow, someone might recognize her.

And now here she was, at a famous Boston landmark, surrounded by tens of thousands of strangers . . . and television cameras.

She was vaguely conscious of the crowd roaring as the Yankee batter swung . . .

Panic was surging through her.

She was a fool to stay here, at a baseball game.

They loved baseball . . .

They would never miss a playoff game . . .

"It looks like a foul!" Tony shouted, leaning forward in his seat and spilling popcorn over his lap. "Here it comes!"

Oh, God, what if they were watching?

What if the cameras somehow captured her, somehow lingered upon her face long enough to flash it across the country?

I have to get out of here.

Seized by the uncontrollable urge to flee, Lia stood, blindly turning toward the aisle, thinking that she'd tell Tony she was going to the ladies' room and just *leave*, just *go*, just—

"Look out!"

Tony's warning, echoed by the handful of spectators surrounding them, came too late.

Lia heard him, turned toward the field . . .

But she never saw the ball before it hit her.

She never saw it slamming into her shoulder and sending her sprawling toward the ground, her fall broken by the seats and strangers' arms that grabbed for her.

She never saw the cameras that zoomed in, projecting a close-up of her dazed expression to millions of viewers nationwide.

There were five men gathered around the projection-screen television in the airy den of the Spanish-Mediterranean–style mansion just off South Miami Avenue, not far from the historic Vizcaya.

Outside, darkness had descended over the choppy waters of Biscayne Bay, bringing with it the ire of a tropical storm that had raged through the Caribbean early this morning. Torrential rain and wind beat against the lush jungle of tropical foliage that served to conceal the thick stone walls topped with barbed wire that surrounded the grounds.

Inside, the men munched on conch fritters and blue

tortilla chips with guacamole, intent on the televised Boston—New York playoff game.

The Art Deco—style floor lamps flickered.

"Maldito sea!" cursed the imposing, black-bearded man on the white leather couch, glancing at the rain-beaten window.

A power outage now would infuriate Victor Caval. He had bet an enormous amount of money on this playoff game, positive that the Yankees would annihilate the Red Sox. His stepfather's godson, Pablo, was a third baseman for New York, called up from the minor league team this past August.

But long before that, Victor had followed baseball. Even as a boy in Colombia, he had passionately embraced the sport, dreaming of one day going to America and becoming a wealthy, powerful baseball star. Everyone said he had talent. He was a decent fielder and batter, good enough to stand out on those skills alone. And he had a tremendous pitching arm.

But it was his feet that made him a star. The sure-footed, slightly built boy could move faster than anyone on his school team; he was a whiz at stealing bases.

Then, at fifteen, came the motorcycle accident that left him with a shattered ankle and shattered dream.

It wasn't long afterward that he discovered baseball wasn't his only ticket to America; to wealth and power.

Victor shifted his weight on the couch and turned his attention back to the game. He frowned intently as the Yankee batter swung, connecting with the ball and sending it sailing toward third base . . .

The cameras followed it up . . .

Up, into the packed stands, where spectators leapt in futile attempts to grab it . . .

Time seemed to stand still as the ball and the cameras closed in on an unsuspecting target, a young woman who stood with her back to the field, oblivious until the last moment . . .

Then she turned, and the lens caught her startled expression in the split second before the ball knocked her from view.

The men in the room erupted in a simultaneous outburst of English and Spanish.

"Es decir ella!"

"That's her!"

Only Victor was silent, leaning forward, his glittering black eyes focused on the screen.

There was no outward sign of the shock that careened through him. Victor Caval was a man who had long ago learned to conceal his emotions.

It was easier that way.

He remained motionless, but his heart pounded wildly as he waited for the inevitable replay.

He wasn't seeing the knot of spectators clustered around the fallen victim; he wasn't hearing the announcers' booming voices as they discussed the play.

No, he was seeing an exquisite face he hadn't glimpsed in a year; hearing a flirtatious drawl he hadn't heard in a year.

She had filled his thoughts, encompassing him in a tide of memories . . .

And hatred.

He was certain, even before the camera replayed the close-up of the woman at Fenway Park, that it was her.

"Parece mentira!" breathed his cousin, Alberto Manzana, seated beside him, as everyone in the room gazed at the paler, rounder, yet unmistakably familiar face on the television screen.

"No, it's not impossible," Victor retorted, turning on Alberto, his eyes blazing. "I've told you all along that I never believed she died that night."

"And you were right, Victor," his cousin said quickly, in heavily accented English. "She's obviously alive."

"*Por el momento,*" Victor responded, rubbing his bearded chin thoughtfully.

Yes, she *was* alive . . .

For the time being.

A five-minute drive from Victor Caval's mansion, on a quiet side street lined with palm trees, family-style cars, and small, pastel Florida bungalows, another man stood, transfixed, watching the television screen in his rented house.

The close-up image that had caused him to gasp and leap from the couch had been replaced by a long shot of the field at Fenway as the batter stepped up to the plate once again.

According to the announcers' voice-over, the spectator didn't appear to have been seriously injured by the foul ball. She had refused medical treatment and had reportedly left the stands. Meanwhile an ecstatic little boy seated in her row had scooped the ball from beneath the seats and waved it triumphantly over his head.

The announcers cheerfully turned their attention back to the game.

Marco Estevez didn't.

He remained frozen, standing midway between the ugly, nubby beige couch and the television, lost in incredulous wonder . . .

Not just that she was *alive*, but that fate had delivered the news to him in a way that made him certain he was *destined* to find her.

He shuddered to think of how close he had come to missing her.

If he had arrived home just a few moments later, he wouldn't have seen her.

After all, he had just barely turned on the television and settled in to watch the game when O'Neal had hit that foul ball into the stands.

If he had lingered at Winn Dixie even a mere minute longer . . .

Or if one more person had been ahead of him in the express line . . .

Or if he'd run into one more red light on the short drive home . . .

Or if he'd stopped to put the groceries away, instead of dumping them on the already cluttered counter in the kitchenette . . .

He would have missed her.

But, he thought with a shuddering sigh of relief, none of those things had happened.

He had arrived home, and he had turned on the game, and he had seen her.

She wore glasses, and her hair was brown, and her face had lost its angular, sun-kissed appearance.

Yet there was no mistaking it. The instant she had turned her head, startled, he had recognized her.

Funny . . .

That pose, that expression . . .

It was almost identical to the way she had looked the last time he had glimpsed her, on that terrible night.

She had been looking back over her shoulder then, too, her features caught in that same wary expression that had instantly turned to shock and fear.

The only difference was that tonight, it was merely a wayward baseball that had startled and frightened her.

That other night, it had been *him*.

She had unexpectedly caught sight of Marco Estevez lurking in the shadows at Victor Caval's bayside mansion, and it had sent her fleeing for her life.

So.

Now, after a year of wondering, he knew.

She was alive.
She was in Boston—
At least she was there tonight.
Marco sprang into action, heading for the phone.
It rang before he could pick it up.
And he knew who was calling.

Chapter Two

Tony didn't attempt to kiss Lia when he deposited her politely at the door of her small rented cape.

She wasn't surprised. That was the last thing she wanted.

"Are you sure you're all right?" he asked.

"I'm fine," she assured him for the millionth time. "You really didn't have to leave the game. I could have taken a cab home."

"I wouldn't just dump you in a cab," he said. "Not after what happened. You're lucky that ball didn't slam you in the head."

"I know . . ."

"Or that you weren't seriously hurt."

"I know."

"Well . . ." He glanced at his watch with a subtle movement that told her he was anxious to get out of there.

And who could blame him?

He'd gone to the trouble and expense of getting seats

for the biggest Red Sox event of the year, and she'd ruined it before the first inning was over.

Once he'd been convinced that the ball hadn't caused a significant injury to her shoulder, he'd even suggested that they stay. But she'd already been fighting her way through the crowd, desperate to flee Fenway Park.

All she could think was that she'd been hit by a foul ball, and everyone knew the cameras at a televised baseball game followed the ball.

Had her face been on television?

If it had, was she recognizable?

If she was, had anyone from her past been watching?

Allowing herself to dwell on those frightening thoughts delivered her to the verge of panic, so she had done her best not to let it happen.

The whole walk back to the car, and the entire drive back to her suburban home, she had struggled against the surge of frantic impulses within her. She wanted to scream and cry; to jump out of the car; to run . . .

As if running would provide an escape.

A year ago, that had almost seemed possible—that she could somehow run fast enough, far enough, to elude their grasp.

Now the mere idea seemed futile.

She couldn't run.

She couldn't hide.

Sooner or later, they were bound to find her.

If not after tonight's fiasco, then some other way, some day in the future.

No! her inner voice screamed, drowning out whatever Tony was saying.

Don't think that way. You can't afford to be afraid again. You can't live like that.

No, she couldn't just sit here, quaking in fear, waiting to be discovered and destroyed.

But you can't run, either, she reminded herself. *You've*

just created a whole new existence, and so far, … *suspected a thing. If you're going to go, it has to be* … *way. You have to plan for it, do it right.*

There was no real reason to pick up and run again, not yet; not when there was a good chance—hell, a *great* chance—that the cameras had never caught her face on film.

After all, she'd had her back turned, and then she'd fallen as soon as the ball had hit her . . .

And even if she had been facing the field for a split second, there was no way the viewing audience could have gotten a good look at her.

No, she couldn't freak out over this.

She *couldn't.*

Not when she'd worked so hard to rid herself of the paranoia that had haunted her for so long.

Not when there was nothing she could do about it, anyway.

She couldn't change what had happened.

And she couldn't—*wouldn't*—run like a doomed fawn scrambling away from rustling bushes that might—or might not—conceal a hunter.

"Lia?"

She blinked at Tony, who was watching her in the dim light from the bulb over the porch.

"I'm sorry," she said, "I'm kind of . . . out of it. What did you say?"

He simply thanked her for joining him and told her vaguely that he'd see her again.

Not, *Can I see you again?*

She wasn't surprised, nor was she disappointed.

All she felt was colossal relief that her charade was over. She was free to go back to her solitary existence, away from prying eyes and probing questions.

Lia couldn't get inside the house quickly enough, and

sensed that Tony felt the same way about getting back to his car, which he'd left running at the curb.

She didn't bother to watch through the window as he pulled his Honda away from the curb; she knew he wasn't looking back in the rearview mirror, either.

The evening was over, mercifully, and now Jaime would surely leave her alone.

So at least something positive had come of the date.

She forced her thoughts away from speculation that something else might have come of it.

Something negative.

Something deadly.

After carefully and swiftly locking the door and sliding the heavy bolt into place, Lia pulled off her brown suede flats and padded through the small living room, turning on a floor lamp as she went. It cast a cozy glow on the floral chintz furniture she'd bought secondhand, and she looked around, thinking that she was fortunate to have rented a place that had so much charm.

There was a fireplace on one end of the room, with built-in glass-fronted cupboards on either side. She'd filled the shelves with thrift shop books and knick-knacks, just as she'd accumulated a clutter of kitchen-ware and framed wall prints and even clothing from yard sales and the local Salvation Army shop. The place looked lived-in as a result.

No one would ever guess that Lia Haskin had come to town with only the clothes on her back and an enor-mous wad of cash in her purse.

In the bedroom, she flicked on another lamp and took off the horn-rimmed glasses that always felt heavy on her nose after a while. She tossed them onto the bedside table. She rarely wore them at home; there was no reason to. Her vision was twenty-twenty and always had been.

She crossed to the closet, pulling her beige mohair

sweater over her head as she went. She draped it carefully on a padded hanger, then slipped out of her long
skirt with its floral pattern in burgundy and gold and
chestnut colors. That, she tossed into the hamper, along
with her tights and bra.

As she walked over to the dresser, wearing only a pair
of white lace panties, she suddenly felt goose bumps
prickling her flesh. Not just because the room was chilly,
but because she was suddenly spooked, as though someone were watching her.

Her eyes darted to the window.

The blinds were drawn, just as she'd left them earlier.
No one could see inside, even if someone *were* lurking
in the yard . . . a thought that filled her with terror.

It happened every night . . .

This eerie speculation that would undoubtedly follow
her for a lifetime.

Tonight it was stronger than usual, but that was just
because of what had happened at the game. And what
had happened was a fluke. The chances of it leading
to her being discovered were so slim that she refused
to devote any more time to paranoid thoughts.

Shivering, she yanked open the top drawer of her
bureau and pulled out a long nightgown. Even after it
had swished around her ankles in a billowing cloud of
white cotton, she felt naked.

Frowning, she again glanced toward the window.

No, it was impossible for anyone to see in.

She was alone.

Alone, as always, and that was how she wanted it.

No . . .

That was how it had to be.

She went into the small bathroom off the hallway. As
she used cold cream to remove the minimal makeup
from her face, she stared at herself in the mirror.

It was hard to remember what she'd looked like only

a little over a year ago. She'd worked so hard to change her appearance. That was why she wore the glasses; why she religiously dyed her hair this dull chestnut color and kept it cut in a neat, shoulder-brushing pageboy; why she made sure to keep an extra fifteen pounds on her frame.

Ironic, wasn't it, that she'd battled with her weight for so many years, struggling to keep herself bikini-thin. That was necessary in South Beach, where it was summer year-round.

Back then, she'd always loved to eat, and it had taken all her willpower not to indulge in the southern foods she loved most: conch fritters, and southern biscuits with sausage gravy, and key lime pie; not to mention frozen piña coladas and margaritas.

Now, though, it was an effort to keep weight *on;* she rarely had an appetite these days, and most of the time she had to force herself to eat.

The extra padding concealed her high cheekbones and what had once been a willowy figure. Thanks to the extended northern winters, she could keep her long-legged body hidden beneath bulky wool and corduroy. The weight had settled in her bust and on her hips, rounding her figure in a way that attracted appreciative stares and comments from men on the street, much to her surprise . . . and dismay.

She didn't *want* to be noticed; she didn't *want* to be attractive. What she wanted was to fade into the drab New England landscape, to be just another number in the overpopulated northeastern seaboard.

Here people had less time and attention for each other than they did in South Florida's warm, easygoing climate. A mousy, slightly overweight newcomer could slip into the mix with little heed from others; could disappear into the bustle of suburbia.

At least that was what Lia had hoped to do.

What she *had* done, so far.

She finished washing her face and ran a brush quickly through her hair. Gone forever were the long, sun-streaked tresses that had once hung nearly to her waist. This hairstyle was far more . . . *Boston.* It was sensible, making her look like a teacher or a banker.

In fact, she wasn't either of those things. Though she adored children and she was good with numbers and finance, both of those careers would demand too thorough a background check, and she couldn't afford that.

No, she had taken a job with a credit card company's collection division. Her days were spent in a tiny cubicle, calling strangers to ask for the money they owed. Some people reacted in surprise, claiming they hadn't realized their accounts were overdue. Others poured out hard-luck stories, sometimes sobbing as they explained why they had fallen behind in their payments. Others—most of them, actually—lashed out at her in anger.

That was fine with Lia. She knew that to them, she was just a disembodied voice on the phone.

It certainly wasn't the most pleasant job in the world, but dealing with the verbal abuse of harried strangers sure as hell beat the alternative.

Like coming face to face with the fury of her ruthless enemies.

One man in particular.

Suddenly feeling exhausted, she turned off the bathroom light and walked the few steps back to her bedroom. Turning toward the door with a sigh, she froze as she heard a faint sound.

A thump.

Her heart attempted to launch itself out of her rib cage and her eyes grew round with the stark fear that seized her from the gut, wrapping around her like a thousand tentacles, rendering her unable to move, to speak, to breathe . . .

And then the doorbell rang.

Lia's legs turned to liquid as she heard Jaime's familiar voice calling to her from the other side of the front door.

"Hey, Lia, it's me!"

For a moment she couldn't move, simply stood rooted to the green bedroom carpet as relief coursed over her.

"Lia, come on! I know you're home . . . I saw you come in!"

For the first time ever, Lia welcomed Jaime's intrusion. At least it explained the sound she'd heard. It meant she was safe, that *they* hadn't found her.

Not yet.

Stop that, she scolded herself as she walked back down the hall to the door. *They're never going to find you. They're long ago and far away, and they've got better things to do than track you down.*

That was what she had told herself every day of her life for the past year, but it hadn't yet sunk in.

Now she believed it never would.

She was condemned to a lifetime of looking over her shoulder.

If so, it was a small price to pay for being alive.

"But Victor, how the hell am I supposed to find her?"

"That's up to you."

"She could be anywhere."

"What are you, an idiot? Up until half hour ago she was in Fenway Park."

"But the television announcer said she'd left the stadium."

"So? She has to be somewhere in Boston, or just outside of the city."

"Do you know how big Greater Boston is?"

"I don't care," Victor hollered into the phone. "You

found that bastard who was stealing from me last year when he thought he was so sneaky, hiding in Rio. You can find her. You *will* find her," he added, lowering his voice to a menacing growl.

And when you do, he added mentally, *I'll do to her what I did to the greedy bastard in Rio.*

No, I won't even be that merciful.

In fact, I'll make what happened to him seem like a day at the beach compared to what's going to happen to her.

"I'll do my best to hunt her down, Victor," his telephone associate was promising anxiously.

"If you don't, I'll hunt *you* down. Do you understand what I'm saying?"

"I understand. Don't worry. We have several reliable associates in Boston. I'm sure one of them can—"

"Get right on it," Victor interrupted tersely, then slammed down the phone.

George Enceladus was fuming.

Mainly because the Red Sox had lost the game after managing to tie it up in the bottom of the ninth. They'd held on through three more innings, until some Yankee newcomer had hit a grand slam.

That wasn't the only thing that had George pissed off, though. It was past one in the morning, meaning he wouldn't be getting much sleep before he had to rise for his job with the sanitation service.

On top of that, the accountant guy who had been sitting behind him owed him fifty skins ... and he'd vanished after that foul ball had smacked his girlfriend in the head.

George could have used the money. Snacks and drinks at the game had set him back more than twenty bucks, and Iris was already on his back about needing cash to pay the paperboy. He'd have to swing by OTB tomorrow after work and see if he could come up with a win or two.

"Excuse me, sir?"

George kept walking. No one called him sir.

But the guy moved doggedly after him, tapping him on the shoulder.

"Yeah?" George turned around. "You talkin' to me?"

"Yes. You were seated in the stands near the woman who got hit by the ball in the first inning, weren't you?"

He grunted. "She was right in back of me. That ball should'a been mine. It brushed my fingers before it hit her. She didn't even get to keep the damn thing. Some kid grabbed it when it hit the ground."

"I know, I just spoke to the kid."

George narrowed his eyes at the guy, wondering what he was up to. Despite his smooth manner and casual way of talking, he seemed a little edgy. "Why'd you talk to him?"

"I actually wanted to talk to the woman, but—"

"She took off after it happened," George cut in.

"I know."

"Why'd you want to talk to her?"

"I'm a sports reporter. Doing a story on people who get hit by foul balls."

George raised a dubious brow.

"You know," the reporter went on, "I'm trying to find out whether it's a good omen, like they say."

"Who says that?"

"It's one of those superstitions. Didn't you ever hear it?"

George rolled his eyes. "I ain't superstitious, buddy. But if you track down that woman, tell her that her boyfriend owes me fifty bucks."

"Her boyfriend?"

"The guy she was with. The accountant."

"He's an accountant? You didn't happen to get his name?"

"Yeah. Just his first name. I got hers, too."

The reporter looked ready to pounce on him. "What was it?"

"Hers? Lisa. No, wait . . . Lia. I heard him calling her that. And his was Tony."

"Sir, is there anything else you can recall about either of them?"

George decided that he liked being called sir.

He thought hard, trying to come up with something else to tell the reporter. Finally he just shrugged and said, "Nope, nothing else."

Then, too late, he realized the guy might have been willing to pay for the information he'd just provided for free.

He was about to tell the reporter that there *was* more, but that he'd have to come up with some money to find out. He figured he'd just make something up.

But then the guy said, "Okay, thanks for all your help," and started to walk away.

"Hey, do you think really you're going to find her?" George asked curiously.

The man nodded and smiled. "Thanks to you, sir, I'm pretty confident that I am."

"It's me," the man said quietly into his cellular phone, standing slightly apart from a group of disgruntled Red Sox fans who were standing on the corner outside the stadium, waiting for the light to change.

"What do you have?" asked a grim voice on the other end of the line.

"She's using the name Lia, and she's with an accountant named Tony."

"Lia?" came the tense echo.

"Does that mean anything to you?"

"Her mother's name was Aurelia ... It's her. It's definitely her."

"But I thought you already knew that."

The light changed and he stepped off the curb, holding the phone against his ear as he crossed the street. He walked past a discouraged hawker packing unsold stacks of Red Sox pennants into a cardboard box, and turned toward the parking garage where he had left his car only an hour earlier.

"I was ninety-nine percent sure. But maybe there was some part of me holding out ... wanting to believe the woman on TV just looked incredibly like her."

"Why?" he asked incredulously, suddenly curious about the man on the other end of the line. He knew him only professionally, and had thought his motives for locating the missing woman were also professional.

Now he wasn't so certain, especially after he heard the hollow reply.

"Because if she was dead, or still missing, things would be so much easier." The sigh that followed was one of resignation. "Go ahead. Track her down. I'm getting on a plane. By the time I land, I want to know exactly where to find her."

"You will," he promised, checking his watch and picking up his pace.

The best thing Tony Lanzone had done when he'd bought the new condo in the Back Bay was equip his bedroom with a thirty-five-inch television set and a mini-fridge—left over from his dorm days at George Mason. There was nothing better than lying back against a mountain of pillows in his brand new waterbed, snug beneath the zebra striped bedspread, with the remote control in one hand and a cold beer in the other. He could reach the fridge from the bed, so there was no reason to get up.

And he sure hadn't—except once to visit the bathroom—ever since he'd settled here hours ago, to watch the rest of the Red Sox playoff game on television. Not that this beat sitting in Fenway, watching the action in person, but several bottles of Molson Ice had taken the sting out of his disappointment over that fiasco—and the fact that the Sox had lost after tying up the game.

Besides, if he hadn't left the stadium, he would have had to pay fifty bucks to the fat oaf sitting behind him. And he might not have found out until after a few dates that Lia Haskin wasn't his type. That foul ball had saved him more than fifty bucks—it had saved him all the cash and time he would have spent wining and dining his sister's next door neighbor.

The first time he'd met her, he'd sensed that there was more to her than the prim glasses and dull school marm clothes revealed. If you really looked at her, she was beautiful—and there was a hint of sensuality smoldering just beneath that surface reserve.

Of course, it had been obvious that she was skittish when it came to dating. But he'd written that off as inexperience—or maybe she'd been burned badly in the past. He hadn't realized she was a bona fide nut case. She'd been a nervous wreck the whole time they were at the game, and getting hit by that ball had really done her in. At first he'd felt sorry for her, thinking she'd really been hurt by the wallop. But gradually, he had figured out that she wasn't freaking out because of the pain. She was freaking out because . . .

Well, who knew why?

And why did every woman Tony dated turn out to be a quivering wuss? Maybe not as extreme as Lia Haskin, but none of them had any flair, any guts.

The only woman who had ever made any sense to

him was his sister. Give him a sassy, brassy babe like Jaime, and he would marry her in a heartbeat. He'd never understood why his brother-in-law had wasted so much time committing to her—especially when you considered the way Billy was always implying that Jaime was as much a spitfire in bed as she was out. Not that Tony got off on imagining his sister's sex life. No, he got off on . . .

He flicked the remote control to Showtime and found a late night movie in progress, with a love scene in full swing.

Now *that* turned him on.

He set his beer on the nightstand and tossed the remote control aside, then focused his attention on the screen.

"Mmm, that feels so good," murmured the actress, a blonde with thinly plucked eyebrows and the largest breasts Tony had ever seen. She threw her head back in ecstasy as her lover, a redhead, licked her nipples and caressed her between the legs.

Tony squirmed on the bed and slid his right hand inside the folds of his boxer shorts.

Too bad Lia hadn't turned out to be a little more exciting, he thought as his eager fingers found his throbbing arousal. It had been weeks since he'd been with a woman . . .

He closed his eyes and Lia and the large-breasted actress rolled into one, and it became her hot, wet mouth moving up and down on Tony.

The ringing telephone startled him just before the point of no return, and he paused in mid-stroke, cursing and glancing at the digital clock on the bedside table.

Two eighteen.

Who the hell would be calling him at this hour?

Pop . . .

It had to be about his father. Pop's heart disease had

taken its toll on him recently, and everybody knew it was only a matter of time.

This is it, Tony thought, sitting up and reaching for the receiver.

He braced himself for the news as he said, "Hello?" and wondered, in the split second before he heard a reply, who was calling him with the news. Would it be Ma? Nah, she would be a nervous wreck. She would probably have to move in with Aunt Frances now—she could never live alone.

It was probably Jaime, he decided.

But it was a male voice—and an unfamiliar one—that said, "Is this Tony Lanzone?"

"This is," he said, thinking wildly that it must be one of Pop's doctors. "Are you calling about my father?"

"I'm calling about the young woman who accompanied you to the Red Sox game earlier this evening."

"You mean Lia?"

"May I have her last name, please?"

"It's Haskin . . . who is this?"

The line had gone dead.

Puzzled, Tony glanced at the receiver, then carefully returned it to its cradle.

"What the hell was *that* all about?" he muttered aloud.

He sighed, lay back in bed again, noticing that the writhing, naked lovers on the television screen had been replaced by a boring scene between some bearded guy and his shrink. And his own powerful erection had shriveled away at the thought of something happening to his father.

Well, at least Pop was all right.

And as for Lia Haskin—why would someone call *him* in the middle of the night just to find out her last name?

Maybe I should call her and make sure everything's all right, Tony thought briefly, then, yawning, dismissed the idea.

It wasn't as if anyone had threatened her. The person had merely asked for her last name.

But who? he wondered vaguely. *And why?*

Suddenly feeling weary, he grabbed the remote control, flicked off the television, and rolled over to get some sleep.

He was just drifting off when a sound in the next room jerked him back to awareness.

One of the windows facing his small terrace was sliding open.

Somebody was breaking into his apartment.

On Saturday morning, Lia dragged herself out of bed feeling as though she hadn't slept at all. She must have dozed on and off through the night, she reasoned as she took a hot shower, but she had spent most of the past ten hours restlessly thrashing on the mattress, going over what had happened at the game, and the possibilities that she was now in danger.

In the darkness of her lonely bedroom last night, that had seemed very likely.

Now, in the bright Saturday morning sunshine, she felt safe.

Maybe it was a false sense of security, but she clung to it as she went about her morning routine. She dressed in a pair of pleated navy gabardine trousers, pumps, and an off-white blouse that buttoned to her throat.

Boring, she thought, surveying herself in the mirror after she had blown dry her shoulder-length hair, pulling it back into a severe twist at the nape of her neck.

She was suddenly swept by a rush of longing for her old lighthearted self. She yearned to let her hair down, to wear something pretty and flirty, a bare floral sundress that would reveal her smooth, tanned skin and taut, slender limbs . . .

Except that she was no longer tanned or toned.

Her hair was no longer a sun-streaked mass of shimmering gold that tumbled to her waist.

And she would never be that carefree girl again.

She sighed, put on her horn-rimmed glasses, and a pair of small gold post earrings.

Then she went to the kitchen for a quick glass of orange juice.

As she poured it from the carton, she couldn't help thinking of the fresh-squeezed Florida juice that had greeted her every morning at Victor Caval's mansion.

And as she picked up her purse and headed out the door to work, she was reminded of those sunny days, not so long ago, when her job hadn't entailed sitting in a tiny cubicle, making collection phone calls for hours on end.

But there was nothing she could do to change the path her life had taken.

She locked the back door carefully behind her, then walked briskly to the small used Hyundai she'd bought through a newspaper ad for cash several months back.

As she pulled out of the driveway, she glanced at the house next door. The shades were still down. Jaime and Billy usually slept in on weekends; she never glimpsed them until well past noon. Jaime liked to hint that they did more than sleeping on those lazy Saturdays in bed.

The last thing Lia wanted was to hear details about their newlywed exploits.

It wasn't that she was a prude.

Far from it.

She just couldn't bear to be reminded of what it was like to be so in love you couldn't get enough of someone.

So blinded by desire that you didn't see the truth . . . until it was too late.

Not Jaime, of course. She and Billy were blissfully married, and probably always would be. No wonder she

had made it her mission in life to see that everyone was
as happily matched as she was.

Last night, she could hardly wait to hear about Lia's
date with Tony.

"What are you doing home so soon?" she had
demanded the instant Lia had opened the door. "Do
you like him? Do you think he likes you? Did he ask
you out again?"

Jaime's questions were endless, and when Lia finally
managed to get a word in, she told her about getting
hit by the ball, and how they'd left the game.

"Why did you have to come straight home?" Jaime
wanted to know. "Were you hurt that badly?"

"Badly enough not to feel like hanging around the
stadium for hours," Lia said curtly.

She managed to change the subject, but one-track
Jaime swiftly slid back to her matchmaking scheme,
wanting to know if Lia saw a future for herself and Tony.

"A future? As in another date?"

"As in marriage."

"Oh, geez. Why are you so eager to marry *him* off?"
Lia had asked.

"Because he's thirty-three, and my father's heart is
bad," Jaime had said cryptically.

"Excuse me?"

And so Jaime had explained that as the only son in
the family, it was up to Tony to carry on their father's
name. Tony Lanzone Senior had been suffering from
heart disease for several years now, and Jaime said that
he didn't have much time left. "It would make him so
happy if my brother would get married and have kids
. . . a son," she'd told Lia.

"What about you? You're married. You can have
kids."

"It wouldn't be the same. My father's from the old

school. He wants to be sure the family name won't die out."

"Well, I really wish I could help you out, Jaime," Lia had said, half-amused, half-touched by her friend's tale. "But it doesn't look like Tony and I will be getting married, so you'll have to fix him up with someone else."

"Why?" Jaime had asked, turning searching eyes on Lia.

"Because we just didn't seem to hit it off."

"No, not that. Why are you so afraid to get involved? Why do you avoid people like they're contaminated with some horrible disease?"

"I don't—"

"You do. You don't go out, except to work. You don't have friends. You don't date."

Taken aback, Lia had abruptly said, "I'm just not the social type."

"Sure you are. Once you loosen up, you know how to have fun. But you hardly ever do. It's like you're always on guard."

Lia shrugged, forced a yawn. "I'm really tired, Jaime . . ."

Surprisingly her neighbor had taken the hint. She left, but only after inviting Lia to an Oktoberfest party she and Billy were throwing in two weeks.

"You have to come, Lia. If you don't, you'll be up all night because of the noise anyway. So you might as well join us."

Lia had said that she'd consider it.

Now, as she drove past the MacGregors' house, she decided that she'd simply feign some sort of illness the day of the party.

There was just no way she was going to risk going blindly into a crowd again—even on a much smaller scale than the one last night.

She drove through the small downtown area, then out onto the highway, past the Super Stop and Shop and Wal-Mart and the commuter train station. At the edge of the business district, she turned into a parking lot and pulled into a spot not far from the nondescript two-story office building that housed the credit card company.

The place was quiet, as it always was on Saturdays. Unlike her colleagues, she never minded working this shift. It was a relief to be one of the only people in the building, not to have to dodge quite so many strangers when she ventured to the bathroom or to the McDonald's across the road to grab lunch.

She took the stairs to the second floor and let herself into the large suite at the end of the corridor. She checked her watch and saw that she was early; twenty-five minutes early. She wasn't allowed to start making phone calls until ten, so she made a pot of coffee in the break room, then settled in at her desk and pulled out a paperback romance novel she kept in her top drawer.

Escapist reading, she thought fondly, glancing at the cover, which depicted a virile blond cover model embracing the slender waist of a half-dressed young temptress.

There had been a time when she herself had lived a torrid affair.

Now she could only read about them.

Now she could only fantasize that someday, somehow, she might once again experience the kind of passion she had with—

"Hey, Lia!"

She looked up and saw Kaneesha, a pretty middle-aged woman who had started work last month.

Under normal circumstances, Lia would have become friends with her; she liked the woman's easygoing, casual attitude and her sharp sense of humor. And Kaneesha was from Florida, too—Jacksonville. She was homesick, always talking about how she missed the South, about how hard it was to be a southerner in Yankee territory, unaware that Lia secretly shared her plight.

But Lia had forced herself to remain standoffish—not that that daunted Kaneesha. She was nice to everyone, Lia included. And though Lia never took her up on her daily invitations to eat lunch together, Kaneesha didn't stop asking.

"Oh, hi," Lia said, offering a smile that she hoped was pleasant but dismissive. She started to turn back to her book, but Kaneesha stopped her.

"Are you all right, girlfriend?"

"What do you mean?"

"I saw you on TV last night. That was some wallop y'all took from that foul ball."

I saw you on TV last night.

A roar filled Lia's ears, and though she was focused on Kaneesha's concerned face, and though the woman continued to speak, she heard nothing.

Nothing but an echo of those dreaded words.

I saw you on TV last night.

"I . . . excuse me," Lia flung out, and turned blindly, moving toward the hallway.

She didn't stop until she was back in her car.

Her hands trembled so badly that she had to try several times before managing to jam the key into the ignition.

I saw you on TV last night.

She drove out of the parking lot, back toward town, heading toward home because where else could she go?

She had to be alone, someplace safe, so she could think . . .

I saw you on TV last night.

What the hell was she going to do?

Okay, she had to get out of here; that was the most obvious thing. She had to vanish, just as she had last year, in Florida. She had to get home, get the meager sum of cash she'd been stockpiling just in case, and take off. There was no time to waste.

According to the clock on the dashboard, it took her exactly four minutes to reach the familiar white cape on Hawthorne Street.

But it felt like hours.

And when she finally pulled into the driveway, all she could think was that she had to hurry. The more time she lingered, the more time they would have to track her down.

What if they already had?

The thought struck her as she scurried toward the back door, stopping her dead in her tracks.

No. They couldn't possibly have found her so soon. Not even with their powerful connections. Even if they had seen her, and recognized her, and knew she was in Boston, it would be a challenge to pinpoint her location.

There were nearly four million people in Greater Boston. Finding her among the throng would be like trying to locate the elusive Waldo cartoon in one of those children's books.

But still . . .

She took a deep breath, unlocked the door, and walked in.

The shades were still drawn, the rinsed orange juice glass was in the sink, and everything was just as she had left it . . .

But.

But something seemed *wrong*.

As Lia moved across the kitchen to the hall, she was struck by the sensation of being watched.

It's just your imagination, she told herself, looking around.

She was alone. As always.

She went to her bedroom and pulled a suitcase from the closet, then began haphazardly tossing things into it. Not clothing—not much anyway. She loathed her Boston wardrobe.

She would buy new clothes, more suitable for the next place she lived . . .

Wherever that might be.

Not the Northeast; that much was certain.

She had gone to college in New England and had never liked this part of the country; couldn't tolerate the cold or the endless gray winters.

She had once told Marco she wouldn't move to New York or New England if her life depended on it.

She had never dreamed that that innocuous statement breathed a tremendous foreshadowing.

And when the time came to disappear, she had been counting on Marco's amazingly sharp memory. He would remember her words, as he tended to remember other seemingly insipid day-to-day details. He would assume she had fled to a place with a climate similar to Florida's—maybe that she had left the country and was living on some lush island in the Caribbean.

That had been their private fantasy, hers and Marco's.

They used to daydream about a tropical paradise where they would spend long, languid days on secluded beaches, their bare skin soaking up the heat of the sun . . . and each other's caresses.

So much for that, she thought abruptly, with a hint of her old sense of bitter irony that had never really left her.

She filled the suitcase with things she couldn't bear to leave behind—books, mostly, and trinkets, and odds and ends that had made this place feel a little more homey.

When the first bag was full, she reached for another

one, a black canvas duffle she'd brought with her from Florida that steamy night a year ago.

She unzipped it and left it open on the bed, then went into the living room and opened the glass screen on the fireplace. Reaching up inside the chimney, she felt around until she located the nylon sack hanging there. A quick peek inside the drawstring opening confirmed that the money was still there. Several hundred dollars.

Not much, but at least it would be enough to live on until . . .

Until she'd established herself again, in some new town, with a new identity and a new job and a new home.

A home that would never truly be home.

How could it be, when she lived there alone, and knew that she always would?

Refusing to give in to the tears that crept into her eyes, she returned to the bedroom and shoved the nylon bag into the duffle, zipping it closed and slinging it over her shoulder. She picked up the suitcase and took a last look around.

Again she was struck by the eerie feeling that she wasn't alone.

It's just nerves, she told herself. *Everything is going to be fine. There's nothing to worry about. You're getting out of here long before they could ever find you . . . even if they're looking.*

So this was it.

She was off.

"Goodbye," she said softly to no one, and reached for the doorknob with a shaking hand, thinking that it really hadn't been so bad, living here.

A rustling sound in the room broke into her thoughts.

Panic washed over her and she opened her mouth to scream just as a hand clamped down over her lips.

"Going someplace?" asked a low voice.

The voice, the unmistakable Hispanic accent, of a man she knew all too well.

The man who had filled her thoughts with memories of forbidden pleasure . . . and dread.

The man from whom she had been running for the past thirteen months.

Marco Estevez.

Chapter Three

She was different.

That was the first thought that struck him when he turned her to face him, keeping one hand over her mouth so she wouldn't scream.

So drastically different from the girl he had loved in that faraway place, that fleeting time that seemed so long ago.

She had been young then, headstrong and brazen, yet somehow naive. Her body had been lean and hard, her skin bronzed, her hair a wild cascade of sun-kissed waves.

The almost-stranger standing before him was a woman. Everything about her spoke of restraint, from the lackluster clothing to the dark hair worn severely pinned back from her face. She had a woman's gentle curves and milky skin; he found himself longing to release his grip on her, to run his hands over the voluptuous flesh that hadn't been there when he'd last touched her.

Two things stopped him.

One was a sense of urgency; there was no time to waste.

The other was the look in her brown eyes, behind the dark-rimmed glasses. Her gaze collided with his own, betraying her hurt, and fear . . . And something else.

Hatred.

She detested him; the fact was as plain as if she had spoken it aloud, and he had no doubt she would if he removed his hand from her mouth . . . The mouth he had, not so very long ago, claimed with his own, in endless, hot, sweeping kisses. The mouth that had teased and pleasured his most intimate places; then whispered seductive words of love, and passion, and trust.

Those feelings were dead.

Now there was only hatred on her part; weary obligation on his.

And so Marco Estevez would do what he was bound by duty to do, and when it was over, he would never look back.

Never again.

Not the way he had these past thirteen months, when he'd agonized over memories of her, tormented by the realization that she could actually be dead, hunted down and killed by Victor's posse . . . Or that, if she wasn't, she might as well be.

She was lost to him now; but then she had been all along, ever since the chilling instant when she'd glimpsed his face in the shadows that bloody September night at the mansion off South Miami Avenue.

He set his jaw, staring at her, forcing himself to betray nothing, to absorb her loathing, to take strength from it.

"You'll have to come with me now," he said when he could speak. He marveled that his voice was cold, miraculously devoid of emotion.

She shook her head, boldly protesting with her glaring dark eyes, as if daring him to force her.

A humorless, bitter sound spilled from his lips—born of despair, yet emerging as a chuckle and not a sob.

Lord knew, he hadn't wanted it to be this way.

He tried again, willing her to acquiesce, yet knowing even as he spoke that it was futile.

"Come with me. Now." He lifted his hand from her lips to allow her to reply.

"You're out of your mind if you think you can order me around." Her voice blazed with maddening defiance.

And so, despite the outward differences, the most fundamental thing about her hadn't changed. She was still the most willful woman he had ever known.

And he would do what he had to do in order to convince her that he was, indeed, in charge of her destiny.

He reached into the pocket of his black jacket.

"I'm afraid you don't have a choice," he said, removing a small pistol from his pocket and nudging the barrel into the soft flesh at her waist. "Let's go."

Run!

The command echoed in her mind, just as it had so many months ago, the last time she had unexpectedly confronted Marco Estevez.

He'd had a gun then, too . . .

But somehow, in those initial moments of disillusionment, his weapon hadn't rattled her the way it did now.

Then again, it hadn't been aimed at her, actually touching her skin the way it was now.

This time, he meant business.

Would he actually shoot her?

He hadn't before. He could have, as he chased her

through the hot Florida night. He could have stopped, aimed, and fired at her back. He must have had the opportunity.

Maybe he had been too startled to seize it—still reeling from the shock of seeing her there, just as she had been utterly stunned to glimpse him.

This time, though, there was no hint that he was unnerved. He had prepared for this moment. He was as cold and ominous as the gun in his hand, and something told her he would use it.

Run!

No.

This time, she couldn't.

Maybe because the long months of anxious hiding had robbed her of the feisty electricity that had sent her spontaneously into motion that terrible night.

Maybe because she was no longer A.J. Sutton, a young woman who had already, in her short life, faced calamity and beaten it with her spirit intact.

For too long now, she had been haunted Lia Haskin, fleeing, looking over her shoulder.

Yes.

That was it.

She had never *stopped* running, never once, since that night. Suddenly, she was exhausted. She couldn't go any further.

She had tried to escape him, had given it her best shot, everything she had.

And she had failed.

He had caught her at last, tracked her to her home and trapped her like a cunning snake hovering over a timid field mouse's hole.

She couldn't possibly get away from him, not this time.

It was all over.

There was nothing to do but allow Marco Estevez, and his gun, to take charge.

Jaime MacGregor rolled away from the sweaty, nude, snoring body of her husband, wondering how he always managed to fall back to sleep after their vigorous Saturday morning lovemaking. *She*, on the other hand, was energized, especially today . . . Especially knowing that at this very moment, deep in her core, Billy's sperm were swimming furiously, and perhaps joining with her own egg to create the child she wanted so badly.

It was time, she reasoned as she headed for the bathroom. Whether Billy thought so or not.

She had always sworn she'd be married by twenty-five and have her first child before she turned thirty. Though she'd met Billy in grad school, she'd been considerably late on the marriage deadline, unable to get him to commit to anything beyond living together until he'd finally proposed on her twenty-eighth birthday.

It figured that he'd be equally reluctant to start a family. With thirty looming and no sign of Billy having a change of heart, Jaime had resigned herself to the knowledge that it would be her job to take the initiative and get pregnant.

She knew he'd realize later—*if* she decided to tell him it wasn't an accident—that she'd done the right thing.

She'd take a fast shower, then go out for a jog, she decided. Billy always told her she was nuts to shower *before* she exercised, since she just had to take another one afterward. He didn't seem to understand that she just couldn't stand feeling stale and unwashed, ever.

Sun streamed in the bathroom window, which faced east, toward Lia's house next door. Jaime looked out and saw that her neighbor's car was in the driveway. That was odd, because Lia always worked Saturday mornings.

She considered running over to make sure everything was all right, but decided against it. Lia hadn't been very friendly last night, when Jaime had popped in for the report on her date with Tony. In fact, she'd seemed distracted and almost rude, making a big point of being tired.

It was just as well that things hadn't worked out between her neighbor and her brother, Jaime decided, dropping the lace bathroom curtain and turning away from the window. She was way too uptight and aloof.

Jaime opened the medicine cabinet and pulled a bottle of Listerine from its spot on the shelf . . . right next to the diaphragm she had supposedly inserted when she'd dashed to the bathroom in the middle of foreplay an hour ago.

Now, feeling not the slightest prickle of guilt over the deception, she brushed her teeth and turned on the faucet in the tub for a long, hot shower.

As she waited for the water to warm up, she glanced out the window again and saw that Lia Haskin's back door was just opening.

Curious, she watched as her neighbor emerged—followed by the most incredibly handsome man Jaime had ever seen.

He was a god, she thought breathlessly, staring.

The man had a mane of tawny hair that flowed past his shoulders, catching the sunlight and blowing back slightly in the gentle breeze that rustled the trees. His strong features were exquisitely sculpted, with a rugged jaw and aquiline nose, and piercing eyes whose color she couldn't discern from so far away. He wore a snug-fitting pair of black jeans and a brown leather jacket, and his height and broad-shouldered build were imposing.

He kept his arm tightly around Lia as he swept her,

with purposeful strides, down the driveway toward the street.

"That little bitch," Jaime murmured, shaking her head.

She had always suspected Lia was hiding something, but had never considered that it might be a secret lover. Everything about her neighbor had seemed to speak of solitude, even loneliness. And she always seemed so tense and standoffish that Jaime and Billy had a standing joke about her needing a good screw.

Who would have dreamed that Lia was obviously involved with the most provocative man Jaime had ever seen?

And why hadn't she let on?

Wait a minute . . . Was he married?

Of course. He must be, judging by the furtive bearing Jaime had sensed in his hurried walk.

Jaime decided he must have snuck over to Lia's shortly after Tony had dropped her off last night. Maybe he'd even been there, hiding in the bedroom, when Jaime herself had stopped by. No wonder Lia had been so edgy, so eager to get rid of her.

Pulling up on the lever that started the shower, Jaime stepped in and closed the glass door behind her.

The next time she saw Lia, she decided, reaching for the shampoo, she'd tell her exactly what she thought of her lies and her sneaky little affair.

Outside in the open, as they scurried down the short driveway toward the street, Marco's entire body tensed and droplets of sweat beaded his forehead beneath his hair.

Someone could come along any second now . . .

Lia could scream for help . . .

But there wasn't a pedestrian or a passing car to be seen.

A Saturday morning hush hovered over the neighborhood, and the only sound that reached Marco's ears was the hurried tapping of his shoes and Lia's against the hard pavement.

Still, he felt a strange vulnerability, and it rendered him rigid with trepidation.

As he ushered his captive toward the waiting car, his forearm against her waist and the gun jabbing into her side, he knew the risk of being seen wasn't the only thing causing his tension.

It was . . .

Being near her.

Touching her.

Inhaling the faint, clean scent of her hair and skin.

He found himself filling his lungs with her, then exhaled sharply and was dismayed to note a tremor in his breath.

Had she noticed? Did she have any idea what she was doing to him, just by being here, alive?

Of course she had no idea.

She thought he loathed her.

If only that were the case.

Emotions he had struggled for so long to bury flitted over Marco and began to jab at him like a swarm of hungry mosquitoes, stinging his flesh and his soul.

He couldn't do this.

He ached to haul her into his arms and tell her . . .

Tell her what?

The truth?

About how he felt?

About who he was?

Both options were off-limits.

There was nothing to do but continue steering her toward the waiting car, and steel himself for what lay ahead.

Victor winced as he paced across the floor of his living room, the telephone in his hand. His bad ankle was killing him. It always acted up when he got agitated.

He swiftly dialed the number for the Quincy, Massachusetts seafood distributor that was a front for the New England branch of his business. He needed to talk to the man who had located A.J. Sutton for him, just to make sure . . .

Just to see that no one was going to get to her before his men did. Alberto and the others were on their way now, but Victor had an unsettling feeling that . . .

"Lighthouse Seafood. This is Maria speaking."

"This is Victor Caval. Give me Francisco," he said to the Spanish-accented voice that answered the phone.

Moments later, someone picked up and said, "Victor, *hola.* This is Francisco. How did you like the way I tracked down—"

"I need to know exactly how you found her," he interrrupted.

There was a pause, and then Francisco told him, "I talked to someone who was sitting next to her at the game. He asked if I was a reporter, and he said he wanted cash. I should'a smashed his face in, but I paid him—"

"He wanted cash?"

"Yeah. Said some reporter had just asked him about the woman who had gotten hit with the fly ball, and what the hell did he look like, a free information service? So I said . . ."

Francisco was still talking. Victor half-listened, his

mind whirling at the implications. Someone else was on her trail. Could it be . . . ?

"So anyway," Francisco went on, "he finally told me she was with an accountant named Tony. From there it was simple. I used the Internet."

"How?"

"I located every Boston area accountant named Anthony, Tony, Antonio—you'd be surprised at how many there are, but I found them all, Victor. Then I accessed the records of their license plates, which I cross-referenced with the parking garages near Fenway—they keep records of plate numbers when you park, and the attendants are willing to talk for a few bucks. I did it on the off-chance that whoever it was had parked his car there, and guess what? There he was. Tony Lanzone," Francisco said, sounding pleased with his own ingenuity.

"So you found this accountant," Victor prodded. "And you went to see him?"

"Yeah. Me and Nardo got into his place through a window—it was easy. He flipped out when he saw us, man."

"I'm sure he did," Victor said dryly, knowing Nardo was as wide as he was long, every inch pure muscle. "Tell me everything he said."

"Not much, if you know what I mean. He was scared to death. He kept begging us not to kill him . . ."

"You didn't, did you?"

Francisco hesitated. "Nah. Just beat him up a little. But only *after* he told us what we wanted to know."

"And that was . . . ?"

"Her last name. Haskin. Her address. It's—"

"That doesn't matter. I'm already on that. Did he say anything else?"

"No . . . yeah. He did, actually. He said something about how everyone suddenly wanted to know about that woman."

Victor clenched the receiver. "You mean, you weren't the first one to look into her whereabouts?"

"I guess that's what he meant, yeah."

"Damn," Victor cursed softly, shaking his head.

Maybe he was mistaken. Maybe it really was a reporter sniffing around A.J. Sutton.

No.

No, he knew precisely who else was on A.J. Sutton's trail.

And he didn't like it at all.

A thousand questions jumbled in Lia's mind, but she was too numb, too shocked, too furious to voice any of them.

She huddled silently in the front passenger's seat of the sleek black sedan—a rental, of course. Marco's taste in automobiles was much more flashy. He had always driven a cherry-red Jaguar in Miami.

"Don't make a sound, or you'll be sorry," he had muttered as they had crossed the street to the car he'd parked against the curb.

For the first time, Lia had regretted choosing to live on a quiet lane instead of a main thoroughfare, where he never could have abducted her without someone noticing.

Here even her nosy neighbor Jaime was nowhere to be found, and Lia had no hope of escaping. She didn't dare scream or try to run; not with Marco's gun nudging into her side, concealed by what looked like a protective embrace.

He won't kill me, she thought again now, glancing at the gun he still held at the ready as he steered the car with one hand.

The Marco Estevez she had loved wasn't capable of hurting any living creature.

She remembered the time a hairy grove spider had turned up on the bedroom floor, sending her skittishly into the next room on some pretense, though she wouldn't admit to Marco that she was afraid. When she dared return, she had found Marco gently scooping the heinous creature into a newspaper and lightly depositing it on the grass outside.

He won't kill me, she thought again, keeping her hands flat on the dashboard, as Marco had commanded, so that he could see them.

No, she amended, the Marco she had known long ago wouldn't have killed her.

But this man—this stranger—who knew what he was capable of doing?

She had already glimpsed the proof that he wasn't what he seemed, that night a year ago when she'd seen him lurking in the shadows, a gun raised straight up above his shoulder, poised against his cheek in a telltale, practiced pose. He was no frightened accidental witness to the horror at the mansion, the way she had been. He was a part of it, and the knowledge had sent her on a desperate journey to escape not just the danger, but her unsettling memories.

How could she have been so wrong?

How could she, even now, doubt that he was a ruthless man who would kill if he had to?

I have to get away from him, she thought frantically as he turned the car onto the ramp leading to the Massachusetts Turnpike heading west.

The toll booths lay ahead.

Salvation, she thought, and braced herself as he moved his foot to the brake to slow the car.

"If you say one word, or make one move, I'll kill the toll clerk," he said in a low, controlled voice, as if he'd read her mind. "And then I'll kill you. Do you understand?"

Her heart pounded as she nodded.

She swallowed hard as they drew up in front of the booth, where a smiling, white-haired man handed Marco a toll ticket and called, "You folks have a nice day," as they sped off.

The entire interaction had taken a second, maybe two. There had been no opportunity for Lia to take a chance and make a break for it, even if she had dared.

In a matter of moments, she knew, the car would accelerate to a speed that would make it deadly for her to jump out, chancing that Marco's bullets might miss their target.

She was trapped, unless she acted now—

"Stop!" he barked, not even turning his gaze from the road as he brandished the gun at her.

"I didn't—"

"You moved your fingers. Stop that, or you'll regret it. Keep your hands flat and still, on the dashboard."

In despair, she gave up her plan. She would be dead before she could reach for the door handle. She had barely flinched a moment ago, and he had again reacted as though he'd read her mind, knowing exactly what she intended to do.

But then, he'd once claimed the ability to do just that, hadn't he?

"I know what you're thinking," he had said in that seductive, faintly Hispanic accent of his, looking deeply into her eyes the night they had met.

"No, you don't." She had laughed and squirmed.

"Oh, yes, I do. I can read your mind perfectly."

"Really? Then tell me what I'm thinking," she had challenged him.

Only moments earlier, she had been giddy from too much sangria and the steamy Miami moonlight. But staring into his seductive blue gaze, she had suddenly felt oddly centered, fully aware of what was about to happen with this enigmatic stranger she had known for mere hours.

"You want me to kiss you . . . and not a chaste, gentle first kiss either, huh, Lia? You want me to sweep you into my arms and claim you. You want me to use my tongue in your mouth and my hands on your body. You want—"

"I just want you," she had interrupted in a whisper, moving forward and pressing herself against him as she lifted her face and waited to taste his passion.

She glanced at him now, at his familiar profile as he watched the road through the windshield, and she wondered how this could have happened; how her own desire had turned to dread.

And as she did, she realized that somewhere deep in her heart, where she had banished memories of the intensely intimate bond she had shared with Marco Estevez, something was stirring.

She fought it, but was seized by a sudden, fierce longing to speak his name, to reach for him, to stroke his face the way she once had.

He turned his head, as if feeling her gaze, and she swore she saw a trace of pain in his blue eyes before they hardened.

"How did you find me?" she blurted, when he looked back at the highway. She noticed that he was careful to keep the speed just above the limit. There would be no chance of salvation from a radar-equipped trooper hidden along the road.

For a moment, Marco didn't respond.

Then he shrugged and said, "Shouldn't you be wondering *why* I found you, and not how?"

"I know why." *So that you can kill me because of what I saw that night.*

"Oh?" He glanced at her again, a flicker of amusement in his gaze. "You always did think you knew it all."

She frowned, hating the mocking tone of his voice. "What do you mean by that?"

"You were so sure of yourself," he said, shaking his head and looking straight ahead. "So stubborn. Too stubborn for your own good."

How many times had she heard that before? And not just from him.

"No aflojar un pelo," her mother, Aurelia, would sigh.

"She's as stubborn as they come," her father, Jack, would agree with a grin. "And it's no wonder."

She got her headstrong genes from her mother's side of the family, she knew—from her fiery Cuban bloodline.

Her father, Jack, was as unruffled as they came, with a stolid midwestern reserve that belied a warm, generous heart.

It was that sensitivity that had drawn him to Aurelia in the first place. Lia's mother had left Havana at eighteen, setting out to cross the Atlantic in a leaky, crowded raft with dozens of young men and women, among them, her fiancé, Carlos. He had drowned in the storm-tossed sea several days into the journey.

But Lia's mother had been rescued by an American ship off the coast of Key West. Jack Sutton had been a young naval officer on board, and he had somehow taken the bereaved, bewildered young girl under his wing—and presumably into his heart.

It was Jack's brother, Uncle Bruce, who had finally shared the particulars of her parents' meeting, and not until years after they were gone, when she had yearned to know more about her past.

Of course, lacking his brother's warmth and affection,

Bruce had spared the emotional details. But it hadn't been hard to imagine the attraction between the quietly gallant man in uniform and the exotic, courageous teenage beauty who found herself alone in a strange land.

They had married mere months after they met, and had their daughter a year after that. Jack had insisted that she be named for her mother, and so she was christened Aurelia Jane Sutton.

She had simply been A.J., though, from the day she was born until that horrible night last September, when she had fled Miami—and Marco Estevez and Victor Caval—to become Lia Haskin.

The last name, she had picked simply by randomly opening the phone book in a bus stop somewhere in Virginia.

As for the first, it had been an echo in her mind through all the hollow years since her parents had been killed when their plane had crashed en route to Bimini, where they were planning to celebrate their tenth anniversary.

Lia.

It was what Jack Sutton had called his wife, an affectionate, shortened version of the full name she shared with her daughter.

Lia . . . The name was her sole link to the distant, happy past before she had been orphaned and sent to live with her only living relative—the only one in this country anyway: her father's brother, Bruce.

A recently divorced workaholic government attorney, he wasn't exactly ripe for raising a nine-year-old niece he barely knew. He had two daughters of his own, Cindy and Debbie—one a few years older than Lia, the other a few years younger.

Both were round-faced, chubby, sullen girls who

resented having to share their father's meager attention with their beautiful cousin. They delighted in reminding Lia that their father hadn't wanted to take her in; that he had spent considerable time and effort trying to locate her dead mother's family that had been left behind in Cuba.

But despite his government connections, Uncle Bruce hadn't been able to cut through the red tape and track down Aurelia Santiago Sutton's parents, sisters, and brother. They seemed to have vanished.

Lia had been devastated when she'd realized that she would never meet her grandparents, aunts, and uncle; that she was condemned to live in Uncle Bruce's cold, lonely household. She had grown up listening to her mother's tales of a rollicking, close-knit family, had believed her mother's promises that one day, they would all be reunited. She had seen her mother weep many times for her lost loved ones.

"Why doesn't Mama just visit them?" Lia had once asked her father.

"It's not that simple, A.J.," he had replied. "People don't just go to Cuba for a visit."

"Well then, can't she call her family on the telephone, or just write them a letter?"

Her father had explained that because of a scary man named Castro, there was no way to reach them, and there probably wouldn't be for a long, long time.

"Well, why did she leave them in the first place?"

"She wanted a better way of life," he had said sadly. "And if she had never left, she wouldn't have us."

"I'll never leave you and Mama, Daddy. I promise."

He had chuckled. "Someday you will, little girl. Everyone has to leave home."

"But not forever, the way Mama did. She'll never leave us, will she, Daddy?"

"No, she never will."

"And you'll never leave, either, Daddy, will you?"

"No, I promise I won't leave, little one." He had shaken his head and caught her close in his arms, hugging her against his strong chest.

Mere months later, he was gone, and her mother was gone, and Lia was alone and unloved.

Those early years of pain and solitude in Uncle Bruce's household had prepared her well for the past thirteen months. Self-sufficient and an expert at hiding her emotions, Lia had twice before proved she was a survivor.

And you'll do it again now, she warned herself, despite her certainty that Marco Estevez was transporting her to her doom. *No matter what he has in store for you, you won't go down without a fight.*

As they headed west through Massachusetts toward the New York border, driving in silence, Marco kept thinking of another road trip he had made with Lia, one long weekend in the heart of that hot Florida summer.

"We have to escape," she had told him spontaneously a few days earlier, sidling up to him at the mansion when no one else was in earshot.

"Escape what?"

"Just . . . everything. We need to be alone together, Marco, away from Victor and everyone. And I have the weekend off."

"Where do you want to go?"

"Paradise," she had said with a twinkle in her eye.

So they had crossed the state in his cherry-red Jaguar, laughing and talking in cozy companionship as they drove west along Alligator Alley.

They had chattered about everything and nothing . . . so different from the stony silence that hung in the car today.

He remembered thinking, as they drove through the wildly beautiful and desolate Everglades, that he had never felt so serene, that he wouldn't care if they never reached their destination, just so he could sit here beside the woman he adored with the sun streaming in the windows and her lighthearted laughter ringing in his ears.

But eventually, they had reached the crystal waters of the Gulf Coast. There, they had crossed a bridge and found themselves on the shell-covered shores of Sanibel Island.

They checked into a whitewashed cottage with a red tile roof, and spent the next three days eating and drinking too much and making love in between meals and all night, every night.

Balmy mornings were spent walking along the beach, where A.J. picked the prettiest shells from amidst the thousands washed up by the most recent tides. They ate lunch every day at the open air Tiki Bar, lazily sipping frosted drinks into the afternoon. Then they splashed in the surf or laid on pastel lounges by the pool, where Marco constantly felt consumed by the need to rub tanning oil over her already saturated skin, invariably taking his time as he smoothed the warm liquid over the curves of her sun-warmed flesh.

"I'm greasier than a french fry," she teasingly complained once, lying face-down on her chaise and writhing slightly under his touch as he sat beside her.

The romance novel she had been trying to read lay tossed aside at his bare feet; real life, she had informed him, suddenly seemed a lot more exciting.

"Do you want me to stop?" he asked, gently kneading

the inside of her lean thigh just below the elastic of her bikini bottom, his fingers brushing lightly and provocatively against the narrow band of thin fabric that stretched between her legs. He felt goose bumps rise on her legs and she squirmed and stretched, as if the tender flesh at her core was straining to find his fingers again.

"No . . . God, no," she moaned. "In fact . . . let's go back to the room, so we can continue in private . . . without these damned bathing suits in the way."

He grinned and teased, "You don't need suntan oil inside."

"No, but I need you inside *me,*" she had whispered wickedly, standing and leading the way back to bed.

Paradise.

Those island days glistened in his mind now like a far-off mirage; had they ever been real?

He glanced at Lia now and caught her looking at him from the passenger's seat.

She held his gaze for a long, deliberate moment. There was no mistaking the contempt and animosity in her eyes.

Maybe Paradise really was a mirage, Marco thought darkly, and shifted his attention back to the gray stretch of highway ahead.

The chartered flight from Miami to Boston hadn't been a pleasant one. The tropical storm that had wreaked havoc on South Florida last night was moving rapidly up the coast, which made for a choppy ride much of the trip.

Alberto Manzana hated flying anyway. When he'd heard what was involved, he had done his best to convince Victor not to send him on this particular mission, but his cousin had insisted. Alberto wondered if Victor didn't get perverse pleasure out of flinging his phobia into his face whenever he got the chance.

Alberto had tossed a vial of Valium into a zippered pocket of his bag before leaving the Miami compound, but when he reached for it just prior to takeoff, it was missing. In its place was a note in an unmistakable, bold dark scrawl: *Sorry, Berto—you must be fully alert for this one. Have a nice flight!*

Alberto had never had a nice flight in his life, and by the time the small propeller plane landed, he was white and trembling. His clothing reeked of body odor; he'd sweated profusely from the time they'd taken off in Miami.

He and two of Victor's colleagues, Ramon and Hondo, were greeted by a car that had taken them out into the working-class suburbs southwest of Boston. The driver worked for a longtime associate of Victor's who handled much of his business in the Northeast, and he had briefed them on the latest developments.

While they were in the air, Victor had been using his powerful underworld network to track the woman whose face had been flashed on television only hours before. It had been surprisingly simple to find her, thanks to a tip from some guy who'd been sitting near her in the stands.

Apparently, when Victor's operative had approached the guy, he had demanded cash for revealing what he knew. He'd said a reporter had just questioned him about the same woman, and what the hell did he look like, a free information service?

Alberto knew what that meant.

Someone else was on her trail.

And it sure as hell wasn't a reporter.

Now, as the car slowly passed the house that matched the scribbled address in Alberto's hand, he wondered, with a sinking feeling, if they might not be too late. He stared at the place through the car's tinted windows, thinking that it looked deserted, with the blinds pulled down and everything shut up tight.

"There's a car in the driveway." Ramon pointed at the Hyundai as they slowed at the curb. "She must be here."

"She must be," Alberto agreed, though something told him that she wasn't.

But even if that were true, it meant nothing.

She might simply have stepped out for a while, to get something to eat or run errands. There was no reason to jump to the conclusion that she'd been swept right out from under Victor Caval's nose by the only other person who would have been interested in learning her whereabouts.

If that had happened, Victor would be livid.

And when Victor got angry . . . Alberto put his hand on the door handle to get out.

"Stay put. I'll go." That had come from Ramon, a bossy little *comadreja,* in Alberto's opinion.

"I'll go," Alberto corrected, already opening his door.

Ramon cursed at him in Spanish.

Alberto cursed back.

"Let him go," Hondo barked at Ramon, as if he were fed up already with the bickering. Ramon had needled Alberto nonstop since they'd left Miami. *"What's the matter, Alberto? Poor baby is afraid to fly? Eh, Alberto?"*

"Cover me," Alberto said, mostly to Hondo, and got out of the car.

His shiny black shoes made a brisk tapping sound against the concrete as he walked swiftly across the sidewalk and up the path to the small cape-style house, his eyes and ears alert for any sign that she was inside.

His short legs carried his portly body up the three steps before the door, and he saw his reflection in the glass. He should have shaved, he thought, noticing the generous stubble covering his swarthy, pudgy face. And his dark hair was unruly as always, not to mention greasy from several days without being washed.

He reached into his pocket with his left hand as he rang the bell with his right.

Alberto's fingers closed over his pistol as he waited, and he repeatedly glanced over his shoulder, nervously checking the deserted street behind him.

Just as he was about to ring the bell again, he heard a voice behind him.

"She's not home."

Startled, Alberto spun around and saw an attractive blonde standing on the lawn. She wore snug Lycra workout clothes, and her hair was caught back from her pretty face in a high, bouncy ponytail.

"Excuse me?" he said, doing his best to keep his accent to a minimum. Behind his dark sunglasses, his gaze wandered downward from her face, lingering at the high swell of her breasts and the slim curve of her hips.

"You're looking for Lia, right? Lia Haskin?"

When he nodded, she said, "I'm her next-door neighbor. She's not around."

Alberto walked down the steps, conscious of a delicious tightening in his groin as he forced his eyes back up, away from her body. Though he was standing a few feet away, he could smell the fresh, herbal scent of her perfume or shampoo.

He could feel himself starting to tremble, seized by the impulse to grab her, to bury his face in her neck, to claw at her clothes until his fingers found her tender flesh ... He managed to control himself, forcing his mind back to the issue at hand.

A.J. Sutton.

aka Lia Haskin.

"Where is she?" he asked.

The blonde shrugged. "She left with some guy about twenty minutes ago."

"What did he look like?"

"He was gorgeous," the woman said, then narrowed her eyes at him. "Why do you ask? Who are you?"

"I'm her brother," he blurted, and instantly realized the alibi sounded lame. Anyone could tell by looking that he was not related to her. A.J. might have Latin blood, as he did, but she was fair and attractive, and a good twenty years younger than him.

The blonde stared at him in disbelief, then snorted and said, "Yeah, right."

Before he could respond, she went on, "You're here because of the guy she's seeing, right? I figured he was married or something. What are you, some detective his wife hired?"

Alberto shrugged, keeping quiet, letting her come up with a believable scenario.

"I can't believe I didn't find out what she was up to before now," she chattered on. "I mean, we talk—but it's not like she tells me anything about herself. She actually lies when she does. She said she wasn't involved with anyone, and then out she comes this morning, parading down the driveway with this golden Adonis. Christ, his hair is longer than mine, and he's better looking, too."

"He had long blond hair?" Alberto asked thoughtfully, just to be sure.

She nodded. "A big, brawny guy with a gorgeous face.

I can't understand why she'd want to hide someone like him, unless she's up to something," she added meaningfully, disapproval flashing in her big eyes. "Like sleeping with a married man. Or maybe he's a gigolo she hired?" she tacked on hopefully.

Alberto shrugged, tense at the realization that Marco Estevez had gotten to her first. Victor wouldn't like that. He wouldn't like that at all.

"I don't know who he is," he lied to the blonde. "Did you see where they went?"

"Nope. I was busy, just getting into the shower when they left, or maybe I would have come outside and checked it out personally."

Her words triggered a titillating image in his mind. She was naked, her slender body glistening with steamy water droplets and slippery soap suds.

Again he felt a stab of lust that threatened to block out everything else.

Remember Victor, he urged himself.

Remember your mission . . .

Deep in his pocket, his fingers clenched the pistol that he knew would allow him to do whatever he wanted with this pretty, sassy woman. All he had to do was show her the gun, bring her to some private place, then tell her precisely what he wanted her to do to him.

She would do it, he knew—they always did. She might beg and plead and cry, but she would eventually get on her knees at his command and she would pleasure him, and then he would rip off her clothes and have his fill of her before he strangled her.

Just as he had done to all the others, back in Bogota, before he'd been caught.

That was when Victor, the family's shining hero, had come to his rescue, no doubt at the urging of his mother, Aunt Maria, who also happened to be Alberto's godmother. Victor had never been particularly fond of Alberto, but he would do anything for his beloved *madre*.

And so he had hired some savvy lawyers, and he had pulled some strings and paid people off—and finally he had gotten Alberto out of there.

Then, to Alberto's surprise, Victor had given him a chance to come to Florida and work for him—on one condition. That Alberto control himself. No more women; no more killing—unless, of course, Victor himself ordered a hit.

He had, several times, but not nearly often enough for Alberto's taste. Anyway it wasn't the same, killing people on someone else's demand. Victor's victims were invariably men, and he was invariably told to execute them swiftly, which meant a few crucial elements were missing for Alberto.

He much preferred stalking and cornering women, hearing them plead and weep, watching his own powerful hands drain the life out of them until they were limp. It had been so very, very long since he'd had a woman, since he'd killed a woman.

Since he'd killed *anyone*.

Victor hadn't even ordered a hit in quite a while.

Not until now.

Not until A.J. Sutton.

She, too, had been a lithe, beautiful blonde, like the stranger standing before him. Many a night back at the mansion, before she had vanished, Alberto had lain in bed imagining her lean limbs wrapped around his waist, her slender fingers clawing at his back, her full lips screaming for him to stop.

Control yourself now, he thought seductively, *and you'll have your chance with her before you turn her over to Victor.*

He allowed his eyes to wander one last lingering time over the blonde's luscious body in her Spandex workout clothes. It was a shame he wouldn't have her.

But A.J. Sutton, he was certain, would be worth the wait.

Victor stared at his reflection in the mirror as he ran a comb slowly through his black hair, slicking it back from his face.

He was a handsome man, he thought contentedly, as he always did, turning his face slightly from side to side to examine all the angles. Handsome despite the newest network of faint lines that had recently worked their way into the corners of his eyes and mouth.

He was getting old before his time.

This business was making him old.

He would retire in a few more years—though he would never truly let his empire slip from his grasp. No, he would continue to keep tabs on things . . . but far enough removed so that the risks would be gone.

The risks of being caught . . .

Or being killed.

There had been a time when those very risks had exhilarated him, and each narrow escape from the authorities or a would-be assassin's hit would leave him feeling indestructible, and even more driven by greed and ambition.

Now, the risks that came with his line of work only infuriated him; robbed him of the ability to sit back and reap the benefits of all he had accomplished.

He sighed and picked up the small pair of gold-plated scissors on the black marble vanity top. He leaned toward the mirror and began to painstakingly trim his mustache, hearing his mama's voice in his ears.

"Always keep yourself well-groomed, Victor," she would say, nodding with approval at his clothes or hair-style. "If you look like you have it all together, people will believe that you do."

Mama had certainly been full of good advice. He wondered if she had ever realized, before she died, exactly how often and in what manner he had applied her words of wisdom to his life.

She might be appalled—and then again, she might have suspected what he was up to all along, he thought with a faraway smile. Mama was no naive fool. And though she was a church-going woman with a strict code of morals, she was also as shrewd as they came. She had always encouraged him to make it big.

She was thrilled that he ran a successful business in America, and never asked many questions about what he did. She just bragged about him to all her friends from the old neighborhood, with whom she insisted on keeping in touch even after he moved her to a stylish house in an upscale development.

Victor sighed, remembering how proudly she had worn the expensive clothes and jewels he had showered upon her as soon as he could afford it. He had buried her in a three-thousand dollar designer dress he bought just for the occasion.

His dear *Madre* was the only woman he had ever loved and respected.

Other women, he used—some for physical pleasure and some to aid him in his business ventures. To them, he was indifferent.

But some women—the few who had dared to cross him—he loathed.

A.J. Sutton was one of them.

Victor snipped fiercely at a tuft of hair and found the scissors slicing into his skin just below his right nostril.

"Ouch!"

He dropped the scissors, leaned closer to see the cut, and cursed in Spanish as a drop of blood fell onto his custom-made white linen shirt.

This, too, he glowered, was A.J. Sutton's fault.

She would pay dearly for everything she had done, Victor thought, narrowing his eyes at his reflection as he dabbed at the blood with a tissue.

Chapter Four

"Are you hungry?"

Marco's words startled Lia. She had been staring out the window at the road that in the past two hours had taken them across the length of the state and into the Berkshire Mountains of western Massachusetts. Traffic was heavy on the Pike as couples and families headed out to view the dazzling foliage that had transformed the rugged slopes and ridges into a kaleidoscope of reds and pinks and golds.

At first, Lia's hopes had been bolstered by the fact that they were surrounded by cars and people. She had thought that if she could just catch the eye of a passenger in a passing car, she might be able to mouth the word "Help."

But no one seemed to see her, and she had finally realized that the windows of the car were tinted.

Marco had thought of everything.

She had resigned herself to the knowledge that she was his prisoner, at least for now. And rather than finding promise in her proximity to other people, she grew more frustrated with every car that passed.

"Are you hungry?" Marco asked again, and she decided she might as well answer him.

She turned away from the window and saw that he wasn't looking at her. He rarely did, as if he didn't want to face her.

"Of course I'm hungry." She deliberately stared at him until he glanced her way, and then she caught his eye and held it as long as she could, glaring at him.

His mouth twitched, and she exulted that she was making him uncomfortable—And then he grinned.

The bastard grinned, and she wanted to throw herself on him and beat at him with her fists.

How dare you? a voice screamed in her mind. *How dare you forget what you and I had? How dare you find amusement in the fact that what I thought was love has changed to loathing?*

"Do you want something to eat?" he asked.

She swallowed the fury that had careened into her throat, threatening to choke her, and she managed to say, "Why? Are you going to stop at a rest area?"

If he did, she knew she would manage to escape. Somehow she would get away from him, even if she had to take the chance that he would fire at her.

Now his grin turned to a chuckle, and he shook his head. "What do you take me for, A.J.? A fool? Of course I'm not going to stop. Those places are crawling with people. But I have crackers in the car if you want them."

Crackers. She almost smiled, then found herself horrified that she had, even for a split second, forgotten that he was no longer the old Marco, the one she had loved.

He had always kept snacks stashed everywhere—in his car, even in his bedside table. Crackers, nuts, granola bars. He used to pull them out and start munching at the strangest times, and Lia used to tease him that he had the appetite of ten men, that if he wasn't careful, he was going to get pudgy.

Do you see an ounce of fat on me? he used to ask around a mouthful of something crunchy. And he would hold his arms up as if in invitation, and she would say, *Hmmm, let me inspect you.*

She would run her hands over his massive, muscular arms, his sculpted, hairless chest and lean, rippling abdomen, down his body to—"Do you want crackers?" he was asking, and Lia tore her thoughts back to the present.

Reality washed over her like a cruel splash of icy water, and she flinched at the pain and outrage of her situation.

"What's wrong?" he asked quickly. The concern in his voice caught her off guard, and again it was almost as if he were the old Marco, and she were the old A.J.

"Does something hurt?" he asked, still watching her. *Does something hurt.*

His words were so ludicrous she would have laughed if a lump hadn't suddenly risen in her throat.

Yes, something hurts, she wanted to tell him. *Everything hurts, because you're not who I thought you were, and even though I've known it for a year, I used to be able to shove the pain aside.*

Now I'm with you again, and it's torture, because I can't for one moment forget that you're not Marco, you're this dangerous stranger who's only going to destroy me.

"I'm fine," she said, and her tone was vicious.

He seemed about to say something, and then he shrugged as if he'd thought better.

After a few moments of silence, he asked, still looking at the road, "Well, do you want the crackers?"

"Okay." She thought that if she tried to put something in her mouth and swallow it, she would gag and choke. But he would have to let go of the gun, at least momentarily, to grab the crackers.

And when he did, she would grab it.

"They're in the glove compartment," he said. "Go ahead. Get them."

"I'd have to move my hands to do that." She couldn't keep the sarcasm from her voice. "And you said I'm not allowed."

"Is that so?" He sounded amused. "Well, in that case, I give you permission to move one hand. Just one. Your left. Open the glove compartment and take out the crackers. Go ahead."

"You bastard," she muttered, shaking her head. She didn't move.

"I thought you were hungry."

"Go to hell, Marco."

"I've been there," he said grimly. "And it's not a place I care to visit again."

Startled, she looked at him, saw that he was focused on the road. She could tell by his expression that he was somewhere else.

Hell.

She knew all about hell.

Uncle Bruce's home in Coral Gables was hell, disguised as a five-bedroom split-level on a manicured, gated half acre. He had money, but money had never mattered to Lia. Her own father had been well-off, and she'd never wanted for anything, not before her parents' death, or afterward.

Except love.

She had been enveloped in warmth and affection the first nine years of her life, when her doting parents showered her with their adoration. But she had been starved for love in her uncle's household, where even the housekeeper, Myra, was detached and callous.

Thankfully Lia had inherited her mother's vivacious

personality, so making friends at school wasn't a problem.

Her wild streak was. Now, looking back, she realized she had been thirsty for attention, any kind of attention.

Skipping classes, getting caught smoking and drinking, breaking curfew—she pulled all the classic teenage tricks. And she was punished. Uncle Bruce took away her television, and he grounded her, and he stopped her allowance for weeks at a time.

But he never once asked what was troubling her, whether she needed help. He never cared.

And after a while, she stopped caring that no one loved her.

She was too busy living it up. Somehow, despite her high school antics, her grades had been high enough to get her into an expensive private college in Vermont. There, financed by her inheritance, she'd had the time of her life while obtaining a degree in business. She'd joined a sorority, had mad flings with various rich boys, and spent a semester abroad, in Madrid, her junior year.

She'd also spent every penny of her father's bequest. All she had left when it was over were her mother's engagement and wedding rings, encrusted with diamonds and sapphires, and worth a fortune. She refused to sell them, but wore them both on a gold chain she'd had permanently soldered around her neck.

After graduation, longing for the sun and sea, she had returned to South Florida, wanting only to have fun. Uncle Bruce—obviously fearing he'd get stuck with her under his roof again—had helped her to get a South Beach condo, and a job as a research assistant in a law office in downtown Miami.

But it wasn't easy to get up and out by 8 A.M. when you spent every night drinking and dancing in the hopping clubs of South Beach. Lia had quickly lost that job, followed by a series of other entry-level positions.

"I'm just not cut out for office work," she had confided in her latest best friend, Juliana, who lived in the condo right above hers.

Juliana, who was around thirty, was stunningly beautiful with an incredible body—not uncommon qualities in glamorous Miami Beach. She wore sophisticated clothes and dazzling jewelry, drove a top of the line silver BMW convertible, and was known by name at the exclusive boutiques and clubs and restaurants frequented by celebrities and socialites.

She also happened to have no visible means of support, which had led Lia to speculate that she was someone's mistress.

How right she had been about that.

"I can set you up with a job," Juliana had promised when Lia had complained about being destitute. "My boyfriend's maid just quit and went back to Jamaica to get married. He's looking for someone, but he's pretty particular. He has to be careful who he hires."

"Maid?" Lia had echoed incredulously. For a moment, she was going to snip at Juliana that she might be desperate for a job, but she sure as hell didn't intend to be someone's household drudge.

"You're desperate, aren't you?"

"Not *that* desperate."

"It pays well."

"How well?"

The figure Juliana named caused Lia to gasp. She couldn't pass up a chance to earn that kind of money.

Juliana failed to tell her two things.

One was the nature of her boyfriend's business.

The other was that she'd be working in paradise.

Lia had never seen a home as lavish as Victor Caval's magnificent waterfront Spanish-Mediterranean-style mansion.

The house itself was a sprawling maze of breezy, high-ceilinged rooms and floor-to-ceiling windows that allowed spectacular views of the crystalline aqua waters of Biscayne Bay. The place was filled with designer furniture in Florida pastels, and Victor's vast collection of modern Hispanic art.

The surrounding grounds were a virtual Eden of courtyards and gardens, cascading fountains and waterfalls, boat slips, and a pool, sauna, and private gym.

Victor Caval insisted on interviewing Lia before hiring her, and she had found him to be an imposing man whose pleasant smile belied dark eyes that spoke of a no-nonsense core. He spoke briefly of his import-export business, which was based there at the house, and of the obvious need to maintain his privacy and the security of his home.

That was when Lia discovered that the meticulous landscaping concealed high stone walls and barbed wire, and that Victor had his own private security force on the premises. The main gate and waterfront were patrolled by armed guards, and the house was protected by an elaborate alarm system.

Lia found that unsettling, but she managed to ignore her misgivings. How could she turn down the terrific money, and the opportunity to work in such a spectacular setting? The work wasn't that difficult, and Victor was often out of the country on South American business.

He had told her she could use the pool and sauna when she was off duty, and to help herself to the constant, sumptuous spread of food in the gourmet kitchen.

Later, when she wondered how she could have been so blind to what was going on, she realized she had simply ignored the warnings in her mind. When she analyzed everything she had seen and heard over the year she had worked in the Caval mansion, she realized she had, of course, suspected all along that Victor's business might include—or *be*—illegal drug trafficking.

She had told herself, then, that it wasn't fair to jump to conclusions simply because he spent a lot of time traveling to and from his other home in Colombia, or because the Miami house was always crawling with burly young South American and Jamaican men.

It wasn't until she met Marco that any of it began to truly bother her. Maybe she sensed the danger that loomed.

But by then it was too late.

She was irrevocably entangled in Victor Caval's shadowy world—never suspecting that Marco himself was part of the drug lord's deadly regime.

Now she was his captive, and she had no doubt that Marco planned to deliver her to Victor like a prize steer to the slaughter. Why else wouldn't he have already killed her?

She looked at him, at his hard jaw set grimly as he appeared to concentrate on driving. But she knew by the way his hands clenched the wheel that his thoughts were on something else, and she couldn't help wondering what it was.

The moon had been full the night he had first lain eyes on her.

Marco remembered how it had bathed the grounds of the estate in soft, milky light reflected off the gently lapping waters of the bay.

He had arrived in Miami only that afternoon, and the hot, humid tropical air had felt sodden, filling his lungs and dampening his hair and clothing. When Victor had suggested that he use the pool once he'd settled himself in his room upstairs, he leapt at the invitation.

After stepping through the French doors that led from his air-conditioned guest room to a secluded terracotta terrace, he descended the flight of outdoor stairs and made his way along a winding path shielded by a jungle of blooming tropical foliage.

It had been late May, and the royal poinciana trees were ablaze with red flowers that seemed to glow like gems in the moonlight. Though the sun had set hours ago, the night air was hot against his bare skin, richly scented with fragrant flowers and the salty sea.

Marco had stepped swiftly through the hedges bordering the kidney-shaped pool, eager to plunge into the sparkling water . . . And then he had stopped and stared.

A beautiful woman was walking to the end of the diving board at the far end. Her hair was pale and flowed down her back; her face, bathed in the white glow of the moon, was breathtaking even from where he stood. She wore a barely there coral-colored bikini that accentuated her bronzed skin and showed off her long, willowy limbs, her lean, flat torso, and her high, full breasts.

Unaware of his presence, she had stood at the end of the board, bouncing slightly, surveying the water as if contemplating a dive.

Or maybe, he had later amended, replaying the memory as he often did, she had realized all along that she had an audience. Maybe she had felt the heat of his gaze; maybe she had enjoyed knowing she was being watched.

It wouldn't be unlike A.J. to tease a little, to play up the moment. She was a flirt, self-confident and brazen, and she'd always seemed to take great pleasure from knowing she was attractive to the opposite sex. Especially to Marco. She had, on more than one occasion after they became lovers, performed a saucy little striptease for him in the privacy of his guest room.

But that first night, she hadn't allowed his scrutiny to linger too long. She had bounced lightly a few more times, then soared gracefully off the board in a perfect swan dive, barely splashing as she hit the pool's surface.

He had strolled to the edge and was standing over her when she surfaced moments later, water streaming through her hair and glistening on her tanned skin. She looked right up at him, then did a lazy backstroke away from him, still watching him.

He was conscious of her eyes taking in his hard, muscular body and black swim trunks. He knew they weren't snug, nor nearly as revealing as the skimpy Speedo-style suits some men wore. But under her gaze he felt nude, not to mention aroused by the realization that this beautiful stranger was boldly evaluating his physical prowess.

"Aren't you coming in?" she had called, gliding effortlessly back into the deep end. "It feels fantastic."

"I bet it does," he murmured, and seconds later he was diving in himself, surfacing to find her on the distant edge of the pool.

"I give you a six," she said, laughing.

"What are you rating?" he'd asked. "My looks or the dive?"

"The dive." She kicked off the wall and swam playfully toward him. "Your looks . . . well, I'll have to let you know."

It wasn't until later, when they were out of the pool, joking and talking, that she'd suddenly interrupted herself, saying cryptically, "Ten."

"Excuse me?"

"Ten," she'd said meaningfully, a sparkle in her eye. "Your looks. I said I'd let you know."

She wasn't the first woman who had found him attractive, but she was the first who mattered.

And he had known, even that first night, that she could—that she *would*—become important to him. That was why he was reluctant to get involved; why he had such a difficult time with the probing personal questions she asked.

And there were countless questions.

"Where are you from?"

"California," he'd lied; the first of many.

"Really? What do you do?"

"I'm in finance."

"What are you doing here?"

"In Miami? It's a business trip, with pleasure mixed in. Especially now," he'd added with a meaningful glance at her.

"How do you know Victor?"

"He's a friend of a friend. We have a lot of the same business contacts, and I'm going to act as a . . . consultant of sorts. He invited me to stay here."

"For how long?"

"As long as I need to. Or want to," he'd added, looking her in the eye.

She'd nodded slowly, her straightforward gaze telling him what even she didn't dare voice. "That might be quite a while," was all she said.

When he'd asked her who she was and what she was doing at the estate, he'd been surprised by her answer. Somehow he hadn't taken her for a member of the household staff.

He had assumed she was one of the leggy beauties Victor liked to have on hand; the master of the house was a voracious ladies' man with several mistresses and a handful of hangers-on. Especially when he had noticed the two gem-encrusted rings she wore on a gold chain around her neck. When he asked her if they were a gift from some lover, and why she didn't wear them on her fingers, she'd told him curtly that it was none of his business.

So A.J. Sutton was simply the maid, and she told him so in no uncertain terms, as if daring him to find fault with that.

He hadn't of course. On the contrary, he'd been relieved to discover that she was apparently oblivious to her employer's extracurricular business affairs, not to mention charmed by her candid attitude and swept away by her beauty.

They had gone out for drinks later that night, slipping away without Victor's knowledge. Marco had insisted they be discreet, and she hadn't argued, though he'd seen an indignant flash in her eyes. She'd been distant, silent as they drove around in his red Jaguar, not melting until he put a CD of Latin music into the car stereo.

He hadn't argued when she'd casually suggested that they go to the ritzy Fontainebleau across the causeway on Collins Avenue, one of the most high-profile nightspots in Miami Beach. He could read her mind; she figured he might dump her tomorrow, so she might as well take him for all he was worth tonight. And she was testing him, wondering if he dared be seen among South Florida's most elite crowd with a woman who so insolently admitted she was a maid.

He didn't dare tell her that he had no intention of leaving her so soon; that if it was up to him, he might not want to leave her, ever.

But it wasn't up to him. And he couldn't afford to talk too much. Or care too much.

And so they'd drunk wine and they'd walked on the beach, past the gigantic pastel hotels and nightclubs with their pulsating Latin beat, and they'd kissed in the moonlight.

And Marco had almost convinced himself, as he had certainly convinced her, that he was just a vacationing businessman looking for some fun and sun.

Lies.

It always came down to lies; he had been telling them for so long that it was nearly impossible to remember where the imposter left off and the true Marco Estevez began.

It no longer mattered anyway, he thought, glancing

at the dark-haired woman beside him now, seeing the pain and fear and loathing mingled in her dark eyes when they collided with his.

She looked away quickly, but he could see her pale hands trembling on the dashboard, where he'd ordered her to keep them.

He'd had no choice, he thought, shoving aside a twinge of guilt. She was quick and clever; if he let his guard down for a moment, she'd escape . . .

Or grab his gun and kill him. .

He had no doubt she was capable of that, though some part of him longed to believe she still loved him. But he knew that was impossible.

Realistically anything she had felt for him would have died thirteen months ago. And in the few hours since he'd invaded her life once again, he certainly had done nothing to dispel her hatred of him.

He clenched his jaw, fighting the urge to open his mouth and say things he would regret. She wouldn't believe him anyway; she couldn't possibly understand. He knew what she thought of him—that he was a shrewd, ruthless liar.

And she was right.

So he would simply do what he had to do, and then he would move on, as he had been trained.

No dangerous distractions; no messy emotions; no looking back.

Not this time.

What he and A.J. had had was long over; dead and buried. That was where it would stay.

This haunted stranger beside him—Lia Haskin, she was calling herself—bore so little resemblance to the woman he had loved that it shouldn't be difficult for him to think of her as someone else altogether.

Except for the fleeting, unsettling moments when something familiar flashed in her eyes . . .

Fire.

Fire and ice . . .

The phrase drifted into his mind like strains of a familiar song from bygones days. It was how he'd always thought of her; had he ever told her, back when they were together? Or had he simply kept his observation to himself, the way he kept so many things to himself . . .

Maybe too many things, but what choice did he have?

Fire and ice.

That was her. All flaming passion—or anger—one moment; frosty detachment the next.

More fire than ice in the past, when they were lovers, but even then she was capable of suddenly donning a mask of cool reserve. It was a protective mechanism, he realized, and one that had caught him by surprise the first time he had witnessed it that first night they met.

He had mistaken her for a freewheeling what-you-see-is-what-you-get type; had assumed she was falling for him body and soul just as he was falling for her.

Only later did he realize that with her, physical intimacy didn't readily give way to emotional intimacy. She might not be guarded with her affections, but she was fiercely so with her emotions. He longed to grasp her, grasp *all* of her; to break down that chilly reserve, to convince her to trust him.

And yet how could he, when nothing he had told her was the truth?

Nothing but that he cared deeply for her.

She told him she felt the same, but he sensed all along that she was holding back.

Throughout that sultry Florida summer, whenever he got too close to reaching past the walls that shielded her heart, she retreated instantaneously. He couldn't blame her in the end; maybe she simply sensed that nothing was as it seemed, that he wasn't who he claimed to be.

And yet it captivated him, the way she could transform so rapidly from spitfire to ice princess before his eyes.

How fitting that she had finally vanished altogether that September night, as elusive in her absence over the past year as she had ultimately been in those fleeting months when they were together.

And now, as Lia Haskin, she was still fire and ice.

Far more ice than fire this time around.

If he let himself, Marco could get caught up in her enigma all over again; he could forget why he was here, why she was with him, that it was against her will.

But he wouldn't let himself forget.

He had a mission to execute, and the unavoidable reality was that it meant he must say goodbye to A.J. Sutton, or Lia Haskin, whoever she was—forever.

Thank God you never went and told him you loved him, Lia thought, staring out the window of the car at the nondescript scenery they were passing.

How many nights had the words found their way to her tongue, only to be forced back by a core of restraint that never failed to take her by surprise? One moment she would be lying there in his arms, swamped in her love for him, on the verge of spilling her emotions. The next, she would force herself back from the perilous precipice, retreating to a private, lonely, safe place.

Thank God she had always kept that ultimate distance from Marco, tempted as she was to cave in, to let him possess her completely. If she had done that, she would have no shred of strength to cling to now.

What was it that had caused her to hold back? As she scanned back over her memory, she was struck by how clearly she remembered certain times they had spent together—like the night they had met, and that idyllic weekend on Sanibel Island.

Yet others blended together into a murky montage of conversations and caresses, woven together with threads of passion—and, on her part, misgiving.

She had never really trusted him—not even in the good times. That much, she remembered. She couldn't pinpoint what, exactly, he had done to inspire her skepticism. But it was more than the fact that he was an incredibly fantastic-looking man who probably had women stashed all over the country.

She had sensed that he was filled with secrets, that with him, what you saw wasn't what you got.

Meanwhile, she had secrets of her own to keep.

She couldn't let him know how badly she had been hurt in the past; how alone she was now; how desperately she longed to find love and a stable future.

So she had guarded her heart, growing practiced in steeling it against Marco Estevez.

And the sooner she got the hang of doing that again, the better.

Victor Caval's cellular phone rang just as the waitress was setting an enormous platter of oysters and stone crabs before him. He nodded briskly at her, then waited until she'd walked away to remove the phone from his pocket and answer the persistent ringing tone.

"Victor," he grunted into the receiver, his eyes darting around the restaurant, which was crowded for noon on a Saturday.

That was fine with him. The more jammed the place was, the less attention people were likely to pay a well-dressed man dining alone in a crowd. He could count on conducting his business in relative privacy, provided he kept his voice low.

"Victor, it's me, Alberto," came over the phone, and then, *"Quiubo?"*

The mere sound of his cousin's voice never ceased to irritate Victor, and today his inane greeting sent fury coursing through Victor's veins.

How dare Alberto casually ask Victor what was up?

He *knew* what was up, must know, too, that Victor had been on edge ever since he'd dispatched his men to Boston, that he *never* put up with useless banalities in the first place.

His cousin sorely needed to be put in his place, but today Victor didn't have the time or energy to waste on Alberto.

He glanced around, then furtively demanded into the phone, "You've got her?"

It was more statement than question, and rage boiled through him when his cousin hesitated for a brief moment, telling him all he needed to know.

"I'm sorry, Victor—"

"Damn you!" he erupted, whispering fiercely, careful not to let other diners overhear. "I told you not to tip her off!"

"We didn't tip her off. She got away—"

"How could you let her get away? Where is she?"

"She's—don't worry, I have it under control. I got a description of the car from a little boy on the corner who saw it drive by—"

"A little boy? A little boy?" he mocked, his hand clenching the edge of the creamy yellow tablecloth. "You're relying on a child to provide—"

"It's all right," Alberto cut in, nerves making his voice higher pitched than usual. "We're right on her trail now, Victor. She's heading west on the Massachusetts Turnpike, and we're closing in on her car—"

"And what car are you talking about? We *have* a description of her car. I don't understand why the hell you'd need—"

"She didn't leave in *her* car," Alberto retorted, sounding smug.

If he had been there, in person, Victor would have cracked him across his fat face.

Conscious of the waitress setting a bowl of lemon wedges in front of him, he managed to control himself, asking evenly when she had departed, "Then whose car was she in?"

"It was a rental."

"A rental? And she was driving?"

A pause.

Victor clenched his teeth, wary of the people seated all around him in the elegant dining room. Miami's finest restaurant was no place for a vehement conversation with that fool Alberto.

He should never have sent his idiotic cousin on this mission . . .

And yet there had been several good reasons to do so.

One was that he enjoyed seeing Alberto squirm at the very thought of flying. He knew that his cousin must have suffered every mile of that overnight flight through a storm on a tiny chartered plane.

Besides, who else could he send on so sensitive a quest? Enrique would have been the ideal choice, but he hadn't answered his page last night. Even if he had, Victor would still have insisted that Alberto go along.

As far as he knew, it had been years since Alberto had raped and murdered a woman. His thirst to kill would have been sated somewhat by the grisly hits Victor had ordered, but his lust for power, for sexual dominance, would be at a fever pitch after so many years.

Victor's mouth had stretched into a grin the first time he had considered the image of A.J. Sutton falling into Alberto Manzana's clutches. Now it did so again, and he felt his anger abating just a bit at the thought.

His cousin was just the man for the job; and of course Alberto knew better than to kill his victim when he was through with her.

That honor would belong to Victor, and he would relish every minute of it, making it last.

Who would ever have guessed that Juliana's "bubbleheaded party girl" would turn out to be Victor Caval's arch-nemesis?

So many times over the past year, he had gone over what had happened, wondering if he somehow could have anticipated the trouble A.J. Sutton had caused him. But he had checked her background thoroughly, and he had been satisfied that she was a safe bet.

So he had hired her.

Who would guess that his *maid* would botch what should have been a simple, routine procedure?

Who would expect A.J. Sutton to slip away without a trace, leaving Victor to fret that one day she would surface to destroy his entire empire?

And his empire had expanded beyond his wildest dreams since he'd added heroin trafficking to his already successful cocaine business two years ago. Victor had always been steps ahead of the other drug cartels; he'd been one of the first to see the potential in bringing premium Colombian heroin to the United States. He had no intention of losing his edge because of some meddling maid.

Ramon and the others had assured him he was merely being paranoid about her, that it was a fluke that A.J. Sutton had been there that night. That she knew nothing about his business—nothing that mattered.

And sometimes, when he went over everything in his mind, he was inclined to believe that.

She had seemed too naive up until that point, too oblivious to what was going on in his home.

But the fact remained that she had been there, and

she had gotten in the way. Victor wasn't taking any chances.

She had to be destroyed.

"She was driving this rental car?" he questioned Alberto again, impatience taking over again and making his Spanish accent heavier than usual.

"No, she wasn't driving."

"No? Who was?" he barked.

There was a moment of silence.

And in that moment, Victor sensed what had happened. He heard the dreaded name in his mind before it spilled from Alberto's lips.

"Marco Estevez."

Chapter Five

"New York," Marco muttered as they passed the welcoming sign at the border. Lia looked up at him, then at the road. They were still passing through mountainous terrain, and the sun had faded to storm clouds that cast the landscape in filmy gray shadows. The traffic had grown more sparse as they headed west toward Albany, and it was well past one o'clock.

Her arms were aching, and her fingertips had gone from pins and needles to numb from the discomfort of remaining absolutely still on the dashboard.

She refused to complain or to let him see that she was suffering.

But if he didn't stop the car soon, her bladder was going to be a problem. She would need to use a rest room in the near future, and resigned herself to the realization that she would have to tell him. She figured he wouldn't be amenable to visiting a crowded highway rest area, but maybe he'd agree to let her go into the bushes at the side of the road. Distasteful as she found the idea, it might just be the chance she needed, to make a break for it.

He would have to stop eventually anyway; he would presumably have to answer nature's call himself at some point. Preventing her escape would be his problem, she reasoned.

For a few moments, she watched the scenery zip by, wishing he would allow the speedometer to creep over the limit so that a hidden state trooper would come careening after them with sirens wailing. He'd always liked to drive fast, she remembered, recalling the hot summer nights when they would dash around Miami in his red Jaguar.

No.

She didn't want to think about the past.

She cleared her throat. "Where are we going?" she dared to ask, surprised to hear herself sounding almost conversational, if not entirely pleasant.

But she was suddenly weary of harboring such intense hostility; it drained her of strength she would need if she was going to survive this ordeal.

For the moment, at least, she was resigned to being the prisoner of Marco Estevez.

"I can't tell you specifically," he said, his own voice equally civil.

To her surprise, he added after a moment, "But you're going to be all right, A.J. You have to trust me on that."

His words stunned her, and she had to fight the impulse to tell him that she believed him, that she would trust him to take care of her.

Looking at him, she thought it would be so easy to conclude that he was still the man she had fallen for so swiftly and so foolishly. Her body remembered what her mind was fighting to forget—how he used to moan when she entangled her fingers in his long, wild mane, how his sandpaper cheek felt against her breast in the mornings, how he turned lazily to take her into his arms and love her again and again . . .

Lord, how he could love her. His virile body had been insatiable; all she had to do was purr softly in his ear and he would be aroused to claim her.

And even after all she had been through, after all the time that had passed and all the bitterness she had endured, she was shocked to realize that she still wanted him.

Physically.

Her body lusted for him, while her heart and mind repelled the very idea. Sitting here, inches from that massive, masculine body, she was battling urges that were so alarmingly primitive, so unseemly and impossible, that her mind was utterly horrified.

And yet some tiny portion of her heart was not. Somewhere deep inside, she clung to the remote hope that this was all an enormous mistake, that Marco wasn't her archenemy, but her hero, as she had once believed.

Fat chance of that.

Face reality, Lia.

"My name isn't A.J., Marco," she snapped tightly. "It's Lia. And my God, you must be joking. Why would I trust you?" She looked pointedly at the gun in his hand.

"This? It's . . . it's for your own good," he faltered, not looking at her.

She seized his momentary lapse in command; she spouted caustic amusement. "Shooting me would be for my own good? You know, Marco, it's funny, but I never looked at it quite that way."

"You don't understand now, A.J.—Lia. But I promise you will someday."

"You *promise*? That's an even better joke. You've never made a promise in your life."

"Not to you."

Startled, she stared at him. "No, not to me. But that's fine, Marco, because I never asked you to make promises, did I? I never asked you to promise you were telling me the truth about your past, and what you were doing at Victor's compound that night. I never asked you to promise not to abduct me or pull a gun on me, and I sure as hell won't ask you to promise not to shoot me now. Is that satisfactory to you, Marco?"

Her voice had become shrill, and she hated herself for betraying her emotions. She felt tears welling in her eyes and cursed them, cursed the lump that threatened to choke her.

And when a sob rose and threatened to escape her, she instinctively gasped and brought her hands to her mouth, as if she could contain it somehow.

Too late, she realized she'd disobeyed his command to keep her hands on the dash.

On the heels of that thought came a defiant *who cares?* She looked at him, still clasping her hands to her mouth, defying him with her eyes, daring him to shoot her.

He didn't.

She could sense his uncertainty, though, and the way his hand tightened on the gun as he said, "Get your hands back where I can see them."

"No."

Her outburst of refusal stunned her more than it did him, judging by the way he glanced at her.

He shrugged. "I'm still the one holding the gun."

"Do you think I'm a fool? I'm not going anywhere, Marco. I don't feel like getting shot in the back just yet. But my hands and arms are killing me, and I can't hold them there anymore. I need a break."

"I'm sure you do, but—" He glanced in the rearview mirror and broke off, cursing under his breath.

"What?" She turned and saw a car on their tail, so close that it couldn't be anything but a chase.

"Duck," Marco ordered, stepping on the gas.

"No!" she shrieked, turning in her seat and waving her hands at the car behind them, forgetting they couldn't see her.

"What the hell are you doing? Get down!" he thundered, wrestling with the steering wheel as they went around a curve at high speed.

The other car had accelerated and was right on their tail. She couldn't discern much about the passengers, except she glimpsed that there were four, and they were men, and they didn't appear to be familiar.

"Help!" she screamed, waving at them. It had to be the police, or the FBI, or something. She exulted that rescue was so close at hand, and unleashed a string of expletives at Marco when he again ordered her to get her head down.

"Go ahead and shoot me, you bastard," she shouted at him. "The police are right there behind us to see you do it."

Almost instantaneously she heard a popping noise.

It was gunfire.

But it wasn't coming from Marco's gun.

It had come from the car that was chasing them.

Lia froze in terror.

Instantly she was carried back to that bloody night last September. Her mind swooped back over the months, reliving the horror of what she had witnessed.

When Marco grabbed her head roughly and thrust her down toward the floor of the car, she didn't resist. Huddled there, vaguely aware of the squealing tires and shots being fired, she closed her eyes, blanking it all out, remembering . . .

* * *

It had started so innocently.

Marco had told her, one afternoon not long after Labor Day, not to wait at the mansion for him after her shift that evening, as she had taken to doing—secretly of course.

Marco insisted that no one, not even her friend, Juliana, know that they were lovers. Though she balked at the notion he might be ashamed of his involvement with a maid, he had insisted that wasn't the case.

He just didn't want to anger Victor, he had claimed—his host might assume she was neglecting her duties, and fire her.

He was probably right, Lia had grudgingly concluded. She had overheard Victor ranting on many occasions, and wasn't particularly eager to be the target of his anger.

And anyway, she had ultimately been titillated by the idea of a forbidden affair—most of the time. She was no innocent, but never in her life had a man turned her on the way Marco did. The fact that they had to sneak around made their encounters all the more exhilarating.

"Why shouldn't I wait tonight? Aren't you in the mood?" she'd teased that fateful afternoon, running her red-painted fingernails lightly down his broad chest.

"I'm always in the mood for you," he'd growled, hauling her into his arms and kissing her deeply—only after making certain they were alone in the upstairs hallway of course. "I won't be back until late tonight, though."

"I can wait. We can go out, my treat. It's payday." She had reached into her pocket and waved the envelope full of cash that represented two weeks' pay. Marco paid her off the books, which was fine with her.

"I'd love to," he said, and she could see his regret, "But I've got things to do. Go back to your condo, A.J. I'll see you in the morning."

And he kissed her again.

The intimate caresses of his lips and tongue had left her trembling with desire. As she bustled about her afternoon housework, she found herself fantasizing about Marco's lovemaking the night before.

He had dared to sneak her into his room for the first time, and there, in his king-sized guest bed, he had pleasured her through the wee hours. It was dawn before they'd drifted to sleep, only to wake an hour later and scramble for their clothes and a brief, temporary goodbye.

As she went about her work that day, she wanted nothing more than to lie naked on his satin sheets again tonight, and feel his big body moving over her, inside her. Tantalizing images darted through her mind, sensual and distracting, saturating her with lust.

When her shift ended, she went to the kitchen to call a cab; her car was in the shop again. The house seemed strangely deserted, which was unusual; though Victor was often gone, there were usually a handful of his cronies hanging around.

She decided to have something to eat before calling the cab, and took her time cutting some luscious mangoes and melons into a fruit salad. When she had finished eating, she again headed for the phone to make her call, yawning as last night's lack of sleep caught up to her.

But somehow she found herself walking right past the phone, up the back stairs to the second floor. After only a slight hesitation, she continued down the hall to the east wing at the back of the house, facing the water, where Marco's spacious guest room lay. She tentatively let herself in, opening the door to the terrace to let in the scented night air. She curled up on his big bed, thinking she was so tired she'd simply lie down and take a short nap before going home.

Sure.

She had known all along that she intended to spend the night in his bed, planning to surprise him when he returned from wherever he had gone.

But it was easier to tell herself, later, that her being caught in the mansion that night was a mistake; that fate, and not her own raging desire, had been responsible for what happened.

It was well after midnight when a sound woke her. Tires on the gravel and a car door slamming; no, several car doors, just below her terrace.

And hushed voices.

Something was going on.

She slipped over to the window and peered out just in time to see several masked men removing two large bundles from the trunk and carrying them toward the house.

Only later would she realize they were the hooded, bound figures of a woman and child.

Her heart was pounding as A.J. crept to the top of the stairs. Two voices were arguing below in fast-paced Spanish.

Her mother had taught her the language when she was a child, and her semester in Spain had made her nearly fluent. She was able to recognize Ramon and Enrique, two of Victor's cronies, and to understand that they were discussing an abduction.

It wasn't until later, through newspaper articles she read during those first days on the run, that she would learn the identity of the victims.

Karen Trask, age thirty-seven, was the pretty young wife of Gavin Trask, a special agent with the Miami DEA.

Tyler Trask, nine, was an only child; his parents' pride and joy.

There were few people in Miami that September who hadn't heard of Gavin Trask. He had the reputation for being a hard-nosed, fearless agent who had vowed not to be frightened off by "cowardly underworld slime."

He'd only come to South Florida the previous spring, as head of a special task force investigating the sudden rise in heroin smuggling through South America. The newspapers were full of Trask's propaganda that summer, about how the stuff coming in from Colombia was "killer pure" compared to Asian heroin, how it was responsible for doubling the number of emergency room OD cases in the past year in South Florida alone.

Apparently not only was Victor involved in the drug trade, as A.J. had suspected, but he was trafficking both cocaine and heroin, and he was none too happy about Gavin Trask's warpath attitude.

She fought the panic that sliced through her and forced herself to remain absolutely silent, listening as Ramon and the others dragged their victims into a downstairs pantry closet.

Crouched at the top of the stairs, she could hear the muffled sounds of a little boy sobbing, and recoiled in horror when she heard a sharp, abrupt sound and Ramon hissing, "Shut the hell up, you brat, or the next time it won't be my fist."

"Easy, Ramon," came Enrique's voice. "Victor wants them alive. He just wants to scare Trask, remember?"

Ramon's muttered reply was unintelligible, and she heard them retreat to the front of the house, still arguing.

A.J.'s mind was whirling.

How could Enrique be involved in the dastardly plot? She had always liked the quiet, mild-mannered young bodyguard.

Besides, he and Marco had even seemed to grow friendly over the past few months.

In fact, a few times, A.J. had caught Enrique looking at her with a knowing gleam in his brown eyes, as though he were aware that she and Marco were involved—and disapproved.

Now she prayed she'd been wrong about that, suddenly terrified of what Victor and his men were capable of doing to anyone who crossed them in the slightest manner.

She couldn't bear to think of anyone hurting Marco—Marco!

What if unwittingly he returned home to the mansion amid the chaos below? For the moment, that prospect was enough to send A.J.'s senses reeling.

Then she was struck by a far more disturbing notion; one that rocked her very core.

What if Marco was actually one of them; *involved* in the abduction plot?

It seemed preposterous, and yet . . .

She had always sensed that Marco Estevez was a man of many secrets, significant ones.

The thought had even crossed her mind, more than once in the months since she'd gotten involved with him, that he might be married. That would explain why he insisted on keeping their relationship clandestine.

There were other clues, too, that he was hiding something.

He wore a pager; nothing unusual about that, but it went off at all hours of the night. He never returned the calls with her in the room, but always sought privacy, and was prone to urgent, whispered conversations.

And he often seemed to get a veiled look in his piercing blue eyes, a look that hinted of secluded, private places existing in his mind, places she dared not seek to venture.

She had private places of her own, and she respected his.

Now, with a sickening feeling in her stomach, she acknowledged that his being married was something she just *might* be able to handle . . .

Compared to the alternative.

As she crouched by the stairs that night, considering that Marco might not be merely secretive, but dangerous, she regretted, for what would be the first of many times, her heart's willingness to overlook his mystery.

As she slipped down the shadowy stairs, spurred by adrenaline and fear, she wasn't thinking straight, her mind blurred by possibilities she didn't want to consider.

If she had stopped to consider her most sensible course of action, she would have returned to the upstairs guest room to call the police.

Or she would have, upon reaching the first-floor hallway, slipped out the back door and, somehow, past the guards who were always on patrol.

She didn't realize her intention until she found herself reaching into the pocket of her uniform for the master key she kept there, the one that opened every door in the house except those leading to Victor's private quarters that were off-limits even to her.

Her feet, clad in their sensible white rubber-soled shoes, carried her across the familiar kitchen and pantry floor plan to the closet, and she swiftly fit the key into the lock, hoping she wasn't too late to free the anonymous victims.

Though she didn't know who they were then, or why they were being held, she had no doubt that they were innocent pawns in some dirty game of Victor's.

The child's earlier cry of pain and fear had pierced her heart, and all she could think was that she had to help and there was no time to waste.

She heard a frightened whimper as she opened the door.

"It's all right," she whispered, hurriedly pulling the burlap hood from the smaller figure, then the larger.

Her eyes met the wide, frightened, identical gazes of a mother and son, and she raised a finger to her lips, shaking her head to indicate that it wasn't safe to speak.

She yanked on the rope binding the little boy's hands behind him, and found it too intricately knotted to be untied. Rapidly she went for a pair of sturdy scissors in the pantry drawer, and cut first the little boy's arms and legs free, and then the woman's.

"You have to go," she told them, her voice barely a whisper. "Out the back, to the water. That's the safest way. I'll let you out."

They nodded mutely, and she mouthed, "Ready?"

Another nod, and she beckoned them to follow her from the closet to the back door several yards across the deserted kitchen. There was a double dead bolt on it, requiring a key to unlock it from the inside as well. She thanked God that she kept that in her pocket, too, and hurriedly pulled it out now.

She was holding her breath as she jabbed it into the keyhole and turned. It stuck for a moment, then responded with a click that seemed louder than a clap of thunder in the silent house.

"Go," she whispered, and they didn't wait to be urged again.

She allowed herself to watch for only a split second as the mother grabbed her little boy's hand and they dashed off into the shadows.

Trembling, A.J. turned and scurried for the stairs, intending to conceal herself in Marco's room again, until morning. No one would ever have to know that the hostages hadn't somehow freed themselves.

She had just put a foot on the bottom step when two chilling things happened simultaneously.

Outside, there was a sudden explosion of noise and action: running feet and shouted commands, mingled with terrified screams and the unmistakable report of gunfire.

Inside, strong arms reached out from the shadowy nook beside the stairs and grabbed A.J. She gasped as she recognized the glint of a pistol and the familiar blue eyes of the man she loved.

"Marco—God, no!" she cried out, wrenching herself from his grasp.

He reached for her again and she impulsively lifted her leg sharply until her knee made contact with the sensitive flesh between his thighs.

She heard his cry of agony as she turned and ran, making her way to the front of the house as the flurry of activity continued out back.

She was out the front door before she heard the footsteps pounding behind her, and never looked back as she dashed out the front gate, temporarily abandoned by the guards as they went after the fleeing woman and child out back by the bay.

Later she was glad she hadn't turned to see Marco chasing her down like a hunter tracking a frightened doe.

She was thankful, too, that there was no moon that night, unlike the night they met.

She was able to slip in total darkness through the deserted streets, crouching behind cars and beneath bushes, trying not to think about the reptiles and other stealthy creatures that might be sharing the tangled tropical undergrowth.

As she made her way through the night, she tried not to think about that poor woman and child being gunned down in cold blood.

And she tried not to think that if he spotted her, Marco might do the same thing to her.

She knew he must be dogging her, though she never saw him. She imagined him stalking her, that steely gun poised beside his handsome face as it had been back at the house, when he'd grabbed her.

Finally, after scrambling through one silent, empty alley and yard after another, she stopped for a rest.

And when she dared emerge into an open space and found herself alone, she realized he'd apparently lost her trail.

At least for now.

She figured he'd assume she'd head back to her apartment sooner or later, and knew she couldn't risk it.

That was when she knew what she had to do.

It hadn't been difficult to find a cab on the outskirts of the thriving Coconut Grove district. The driver didn't speak English—something she'd been counting on—and was willing to take her to Fort Lauderdale when she flashed two hundred dollar bills from the envelope that was still in her pocket.

Miami's bus station was the first place they would look for her, but hopefully they wouldn't think of Lauderdale. Once there, she camped out near two drunk college-age girls who had turned their backs on their suitcases. Stealthily she unzipped the nearest one and managed to remove leggings and a University of Florida T-shirt.

She hurriedly put them on in the bathroom, then hopped on the next bus that was departing, paying for her ticket with cash. She found herself crossing the panhandle early the next day, and was in Louisiana by nightfall.

Even if Victor and Marco tracked her this far, they would assume she had gone on to Texas and left the country.

She had no intention of doing that. Passing through Customs would be far too risky.

New Orleans' colorful, bustling French Quarter was crawling with hookers and transvestites and runaways and junkies, and no one paid much attention to a bedraggled young blonde with a haunted look in her eyes.

Pawnshops were plentiful.

She forced herself to walk into one and show the sleazy looking broker her mother's wedding and engagement rings, dangling from the gold chain soldered around her neck, where they had been for years. She'd had to break the chain to get them off, and her fingers trembled violently as she placed her most treasured possessions in the grubby, eagerly outstretched hand.

When she walked out of that pawnshop, her cash supply was replenished several times over.

Her heart and soul were barren.

She spent the next few days holed up in a seedy hotel, altering her appearance until she was confident she bore little resemblance to the young woman whose photo was splashed across every newspaper in the country.

Victor, Marco, and their cronies weren't the only ones after her.

The FBI wanted to question her in connection with the murder of Karen Trask, who had been shot to death at the edge of the bay behind Victor Caval's compound. The child, Tyler, had escaped into the water when his mother shielded him from the bullets with her own body.

He had identified Caval's maid, A.J. Sutton, as the woman who had freed him and his mother from a closet at the Caval mansion. The poor child was traumatized, unable to say who had taken him, or why.

Victor Caval had claimed no knowledge of the abduction, and had cooperated fully with the investigation, allowing a search of his home. He claimed to have been set up by a rival "businessman" who had planted the hostages on his property, and admitted that though his guards had shot at them as they fled, they'd assumed they were intruders who might have robbed the place. He himself had an airtight alibi for that evening; he had been in Orlando, having dinner with a highly visible local politician.

With no concrete evidence against Caval—not for the abduction and murder nor for drug trafficking—he was a free man.

As for the missing maid, according to the papers, A.J. Sutton was, quite possibly, dead.

An eerie feeling came over her as she read that, sitting in a dingy coffee shop in the French Quarter.

And she realized it was true.

A.J. Sutton was dead . . .

And thus, Lia Haskin was born.

The woman beside Marco was motionless on the floor, and as he steered the car wildly along the winding highway, swerving to avoid the smattering of other traffic, he struggled not to contemplate what that might mean.

Flooring the gas pedal, he managed to put some distance between his rental and the vehicle in relentless pursuit, and when he rounded a wooded curve and spotted a narrow opening between the trees, he seized the moment.

"Hold on!" he hollered to Lia.

With a curse and a prayer, he jerked the wheel to the right, and the car careened over the gravelly shoulder, violently bumping across the short distance toward the dense forest. He clenched the wheel to keep control, hitting the brake several times to slow the car as it narrowly shot between the trees, along a wooded path that was mercifully clear of trees and debris.

Finally Marco brought the car to a rest and allowed himself a shuddering sigh when he realized they'd evaded their stalkers.

Then he reached gingerly toward the woman crumpled on the floor beneath the passenger's seat.

"A.J.?" he said tentatively, and touched her unnaturally dark hair.

"Lia?" he modified, when she was silent.

His massive frame trembled violently as he lifted her limp body from the floor and cradled her in his arms, looking down at the face that in slumber looked heart-wrenchingly familiar at last.

How many times had he watched her as she slept in his arms?

How many times had he stroked her cheek, then let his hand slip down to her breast to feel her beating heart?

Now he did just that, relieved when he discovered that her heart was strong and regular. He examined her and saw that there was no bloody gunshot wound.

She had merely fainted.

For a moment, he was too weak with relief to move. Then, knowing there wasn't a moment to waste, Marco opened the door on his side. He got out of the car and tucked his gun into the holster hidden beneath his brown jacket.

Then he bent and slid his hands gently beneath Lia's back and her thighs, lifting her from the seat.

"We can't stay here," he whispered, cradling her against his chest.

As he set out through the dense forest, his strong arms barely straining beneath their fragile burden, he softly called her name to make sure she was still unconscious.

The only sounds that met his ears were chirping birds and twigs snapping beneath his feet.

Satisfied that she was still adrift in some far-off place, Marco allowed himself to dip his head lower, to plant a single, fleeting kiss on her hair before he turned his attention to the grim journey ahead.

Marco was kissing her hair, holding her in his arms.

Good . . .

Oh, so good . . .

Marco was with her. That meant everything was all right.

Lia had been so scared . . . so alone. Marco had been angry . . . or was he gone? Yes, he was gone, for a long, long time. And she couldn't find him . . . or was it he who couldn't find her?

It was so confusing . . .

Everything was always so confusing.

But, wait . . .

It wasn't real.

She must have had a nightmare.

No . . .

She was dogged by a sense of urgency, of being on the move.

She was *still* having a nightmare. That was it. She was still running, still frightened . . .

Only Marco wasn't chasing her; Marco was running with her. Carrying her.

Did that make any sense?

You're dreaming, her own voice cut into her fog-shrouded mind. *None of it's real. Any second now you're going to wake up and you're going to be in your bed in the South Beach condo, and Marco will be sleeping next to you, and the sun will be streaming in the windows . . .*

Except that wouldn't happen, she thought, bemused, because Marco never spent the entire night in her bed.

He always left, often while she was still asleep, so that she would awaken to find herself alone. And then she would feel that horribly empty sense of abandonment, less acute than it had been in her childhood when her parents had left her, yet still . . .

They'd had no choice.

Marco did.

Why do you always have to leave? she demanded of Marco, frustrated. If she weren't so groggy, she would really be angry. She *deserved* to be angry. Why didn't he want to stay with her?

I should wake up, so that I can ask him about it.

But maybe that wasn't such a good idea . . .

She was still so tired, so very tired . . .

And anyway, dreams were sometimes more pleasant than real life.

So she continued to drift, slipping further into a surreal world that sometimes made more sense than her life did.

Chapter Six

"*Mucho ojo!*"

"Look out!"

"Oh, Christ," Alberto muttered, then closed his eyes and braced himself against the seat in front of him. He clutched his gun, which he'd just reloaded, tightly in his lap and prayed.

The speeding car hurtled forward, narrowly sideswiping a slow-moving truck that was blocking the left lane of traffic, with a Peter Pan bus alongside it on the right.

They bumped over a slight embankment onto the grassy median, nearly hitting a stand of trees before the cursing driver brought the car to a halt.

There was a moment of silence before an eruption of angry Spanish.

Finally Alberto barked, "*Basta!* That's enough!"

The abrupt silence that fell over the car gave him a deep-seated satisfaction that helped—if only a little—to diminish the sick feeling in his stomach. He didn't want to think about what Victor would say when he found out Marco Estevez and A.J. Sutton had given him the slip yet again.

"If we keep going, we can catch up to them," Ramon said, stroking his black beard the way he did when he was agitated. His small, close-spaced eyes were intent on the road ahead, and his small, wiry body seemed poised with tension.

He was tightly wound, that one, Alberto thought. You never knew when he was going to explode. He knew Ramon was a true mercenary, snatched by Victor from the ranks of a notorious Colombian cartel several years back.

The other man Victor had selected for this mission was equally formidable. His name was Hondo, which, as Victor had once significantly told Alberto, was an ancient Egyptian word meaning "war."

Alberto had never once seen Hondo smile in the six months or so he had been around, though he had, on occasion, bared his white teeth in a snarl. He was a sleek, beautiful man, much like a crouching panther—a magnificent yet formidable creature. His mammoth, towering body was sculpted of rippling muscle, his skin the blue-black of asphalt in the sun. He seldom spoke, but his inky eyes reflected a soul that was incapable of compassion.

That, Alberto knew, was what Victor admired about Hondo. Personally, Alberto—who himself couldn't be considered compassionate by any stretch of the imagination—was secretly petrified of the man.

Hondo was a part of the Jamaican posse that collaborated with Victor to fly cocaine—and more recently heroin—by private plane from Colombia to an illegal landing strip in Jamaica. From there the cargo was transferred to boats and transported to South Florida, where Victor's vast underground syndicate took over its distribution.

The posse was notorious even among the narcotic-smuggling underworld, where violence was a way of life. Alberto had heard the stories of torture, mutilation, and grisly murder that went beyond even his own wildest imaginings.

Alberto did his best to stay away from Hondo and the other posse members. He wouldn't dream of letting Victor suspect how badly they frightened him. Knowing Victor, he would find his cousin's fear amusing. He wouldn't balk at using it against him someday; Victor's power depended in part on delving for someone's weak spot and exploiting it.

He thought back to a time when they were both teenagers back in Bogota, when their grandmother's girlhood friend had come to visit from Brazil. With her was her granddaughter, Lydia, a voluptuous blonde who was spilling out of her snug, low-cut minidress. The moment Alberto had lain eyes on her, his trousers had grown uncomfortably snug in front. Victor, of course, had noticed and snickered, drawing Lydia's attention to the situation.

For a week, Lydia stayed at their grandmother's house, and Alberto was beside himself with desire. Of course, at first, he hardly dared hope that a buxom beauty like her would want a squatty, pudgy, acne-faced boy like him. It was Victor, his older, far more handsome cousin, who had planted the seeds in Alberto's mind.

"I think she likes you, Berto," Victor had said one day, and then later, "She told me she thinks you're sexy."

Alberto could have sworn Victor and the other male cousins were laughing behind his back, as they always did. But he wanted so badly for Lydia to want him the way he wanted her, that he started to believe it.

Finally, the night before she was to leave town, Victor

gave him a note he said was from Lydia. It said simply, "Meet me in the garage loft tonight."

Of course he had.

And of course, what he had seen, when he had opened the door to the garage loft, was Victor's naked backside as he pumped furiously into a naked, writhing Lydia. She'd been oblivious to Alberto's presence.

But Victor, as though he'd been waiting for Alberto to show up, had turned his head expectantly. And in the split second before he began to groan with his passionate release, he had flashed a fleeting, sly grin at Alberto.

In that moment, Alberto had been devastated.

And, later, filled with a growing rage that was compounded every time a woman spurned his advances.

But even though Alberto had eventually found an outlet for his anger toward women, he still cowered at the thought of being on Victor's bad side.

Victor's vast power and wealth had saved him when he'd found himself in trouble several years back.

But Victor also had the capability of destroying Alberto.

The mere thought of angering his cousin by botching this assignment made sweat trickle from Alberto's already perspiring brow.

He cleared his throat and barked at the driver, "Get moving. Let's go after them."

The swarthy, pug-nosed man shook his head, explaining in Spanish that they'd already lost the other car.

Infuriated, Alberto said, "If we sit here arguing, some cop is going to come by and stop to see what's going on. We're lucky we haven't run into one yet. And in the meantime, they're going to get even farther ahead."

"Put a move on it," Ramon chimed in from the backseat. "They can't be that far away. We don't have time to waste."

The driver shook his head stubbornly.

Alberto opened his mouth, but before he could speak, he saw a sudden flash of movement from Hondo, who was seated behind the driver. Something glinted in his hand, and he reached forward in a lithe, skillful movement.

A split second later, the driver was gurgling his last breath from a throat that had been nearly severed.

Alberto gasped and recoiled in astonishment as blood spurted over him in the front passenger seat.

"What have you done?" he blurted.

Ramon, too, seemed stunned—but only for a moment. "What are we supposed to do with him now?" Ramon demanded of Hondo. "Dump his body out here in the middle of the highway?"

"Drive," Hondo commanded darkly in return. "You. Go ahead."

Shrugging, Ramon got out of the car and went around to the front. After a moment's hesitation, he shoved the driver's hideous body from its upright position, so that it toppled onto the seat beside Alberto.

Alberto cringed and moved closer to the door, briefly thinking that the blood had better come out of his silk shirt.

"There's blood spattered on the windshield," Ramon observed as he steered the car toward the road again, and commanded, "Clean it up, Alberto."

He wanted to protest, but was conscious of Hondo's stealthy presence behind him. So he found some napkins in the glove compartment and he sopped up the blood, its metallic odor stirring something deep in his gut.

He felt himself becoming aroused, his taut flesh uncomfortable against the straining fabric of his slacks.

He thought of A.J. Sutton, and his mouth curled into a smile.

You can run, he told her, *but you can't hide. Not anymore. And when I find you . . .*

"Drive faster," he urged Ramon, and kept his eyes on the road.

"Marco," Lia murmured, opening her heavy eyes and seeing his face hovering above hers.

She smiled faintly, realizing with enormous relief that it had all been just a terrible dream, and she was where she belonged, safe in Marco's arms.

Then, as she focused her bleary eyes on his ruggedly handsome face, reality crept up and slammed into her. She gasped at the brutal disillusionment.

"No!" she shouted, raising her hands and striking out, pounding furiously against Marco's brawny chest. "Let go! Put me down!"

But she was hopelessly imprisoned in his sturdy arms, and he barely flinched against her vain assault.

"Where are you taking me?" she demanded, seeing that trees loomed all around them, rising on a sharp incline. The sun was gone, and an oppressive gray gloom seemed to infiltrate the unfamiliar forest.

"Shhh," was all Marco said, his eyes darting to her face, then back, intently, at the terrain ahead.

"No!" she protested again, fury sending a shock of adrenaline coursing through her veins.

She attempted to contort and twist her body, to wrench herself from his clutches, but her own burst of fortitude was futile against his weighty strength.

Frustration and rage finally made her cry out, a pathetic wail that humiliated her even further.

"Everything's going to be all right," he said . . . almost tenderly?

Startled, Lia looked up into his face.

She realized, when she saw that his blue eyes were dispassionate as always, that although something in his voice had made her anticipate a hint of leniency in his features, there was none.

She must have been imagining things.

"You bastard," she bit out, her voice taut as her body in his arms. "How dare you lie to me? Do you think I'm a fool? I know everything's not going to be all right—"

"But it is."

"No! Don't give me that! I know what you're going to do to me, you and Victor, whenever we get to where we're going—"

"You're wrong."

"For God's sake, Marco, don't play games with me! The most decent, humane thing you could do is respect my intelligence. Be honest with me for once. You owe it to me."

A shadow crossed over his eyes, and she saw his mouth set grimly.

"I owe you nothing," he said after a moment, never missing a step as he continued on his fleet-footed way through the dense forest.

"You owe me everything, everything you never gave me," she shot back. "The truth, and trust—"

"Trust?" He practically spat the word at her. "Don't talk to me about trust."

"What's that supposed to mean?"

"Why do I owe you trust, when you never gave it to me? As far as I'm concerned, we're even on that count, A.J."

"It's Lia," she insisted, like a petulant, stubborn child. As if it mattered.

"No, it isn't Lia," he said, his voice maddeningly calm. "It's A.J. You can try to pretend to be someone else; you can do your best to hide behind that pasty skin and dark hair. But you're A.J. Sutton, and I would recognize that insolent attitude of yours if you were ninety years old and I were half blind.''

She was silent after his uncharacteristic lengthy speech.

I would recognize you if you were ninety years old and I were half blind.

They were words that, in another time and place, in another tone of voice, might have been reassuring. Words a man might tenderly utter to his lover, words that might send a thrill through her soul.

What was it her mama had once said, so very long ago?

The heart remembers.

That was it.

Lia, looking at tattered pictures of the family her mother had left behind in Cuba, had asked her mother if they looked much different now, years later, the way her own parents looked so different from the dated photos that had been taken with her as an infant.

"I'm sure they do look different," her mother had said wistfully, a faraway look in her big dark eyes.

"But then how would you know them, if you ever saw them again, Mama?"

"I would remember . . . the heart always remembers."

The heart always remembers . . .

Suddenly overcome by sorrow, Lia turned away from Marco's gaze.

The deep-seated sentiment was so unexpected, after she'd run the emotional gamut from rage to pity to determination, that it momentarily stole her fighting spirit.

She shook her head, trying to ward off memories that insisted on haunting her. But she couldn't keep them at bay; she had no choice but to let them wash over her.

She closed her eyes, and she saw Marco as she had once known him—a lively companion, a compassionate friend, an indulgent, tender lover. She saw a teasing glint in his eyes, saw his face contorted in ecstasy, saw him nodding as he listened intently to something she was saying.

For the first time, she truly allowed herself to mourn what she had lost.

No, you never lost him, came the warning voice in her head, *because that Marco never existed. You were blinded by lust, and that's all.*

Yet she knew, even as she acknowledged her constant, all-encompassing desire for Marco Estevez, that there had been more to it. Somewhere, amid the steamy banter, the cat-and-mouse games, the frenzy of passionate lovemaking, there had been a spark of something genuine.

"Maybe . . ." The word escaped her before she could stop it, like a whisper of a sigh, and she saw a trace of intrigue in Marco's eyes.

"Maybe what?" he asked, his voice low.

"Maybe in another time and place," she said slowly, "we could have had something real."

His pace slowed, and when he spoke, he sounded breathless; somehow she knew it wasn't from the exertion.

"Maybe we could have," was all he said.

But in that terse phrase, he told her everything she needed to know.

He had cared about her once; she had been more to him than merely an erotic diversion from Victor's world of intrigue and danger.

Whatever he was doing here now, he was doing because he had to.

And Marco always did what he had to do; his deep-seated, stoic sense of duty was an essential part of his character.

Lia felt a stab of regret that he was somehow so misguided; that he could have channeled all that loyalty and devotion into an ordinary existence, a wife and family. She wondered who he was, really—where he had come from, and what trauma had left him so unwilling to bend away from the difficult path he had chosen.

And she had no doubt that he had chosen it, because Marco Estevez was not a man who let others control him. Nor did he let his emotions control him.

She supposed she should respect him for that.

But right now, once again facing the fact that she was irrevocably imprisoned in the arms that had long ago seemed like a haven, all she could ultimately do was despise him.

For Marco, holding A.J. in his arms, against his beating, forsaken heart, was the cruelest of punishments. Yet he bore it willingly, almost gratefully, knowing it was what he deserved.

He never should have given in to his own desire.

The night he first laid eyes on her by the pool, teasing and seductive, her sexy body glistening in the moonlight, he should have somehow mustered the willpower to turn and walk away.

Instead he had allowed his fierce physical craving to override his better judgment.

He'd tried to tell himself that she was just like the handful of others he'd bedded and left in the long, lonely years since his heart had been battered, then shattered for good. That she was like the women who were easy on the eyes and easy in the sack, women who knew his game and played it expertly.

Besides, it wasn't as if carnal gratification was off-limits for men like him; on the contrary, physical release was a necessity to relieve the tremendous pressure that accompanied his line of work.

Yet he had sensed, the moment he saw her, that she was different—that this was different. Different, even, from the long-ago, long-lost woman who had left an indelible imprint on his soul. The woman he'd sworn he'd never forgive . . .

The woman he'd never been able to forget, even for an instant . . .

Until A.J. Sutton.

The woman was capable of engulfing his senses so that he could see, hear, only her, think only of her . . .

And a woman like that was forbidden to a man like Marco Estevez.

He knew the rules, and he had broken that one with alarming disregard for the consequences.

Now he would pay.

As he had paid before.

And this time, it would cost him far more dearly, because it was A.J.

He shifted her weight in his arms, and saw her hopeful expression when her eyes collided with his own.

"Am I getting heavy?" she asked, feigning innocence. "Why don't you put me down?"

"All right," he said after a moment's pause. "If you think you can walk."

"Of course I can walk," she snapped.

"You passed out. I thought you might still be feeling weak."

"I'm not weak."

No, he wanted to tell her. *You're not weak.*

But I am.

He was so close, so damn close, to giving in, once again, to the temptation that battered his determination like storm-tossed winter waves eroding a crumbling cliff. He wanted to stroke her cheek gently, to tell her the whole story, to tell her that he loved her.

He loved her.

No, you don't love her, an inner voice protested. *You're incapable of loving, because you're incapable of trusting. You never trusted her, and she never trusted you.*

That was what hurt the most, in the end.

The way she had struggled when he'd grabbed her that night by the stairs.

The way she had looked at him with undiluted loathing that had ripped into his heart, even as she had physically hurt him in his most intimate, most vulnerable spot.

She hadn't expected to see him there, in the shadows, and her reaction had been pure instinct. Her instinct had been to flee without a backward glance.

Some part of him couldn't blame the way she'd left; intellectually he knew she'd just been through hell. He could hear the first burst of gunfire echoing from the back of the house as he grabbed her; he was fully aware that she was hearing it, too, that she knew what it meant.

Why, he asked himself, *wouldn't she turn and run?*

Because she should have known that I would never have hurt her, he thought with unyielding conviction. *She should have trusted me.*

Instead she had jumped to the conclusion that he was one of *them,* that he intended to harm her. She had turned her back on him without hesitation.

There were times when he wondered why that had ever surprised him. He had known all along that she wasn't wholly there for him, that she was keeping some significant part of herself from him.

But then he had also, through all his uncertainty, seen glimpses of honest, unwavering emotion. When they made love, when she murmured his name—not in the wild frenzy as she approached release, but in the sweet aftermath, as she lay in his arms—then he knew.

He knew that she cared for him, that she might even love him.

And he knew, when she vanished without a trace, that whatever feelings she'd had for him had dissolved the instant she saw him that night in the shadows.

And no matter how many times he relived that scene, going over everything he could have said, might have done . . .

It always came down to that.

She had left.

Nothing he could have said or done, once she had made up her mind in that tense fraction of a moment, could have changed what had happened.

It had never been up to him to convince her that she could trust him, and love him.

It was up to her all along.

Her ultimate message had been loud and clear.

And so he knew where he stood.

It wasn't meant to be.

And maybe it was better this way, he thought, his arms aching with their precious burden.

But he still didn't know how he would manage to say goodbye to her.

"Put me down," she insisted, nudging him back to the present. "You said you would. This is ridiculous, Marco."

"I'll put you down," he said, stopping and lowering her to the ground, still holding her firmly with one arm as he reached into his pocket with the opposite hand. "But don't think you're going to slip away from me."

"I promise I'll be a good girl," she said, her voice mocking him as he knew her flashing dark eyes would be.

But he didn't look up at her face, just pulled from

his pocket his secret weapon, the one he was grateful he'd had the foresight to bring.

He heard her gasp when she saw it, heard her protest softly, "No. Oh, God, no, Marco . . ."

"Sorry, A.J.—I mean, I'm sorry, *Lia*," he amended. "But this is the way it has to be."

Victor slammed the cordless phone into its cradle in the kitchen and paced.

Then he stopped in front of the marble-topped island with its sparkling all-white designer cabinets below, and yanked open a drawer.

He should have flown to Boston himself, he fumed, rummaging through the jumble inside until he found a nutcracker.

If he had, A.J. Sutton would be in his possession now, whimpering and begging for mercy.

And Marco Estevez would already be dead.

He opened a cupboard and took out a canvas bag full of hazelnuts. Then, still glowering, he made his way up the stairs to his private quarters.

The door leading into his bedroom looked ordinary enough, though it was equipped with several bolts and an alarm system separate from the rest of the house. The bleached wood panels concealed a bulletproof steel core.

The bedroom itself was modeled after one Victor had seen in a James Bond film years ago, when he was merely a poor boy being raised by a single mother in Bogota. Back then, he shared a room with three of his brothers, and could only dream of one day having a space all to himself.

Never, even then, when even the major leagues had seemed accessible, had he imagined owning a home as

grand as his Miami estate, nor sleeping every night in
a room as luxurious as this one.

The walls were covered in hand-painted paper
imported from Europe; the floors in the finest Persian
carpet. The bed was enormous and round, sitting on a
raised platform and covered in a sumptuous white
spread and at least a dozen pillows. Surrounding it,
behind various panels, were state-of-the-art electron-
ics—some for entertainment, others for surveillance.
French doors led onto a balcony overlooking Biscayne
Bay.

Off in the corner of the room, beside the closet door,
was the camouflaged panel that concealed Victor's small
secret inner sanctum. The police hadn't found it when
they'd presumably gone over every inch of his home
last fall, after the botched abduction of Trask's wife and
son.

They couldn't find a shred of evidence to implicate
him for the kidnapping and murder, or anything else.

Good thing Trask's kid had been scared out of his
mind; maybe too scared to notice identifying details
about Ramon and the others, or maybe just too scared—
and smart—to tell the cops who they were.

As far as Victor was concerned, only A.J. Sutton could
do that.

Not that she could implicate him in the Trask case.
He had an airtight alibi for that one, an alibi even she
couldn't destroy.

No, he wasn't worried about the kidnapping, or even
the murder.

It was what else she might know that worried him.

She had been a part of his household for months;
had been screwing one of his men behind his back. For
all he knew, she had a cache of drug evidence against
him.

For all he knew, she could destroy him anytime she felt like it.

That was why he had to find her first; destroy her first.

He sat in his white leather recliner beside a floor-to-ceiling window with a spectacular view of the crystalline bay, and reached thoughtfully for a hazelnut.

How could he have entrusted a mission this crucial to anyone but himself?

It wasn't that he didn't trust Ramon or Hondo—they were loyal soldiers of his empire. But they were just that; soldiers. They had been trained, by Victor himself, to follow orders, not to give them. They were doing exactly what he expected of them.

But when he thought of that bumbling oaf Alberto, of how he'd allowed A.J. Sutton and Marco Estevez slip through his fingers not once, but twice, he wanted to break his fat neck.

And he would, someday soon.

He placed the hazelnut firmly in the jaws of the nutcracker, then squeezed in a swift, practiced movement. The shell promptly shattered. Victor smiled and popped the tasty nutmeat into his mouth.

Or maybe he'd have someone else take care of that nasty little deed for him, he mused, looking blankly out the window as he chewed. Yes, he'd bet Hondo could squeeze the life from Alberto in a few seconds flat . . . and would surely relish the opportunity.

But for now, Victor could only hope that Alberto would prove himself to be worth the trouble he had cost. Victor had seen the way his cousin had watched A.J. performing her household chores in her crisp pink uniform that was professional, yet just short enough to reveal a length of those sleek brown thighs.

Victor himself had selected the uniform, savoring the idea of being surrounded by ravishing women everywhere he went. If he ever found a beauty who could prepare his favorite Spanish dishes as well as Filippe, his paunchy middle-aged cook, did, he'd hire her in a heartbeat.

Or maybe he wouldn't.

Maybe he'd think twice before hiring a lovely, buxom woman ever again. Women couldn't be trusted. And he'd learned the hard way that perhaps his men couldn't be trusted, either. Not when opportunity lay tantalizingly beneath their noses.

Of course Victor, too, had found A.J. attractive. But he had a rule against becoming involved with the hired help. Those days of slumming were long behind him, along with the days of wearing secondhand clothes and eating the thin stew his mother would make from beans and tomatoes and rice.

No, he had never been tempted to lay a hand on A.J. Sutton.

Unlike Marco Estevez, and who knew how many of the others?

He reached for another nut, cracked it expertly, and ate it with the mechanical movements of one whose thoughts are far, far away.

Certainly Alberto had found A.J. Sutton enticing.

And he was positive his cousin would readily give in to transforming his sick little fantasies into a reality . . .

Just as soon as he found her.

And it had better be soon.

As for Marco, his fate lay in Hondo's strong, lethal hands.

How could I ever have trusted him? he wondered darkly.

But then, how could he not? Marco Estevez had come to him as a bodyguard, with impeccable credentials, through the same channels where he'd found Enrique.

One of the most reliable members of the cartel, Enrique moved on the fringes, going about his business without stirring up trouble or talking too much. That was why Victor had recently begun to trust him with more information than he usually allowed his bodyguards; why he'd allowed Enrique to take part in the abduction plot.

Marco had seemed to be the same type; discreet and dependable.

Little had Victor known that his newest bodyguard was sleeping with his maid.

Of course, under other circumstances, Victor might have forgiven Marco that.

He *had* forgiven him, had even, in some remote corner of his being, felt sorry for Marco when he'd told Victor he'd had to kill her because she'd seen too much, even though Marco had shrugged it off as though it were no big deal.

But in another part of his being, Victor harbored a shred of suspicion.

That maybe . . .

Just maybe . . .

Marco had lied about killing A.J. Sutton that night.

After all, Marco hadn't been directly involved in the abduction plot. Victor was careful not to let too many people know too much. And whenever he allowed someone new into the fold, he let them know that any breach of loyalty would result in an excruciating death.

Those two precautions—and the hidden room behind his bedroom walls—had kept his secrets safe from the authorities, who hadn't been able to pin him with anything after the bungled Trask case. They knew, and Victor knew they knew, that he was one of the most powerful drug lords operating in South Florida. And yet without evidence, they could do nothing.

But in the year since, he had lost millions of dollars. Aware that he was under close scrutiny, he had reined in his operation, had entrusted no one but a handful of his closest confidants.

Now the fate of his empire depended on seeing that no one suddenly came forward with evidence.

I should have listened to my instincts about Marco, Victor scolded himself now, as he pulverized another nutshell, *instead of to him.*

Marco had claimed he'd tracked her down when she'd fled the estate that night, and shot her, then disposed of her body at sea.

As far as Marco knew, Victor had taken his word for it. And when Victor had dismissed him from the fold a few days later, he hadn't given a reason.

Marco hadn't asked for one.

Victor had simply decided he couldn't take any chances. There wasn't room in his operation for someone who couldn't be trusted, and he just wasn't sure whether Marco Estevez could be.

Well, now he knew.

Estevez had lied.

He had let A.J. Sutton live.

And now he was out there somewhere, playing knight in shining armor for a doomed domestic servant who must have been something in the sack . . .

But even then . . .

Why would a man like Marco put his life on the line for her?

Victor's eyes were hard and glittering as he contemplated that mystery for a moment.

Then he shrugged and reached for another hazelnut, concluding that it didn't matter. In just a few more hours, if everything went according to his plan, A.J. Sutton and Marco Estevez would never again be a threat to his empire.

* * *

A.J. Sutton was just like the rest of them, Alberto reflected, eyes closed in the front seat of the car as it rolled along in search of her and Estevez.

Just like that pretty blond neighbor he'd encountered earlier.

Just like Lydia.

And the others, back in Colombia, the ones he had actually made love to before he . . .

No, he didn't want to think about that now.

He wanted to think about A.J. Sutton, and the other women *before* their lovely faces had been horribly disfigured and bloated in death . . .

Women who made his blood hot with lust.

All of them undeniably beautiful, with lithe, ripe curves just begging his touch and laughing eyes . . . laughing at him?

Probably.

Why wouldn't they laugh at him?

None of them had been attracted to him . . .

Or had they?

Until now, he had forgotten something that had happened back at the mansion late last summer, shortly before A.J. had disappeared. One afternoon, Alberto had been napping in a chair in a corner of the vast Florida room, shielded by several potted palms. He had stirred, hearing a noise, and seen that A.J. had come in to dust. She was wearing that short uniform of hers, the one that bared her long, tanned legs and revealed the lacy edge of her panties when she bent over.

She'd acted as though she hadn't known Alberto was there, but he was positive she sensed him watching her from the corner. Why else would she have sashayed that way when she walked around the room, swinging her behind and her long, silky hair?

She was doing it for his benefit, he was sure. And as he watched her, his hand found its way down the front of his trousers. He had fondled himself as he watched her work, incredibly excited by the knowledge that she knew exactly what he was doing there behind the potted palm, and was pretending that she didn't see him. She even hummed faintly under her breath, to add to the casual impression.

Her performance was breathtaking.

Reach up high to dust the hanging fern, yes that's it, A.J. . . . are you even wearing panties? Yes, there they are, and oh, Madre de Dio, they're black satin . . .

Now bend down to pick up the leaves around the ficus tree . . . mmm, yes, when you lean forward like that I can just imagine coming up behind you and burying myself inside of you . . .

She was such a tease, that one. Such a beautiful, sexy little tease.

She had left the room without so much as glancing at him as he exploded all over his hand.

But she knew.

And he knew she knew.

And he had decided it was only a matter of time before he confronted her about it, some night when no one was around.

He would say, "How about if you parade around and clean while I watch, like you did the last time?"

And she would say coyly, "What are you talking about?"

And then he would reach out and roughly stroke her breasts, feeling her nipples harden with excitement beneath the fabric of her uniform.

She would say, "Oh, yes, I'll clean while you watch. Only this time, I'll be naked and we'll be alone in your room, Berto . . ."

But he had never gotten the chance to seduce her.

Just as well.

It was probably only a fantasy, he thought abruptly, focusing on the gray world outside the car window.

The reality was that if he made a move on her, she most likely would have slapped him, the way the others had.

A knot of anger twisted in his gut.

Why did she have to be like the others?

Why did all women who looked like her look at him like he repulsed them?

Why was he condemned to this horrible need to possess them all and then make them pay, make them all pay, for what teenaged Lydia had done on that long ago night with Victor?

And why didn't he need to make Victor pay?

He shuddered at the mere thought of confronting his cousin.

But women, they were different. He could control them. He could kill them.

He sighed, watching the first raindrops splatter against the window.

Maybe he just needed to get it out of his system once and for all, he told himself. Maybe, if he could just have one more woman . . . kill one more woman . . . it would be enough.

All he needed, then, to purge his soul of this affliction, was to find A.J. Sutton.

Chapter Seven

"What are you doing? Stop it!" Lia shrieked, trying to wrestle her wrist from Marco's grasp.

"What I have to do," he grunted, his big fingers firm yet somehow gentle in their powerful grip.

"No! Let go of me!" From the corner of her eye, she saw a glint of silver and felt cool metal graze her arm before she heard the telltale click that sealed her fate.

"There," Marco said, staring down at her arm with a pleased expression.

Lia followed his gaze, and cursed aloud at the sight of the handcuffs that encircled her slender wrist and his broad one.

"How could you do something like this?" she asked bitterly, yanking her arm, wanting to see his hand jerk in response. She needed to have some power over him, to show him that he wasn't entirely in control here.

Though he flinched slightly, his hand didn't move, his strong muscles resisting her force.

With his free hand, he deposited the key into the depths of the front pocket of his snug-fitting jeans.

"If I were you," he said mildly, "I wouldn't fool around with these. You'll get an awful bruise on your wrist trying to break them, and you won't even strain the links. They're the real thing."

"Oh, yeah? And what're you, suddenly a cop?" she demanded.

He shrugged. "You wanted to walk so let's walk," he said, and started through the woods toward a clearing several hundred feet away.

She had no choice but to hurry along beside him, trying to match his long strides so that she wouldn't have to break into a run to keep up.

They passed through the clearing and into more woods, and the sky was growing darker overhead. They trudged through thick piles of leaves, and more drifted lazily, constantly down around them. Occasionally there was a scampering in the underbrush, as their footsteps startled some woodland creature or other.

As they walked, Lia was silent, seething at her predicament, far beyond the fear that had tormented her earlier.

But, dammit, she was conscious of their hands occasionally brushing as they walked, of his muscular arm bumping against hers now and then.

And she couldn't help remembering how they used to walk side by side along the beach, their arms joined by warm, entwined fingers rather than by cold, cruel metal clasps.

"Where are we?" she finally asked wearily. Her shoulder ached where the wayward baseball had hit her, and her feet were sore in the sensible blue pumps she'd donned a lifetime ago.

Or was it just this morning?

"I have no idea."

Marco's answer caught her by surprise, and she looked up at him.

"What do you mean, you have no idea? Aren't you the one in charge here? I mean, if you want me to take over, I gladly will, but we're going to have to lose the cuffs."

He smirked—or was it a smile? Nothing seemed simple; she kept catching glimpses of the old Marco in his face, then wondering if she had simply imagined it.

"It's all right," he assured her, a hint of amusement in his voice. "I'll remain in charge, A.J. And we'll keep the cuffs, unless you'd like me to carry you again."

Her feet *were* killing her . . .

And there had been a strange, preposterous comfort in being held against his chest that way . . .

But she refused to let him carry her through this endless forest like some hunter lugging his prey.

So she shook her head and said airily, "I'll walk, thank you very much. But I won't go another step until you tell me where we're going."

With that, she stopped abruptly in her tracks, praying he wouldn't continue on, causing her to stumble, fall, and perhaps be dragged through the twigs and mud.

But he stopped, too, looking at her with an expression that seemed to be part admiration, part irritation.

"I just told you, I have no idea where we're going."

"Is that because we're supposed to be in the car, driving along the New York State Thruway right about now?"

He nodded.

"Then I guess the cops ruined your little plan, didn't they, when they started chasing us?"

"That wasn't the cops, A.J."

"Oh, really?" He must think her an idiot. Who else would come to rescue her from his clutches?

Then again, how would the police have known of her abduction?

She contemplated that, then kept her tone sarcastic as she asked him, "If it wasn't the police chasing us, then who, exactly, was it?"

"It was Victor Caval, or maybe just some of his men. They're trying to kill us both."

She let out a sharp, staccato laugh. "And you aren't? At least, me?"

He let out a heavy sigh. "I'm not trying to kill you, A.J. I swear I'm not."

She wanted to laugh in his face.

Or cry.

But for the first time, she felt a flicker of doubt.

Could he possibly be telling the truth?

For a moment, she didn't speak, carefully trying to organize her thoughts. No matter how she looked at it, the evidence pointed to the fact that Marco Estevez was a dangerous man—and her enemy. And yet . . .

"If you're not trying to kill me," she said carefully, watching him, "then why would you track me down, break into my house, abduct me at gunpoint, and never say a word about why you're doing it?"

He appeared to be contemplating her question.

"All right," he said, after a pause. "Let's just say that after a year apart, with you in hiding, I suddenly showed up on your doorstep and rang your doorbell this morning, and I said, 'Come with me because I'm going to save you from some bad guys who want to kill you'? Would you have done it?"

"Not on your life," she retorted promptly. "I wouldn't go anywhere with you, Marco, unless you held a gun to my head. Which you did."

"I never held it to your head."

"Oooh, I'm sorry. My mistake. You held a gun to my *stomach*," she said tartly.

"And that was the only reason you came with me."

"You bet it was."

"See?"

"See what?"

"You wouldn't have gone with me if I'd asked nicely. You wouldn't have believed it was for your own good, A.J.—"

"It's Lia, Marco. Remember it. Use it. And let me tell you something. I would never in a million years believe you're trying to save me from some 'bad guys' because *you* are the bad guy. I know about you, remember? I saw you that night."

"You have no idea what I was doing that night." His voice was low, and he'd broken eye contact with her. His blue gaze was fixed on the wooded trail ahead.

"Are you kidding?" she asked incredulously. "A woman and a child had just been kidnapped, and *you* were lurking in the shadows with a gun. What else would you be doing?"

His head jerked around as he looked at her again, and she felt his intense scrutiny even after she tore her eyes away, shifting her weight from one aching foot to the other and wishing she'd never started this conversation.

"You can't think of one other thing I'd be doing, can you?" Marco asked on a bitter laugh. "To you, it was totally self-explanatory. You never questioned what you saw."

"Why would I?"

"Because . . . "

He trailed off, and she looked at him.

For a few seconds, there was silence, as they stared into each other's eyes.

"Because why?" she asked finally. "Why would I question it? Why would I ever think you were innocent when you lied to me all along?"

Still he was silent, watching her, waiting.

Say something, she commanded him mentally, but obeyed her own command as words continued to tumble out of her.

"You lied, Marco." Her voice was becoming ragged, and she struggled against the emotion that threatened to rise and choke her. "You lied about who you were, about what you were doing there, in that house. You never told me that you were anything more than a casual visitor there, a business acquaintance of Victor's, and it's so damned obvious that wasn't the case. How could you not trust me?"

Trust.

There it was again.

As soon as she saw his expression, she wished she'd caught the word before it had spilled from her lips.

"How could *I* not trust *you?*" he asked tightly. "I did trust you. I got close to you, A.J., and I haven't been close to anyone since ... "

"Since what?"

"Never mind." He was closed off again, and she shook her head in frustration.

"Tell me, dammit, Marco! Why do you always have to shut so much away from me?"

"You do the same thing to me."

"I *don't.*"

Oh, Lord, she thought, were they back to this? Back to the childish *did-so/did-not* brand of arguing that had peppered their relationship?

He accused, "You won't tell me anything about yourself, nothing that matters."

"And you will?"

She was breathing hard, her face in his face, her eyes boring into his. And it struck her that they had gone from rehashing history to sounding as if they were dissecting the present.

You do . . .

You will . . .

What a joke. Their relationship should only be discussed in the past tense, because that was the only place it existed.

His voice interrupted her thoughts.

"Will we never stop doing this to each other, Lia?"

She frowned faintly, realizing he'd called her by her other name, just as she'd asked him to do. And the way he was looking at her . . .

"Will we stop doing what?" she asked, suddenly hesitant, unsure of herself.

"Hurting."

It was so unexpected, so vulnerable a word that at first she couldn't respond.

And when she did, her voice was as hushed as the woods around them.

"But you can't hurt someone who doesn't care about you, Marco."

"I know." He moved his head in the slightest nod, his gaze locked on hers.

"I don't care about you," she said hoarsely, "not anymore. And you don't care about me."

Again he nodded.

But his face was closer, somehow, and she felt herself starting to tremble.

Not this time in dread . . .

Nor in anger.

"It's over," she whispered, mesmerized by his face . . .

By his wide, provocative mouth, and the rugged angle of his jaw, and the strands of blond hair that had fallen forward, begging her fingers to stroke them back from his cheek.

"It's over," he agreed, his voice husky.

Why couldn't he disagree with her, rile her into an

argument—anything that would break this dangerous spell.

She swallowed, repeated, "It's over. And we can't—"

"No, we can't," he agreed again, and yet his face was closer, his lips closer, so close that she could almost . . .

With a groan, he bent his head and his mouth lowered over hers.

His lips were pure heat, pressing, alive, daring, delving. Lia was engulfed by a wave of desire that swept her back through time, so that she could do nothing but open her lips to allow his tongue entry, nothing but moan deep in her throat and press her soft breasts and belly against his masculine chest and hips, plainly feeling the rigid evidence of his passion, excited by how much he wanted her . . .

Then she moved her arm—the wrong arm—instinctively wanting to pull his head closer to her, to bury her fingers in his long hair . . .

And just like that, the spell was broken.

Because she found that she couldn't move her arm; it was handcuffed to his.

The fresh realization that she was his prisoner shot through her and she whimpered, pulling back from him and raising her unencumbered hand to her lips as if they'd been seared with a hot brand.

"No," she bit out, shaking her head, glaring. "How dare you touch me?"

"I *didn't* touch you. . . ." If not for his ragged breathing, she'd have thought him utterly unrattled by what had just happened.

"Yes, you did!" she challenged, trying to calm her own racing heart. "You . . . "

"I . . . " he prompted, a maddening glint in his eyes. "Go on, Lia. Say it . . . "

"You kissed me," she hissed, wanting more than anything to turn her back on him, to flee.

But she couldn't, not with her arm fused to his.

"I did," he acknowledged. "I kissed you. And you kissed me."

"No, I—"

"You kissed me," he repeated firmly. "You wanted it as much as I did. And we both wanted more."

She stared at him, wishing she could read the cryptic expression in those cryptic azure eyes of his.

Was he toying with her emotions, getting his kicks out of riling her temper?

Somehow she doubted it.

And that unsettled her more than his merely goading her would have.

She looked away from his face, up at the sky, where heavy gray clouds seemed to hover just above the tree-tops.

"It's going to rain," she observed, in a tone and manner that seemed absurdly casual, even to her.

But he simply nodded and said, "It is. Soon. This is part of the storm that's coming up the coast from Florida."

"Rainstorms in the Northeast aren't like they are in Florida," she told him. "They don't come and go in minutes, with the sun popping out right afterward."

"I know that."

She glanced at him in surprise. "How do you know that? I thought you had never lived anywhere other than Florida and California. Isn't that what you told me?"

He shrugged. "Anyone with a brain knows about the weather differences between the Northeast and Florida, Lia. And if I recall, you had said you would never return to New England because of the climate. Isn't that right?"

She tilted her head at him, and would have offered cynical applause if her wrist hadn't been locked to his. "Very good, Marco. It's so nice to know that you haven't forgotten *everything* about our time together."

"I haven't forgotten *anything* about our time together, Lia," he informed her with an expression she couldn't decipher.

Then, changing his tone abruptly, he added, "Come on. We'd better get moving before it rains."

They had always argued, Lia reflected as she trudged alongside Marco. From the beginning, they had been as prone to fiery flareups as California scrub brush in an August drought.

What had they fought about? she wondered now, looking back on their past encounter—because anything was less unsettling than what was happening between them in the present.

They had fought about everything.

Everything . . .

Yet nothing that mattered. It couldn't have, because they would so readily fall into each other's arms even as bitter words continued to slip past their lips, until one of them silenced the other with a kiss.

Most of the time, anyway.

On a few occasions, either she or Marco would storm off in anger, and it would actually be a day or two before they would manage to reconcile.

Once, Lia recalled, she had come home from a long day of scrubbing all seven of Victor's marble bathrooms, wanting only to collapse in front of the television.

Marco was going to a business dinner in Coconut Grove with Victor and the others, but had promised her he'd come over to her place afterward "for dessert." He had said it with a gleam in his eye, and she had known he wasn't talking about coffee and cake.

Still, struck by a whim, she had painstakingly prepared one of his favorite deserts, a rich flan with homemade caramel sauce. He had mentioned a few days earlier how he missed true Spanish food, the homemade kind his mother used to make.

The entire time she slaved in the tiny condo kitchen, measuring and stirring and drizzling the ingredients, she had entertained herself with visions of how thrilled he would be when he saw what she had done for him.

How he would at last declare his undying love for her.

She had pictured the look of ecstasy on his face when he tasted the first bite . . .

Had even imagined him taking the bowl into the bedroom with them and coating her naked body with the sticky stuff so that he could slowly and tantalizingly lick it off. Mmm . . .

Hah.

Marco had been two and a half hours late getting to her apartment, breezing in with a brusque, "sorry I'm late" and a casual peck on her cheek. He had looked faintly ill when she escorted him into the kitchen and proudly presented him with her concoction.

"I've been eating nonstop since seven o'clock," he told her, rubbing his lean stomach as though it were painfully bursting. "Victor insisted that we have course after course, including fried ice cream and bananas flambé for dessert. I'm stuffed, A.J."

"But I spent hours making this for you, Marco . . . you said it's your favorite."

"It is."

"Just have a little taste."

"A.J., if I had a little taste, I promise you, I would throw up. I'm so stuffed it makes me sick just looking at it."

She just stared at him, livid.

"Sorry," he had said with a shrug, and added, "I'll eat it tomorrow for breakfast."

She had just stared at his nonchalant face, wanting

to scream at him for having put her through such an exhausting evening for nothing.

But spontaneous rage bubbled through her veins and before she could open her mouth to lash out, she found herself lifting the bowl in her hands and dumping the sticky contents over Marco's handsome blond head.

"What the hell are you doing?" he had erupted, his Spanish accent thick the way it always was when he was angry. "Are you *loco*?"

And of course, she had hollered right back at him.

A cliché, she thought sadly now. Had they really been such a cliché? Like some fifties sitcom episode—the woman angry that the man was late, the man oblivious, brushing her off with soothing, casual words.

We had it on the nose, right down to the pie in the face, she thought acridly now, remembering the way he had looked with thick white custard coating his face.

That time, he had been the one who left without making up. He hadn't even bothered to brush the gooey flan from his hair before stalking out the door, slamming it behind him.

She had finally gone crawling to him with an apology, but only after two days of stony silence had passed—days during which she had mentally berated him for being such an insensitive clod and herself for ever thinking she could love a man like him.

Had she really been angry because he wasn't hungry? He couldn't have known she was making the dessert, and even if he had, there was no denying Victor when he had a whim. The man could convince the staunchest teetotaller to gulp champagne if he really wanted to.

Or was the real reason she had exploded due to the fact that Marco hadn't been at her place when he said he would be; that he hadn't even bothered to call from the restaurant or at least from his car?

She remembered watching the clock that night; worrying when the hours slid by with no sign of Marco.

Now she wondered exactly what it was that had her worried.

Had she been frightened that something had happened to him—that he'd had an accident the way her parents had that long ago night?

Or was she afraid he had simply lost interest in her—that he had found someone else or maybe he just no longer cared about her?

Probably a little bit of both.

And maybe she and Marco had constantly clashed about trivial matters simply because it was easier than clashing about the big stuff.

Like the fact that their relationship was temporary, and they both knew it.

But why did it have to be that way? she wondered now, stealing a glance at his strong profile. He appeared to be lost in his own thoughts, unaware that she even walked beside him.

Why couldn't we have cared about each other enough to make it last, Marco?

She already knew the answer to that question.

Because he had been living a masquerade. He couldn't let her get too close, lest she catch a glimpse of the real man behind his appealing mask.

Well, now the mask was off and she was fully aware of who Marco really was, Lia thought firmly. And she wouldn't make the mistake of letting passion blind her a second time.

But do you really see the real Marco, even now? a stubborn voice protested in her mind. *Or is he still hiding, still playing games?*

Something told her the masquerade wasn't yet over.

* * *

With a final, forceful thrust into the woman lying beneath him, Victor collapsed on top of her, feeling as though his entire body had turned to liquid, every shred of stress seeping away . . .

But only for a blissful moment, or two.

Then A.J. Sutton's face flashed in front of his closed eyelids, and tension once again infused his body. With an abrupt jerk, he pulled himself from between her outspread legs and rolled onto the rumpled sheet, sitting up in one swift movement.

"Victor, where are you going?" she protested, propping herself on her elbows.

He didn't bother to glance at her pretty face or her lanky, nude body. She was just another South Beach fashion model, an Australian beauty whose bed he had occasionally occupied in the past. If she hadn't called him on a whim and suggested they get together for dinner, he might never have thought of her again, or even recognized her if he passed her on Collins Avenue.

"I'm busy for dinner, *querido,* but I'll drop by for an hour if you're free right now," he had crooned over the phone, his loins stirring with a sudden need for release. A willing woman was just what he needed to pass the hours until he finally had his ultimate prey in his clutches.

Of course, she had told him to come right over. They always did.

"Where are you going?" she repeated plaintively now, laying a perfectly manicured hand on his thigh.

He brushed it off as if it were a pesky flea and stood to gather his clothes, which he had left folded neatly on a chair by the bed.

"I have business to attend to," he said curtly, stepping into his snug black briefs.

"Can't it wait? You said you'd stay an hour. You've barely been here fifteen minutes."

He smiled faintly. "Fifteen minutes was all I needed."

"You're just going to screw me and leave? Just like that? Like I'm some whore?"

"And you aren't?" he asked, buttoning his shirt and then tucking it into his pants.

"You're a—"

"What?" he asked, spinning around and catching her eye.

He narrowed his gaze, watching her, silently daring her to insult him.

She hesitated, biting her collagen-enhanced lower lip. Then she shrugged and untangled her long limbs from the bedding, standing and strolling across the room to take a pale pink satin robe from the hook behind the door.

He resumed dressing as she slipped into the robe. He buckled his snake skin belt and slipped his bare feet into his Gucci loafers. He examined his reflection in the mirror over her cosmetic-cluttered bureau and, satisfied, strolled to the door.

There he paused with his hand on the knob, turning to look back at her.

"Thank you for everything. Have a pleasant afternoon, Sara."

Victor opened the door, stepped over the threshold, and closed it firmly behind him, chuckling softly as he heard her protest, "It's Susan."

Marco figured they had walked several miles before the woods finally gave way to open, rolling meadowland.

From the fringes of the forest, he surveyed the panoramic view that was bisected by a dirt lane, with a ramshackle farmhouse on one side and an enormous barn on the other. Beyond the barn were several small buildings, including one that appeared to be an outhouse.

"What are you doing?" Lia asked after a moment, sounding impatient.

"I'm checking to see if there's a place where we can spend the night."

There was a pause, and then she said firmly, "I'm not spending the night holed up in some chicken coop with you."

He turned to her, marveling at her impetuous spunk. The woman clearly believed he was her enemy, that he meant to cause her harm—for Christ's sake, she was handcuffed to him and knew he had a *gun* in his pocket—and yet she still found the nerve to tell *him* what to do.

"You're really something," he told her, shaking his head at the obstinate gleam in her enormous dark eyes.

"I'm really something? How do you figure that?"

"You just are. You think that you can stand there and tell me what you will and won't do?"

Her expression remained defiant. "You think you can stand *there* and tell *me* what to do?" she shot back.

This was ludicrous, he thought. Here she was, ostensibly his prisoner, and yet she persisted in letting him know she didn't intend to meekly follow his orders.

But you told her you had no intention of hurting her, that you were doing this for her own good, he reminded himself.

Yes, and she hadn't believed a word of it.

"Lia," he said after a moment, with her insolent gaze still resting on his face, "you really don't have a choice about where you spend the night—and with whom. And I don't have a choice, either."

"Sure you do. Let me go. We'll never have to see each other again."

"Is that what you want?"

She hesitated, only for a split second, but it was long enough to allow his foolish heart to soar.

"I left, didn't I?" was her reply, in a voice that betrayed no emotion. "I *ran* from you, Marco, as fast and as far as I could go. That should give you an answer."

He shrugged and turned his gaze skyward. Dusk was falling rapidly, and the clouds still hovered overhead, now an ominous purple-black, swollen with rain that threatened to spill to earth at any second.

"We need to go down there," he said, motioning at a small building on the far fringes of the farmland, bordering the woods.

"And do what?" she asked. "Are you going to terrorize some poor farmer and his family with your gun?"

He was shocked at her suggestion, and it only proved to him how little she knew of him. Anger surged through him once again, and he clenched his jaw as he said, "I have no intention of confronting whoever lives there. We need a place to spend the night, out of the rain. They'll never know we were there."

"How do you figure that?"

"Do you see that building? It's a shed, and it's hardly convenient to the house or barn. They probably rarely use it. We can go there. Come on."

He waited for her to protest, but she said nothing.

At least she knew where to draw the line, he mused, as they made their way through the trees at the perimeter of the farmland.

"You can uncuff me now," Lia announced breathlessly, speaking loudly above the downpour that beat against the roof of the shed. Using her free hand, she shoved her drenched hair back from her face, and squirmed uncomfortably. The skies had opened up only minutes ago, as she and Marco were covering the last bit of ground between the woods and the shed.

"Absolutely not," was Marco's reply. His back was to her as he surveyed the storage shed in the dim light from a single cracked window. The shelves were lined with ancient household artifacts, like old toasters, lanterns, and even stacks of magazines. Much of the floor space was jammed with rusted farm equipment. Thick layers of cobwebs and dust covered everything, as though the place hadn't been disturbed in centuries.

Marco had been right about no one discovering them here, she realized. There went *that* opportunity for rescue.

"I need to use that outhouse behind the shed," she told him, her teeth clenched. "Very badly."

He seemed to contemplate that, then shrugged. "All right, I'll take you out there, but I'll be right outside the door while you use it."

"I'm sure you will." At this point, she wasn't even thinking of escape, only of relieving her aching bladder.

"Let's go," he said tersely, and opened the door.

Wind and rain blew in, and Lia cringed as the cold rain hit her face again.

"Unlock the cuffs," she told Marco, holding back in the doorway.

"Not until we reach the outhouse. I'm not taking a chance on your making a break for it."

"Are you crazy? I have to go to the bathroom so badly I can barely walk, let alone run. Unlock the cuffs."

Still he didn't move.

Exasperated, she added, "I swear I won't go anywhere."

She never expected him to reach into his pocket for the key and insert it into the lock on her wrist.

But he did, without a word.

The instant her hand was free, he grabbed her arm in his steely grasp. "Come on," he said, "let's go."

They stepped out into the storm and crossed the few feet to the dilapidated wooden structure behind the shed. He tugged on the door, still anchoring her to his side with his other arm, and finally got it open. She balked as he stepped aside, saying, "All yours."

The place was probably filled with spiders and centipedes, maybe even snakes. Despite having grown up in the tropics, where hideous reptiles and multilegged creepy-crawly creatures were commonplace, she recoiled at the thought of being alone in the dark with them.

She almost asked Marco to come in with her, but the very idea of suffering that indignity was out of the question.

"Go ahead," Marco prompted, and let go of her arm.

And a wild impulse crossed her mind.

An impulse to flee, as fast as she could, for the dense cover of the woods several yards away . . .

But the whim dissipated as quickly as it had come.

Even if Marco didn't shoot at her as she retreated, she wasn't crazy about the notion of being alone in the forest, at night, in a storm.

Somehow it seemed much safer here with Marco.

You're insane, she scolded herself as she stepped gingerly over the threshold of the outhouse. *Talk about a false sense of security. The man broke into your home, abducted you at gunpoint, then subjected you to a highway shootout with the cops. And you think he's safe?*

No.

She didn't believe that he was.

She really didn't.

And she refused to acknowledge that infuriating corner of her soul that nudged her to think otherwise.

But until she found a viable way to get away from

him, she was his prisoner. And that meant she'd have to spend the night with him in that cramped storage shed, most likely handcuffed to his side.

"Do you want me to close the door behind you?" he asked, and she realized she was still hesitating in the doorway of the outhouse.

In front of her was a low bench, with a gaping hole in the middle of it. She took a step forward, and something brushed against her face. She jumped, told herself that it was probably just a cobweb. But still . . .

"No," she called to Marco. "Don't shut the door. Just stay right there, okay?"

"Okay."

She went about her business quickly and when she returned to the door, she saw that Marco was waiting in the rain.

"Stay there. I'm going to use it, too," he informed her, as thunder clapped overhead.

"I'll wait out—"

"You'll wait in here, with me," he cut her off, brushing past her in the doorway.

She scowled. "I don't want to—"

"You have no choice. Don't even think of moving. Just stay right there, where I can keep an eye on you."

Irritated, she kept her back to him, staring out into the pouring rain. Again the thought crossed her mind that she could, conceivably, make a run for it. All she'd have to do was get to the woods . . .

Or even to the farmhouse down the hill, where she could see yellow light spilling from the windows . . .

Behind her, she heard the faint sound of Marco unzipping his jeans.

Instantly visions of bolting evaporated from her mind, replaced by a fresh barrage of memories.

She remembered what it was like to lie in bed in her Miami condo, naked in the dark, her body fully aroused from Marco's expert foreplay, waiting impatiently for him to get undressed and come to her.

She remembered the acute hunger that would seize her in those tantalizing moments, when she heard the soft rustle of his clothing falling to the floor around him, when she envisioned his magnificent nude body that would soon join with hers.

He had often suggested that they make love with the lights on, and she had always refused.

"Why not?" he had asked once, sounding bewildered. "You can't tell me you're shy. Not after that little strip-tease you performed in the living room just now."

No, she couldn't tell him she was shy.

That wasn't it at all.

It was just that in the dark, she could avoid looking into his eyes in those profound moments when he became an intimate part of her. In the dark, she could cling to the private part of herself that she'd always shielded from him, the part she would never give to him, to anyone.

Maybe if he hadn't been so secretive, she would have let down her guard.

Maybe, if they had stayed together, she eventually would have anyway.

But in that time and place, she simply couldn't allow herself to let go completely, to face those blue eyes and the knowledge that she was half in love with him . . .

Maybe totally in love with him.

Love wasn't something she wanted, or needed.

Not when love could hurt so badly.

Not when the person you loved would leave you one day, one way or another. No matter what they said. No matter how many promises they made.

I promise I won't leave, little one . . .

Her father's words drifted back to her.

"Okay, let's go." Marco's voice and a hand on her arm made her jump.

She frowned and looked up at him, coming slowly back to the present, and saw that he was watching her closely.

"What is it?" he asked.

"What . . . ?"

"That look on your face. Are you all right?"

"It's nothing. Let's go," she said brusquely, and allowed him to take her arm and propel her back out into the rain, to the shed.

Marco stood restlessly in the doorway, surveying the rolling hills for a sign that someone was lurking, watching them, waiting.

His instincts told him they were relatively safe—at least for the moment—but then, his instincts had been wrong before.

He thought back to one time in particular, on Sanibel Island when, after a languid night of lovemaking, he and Lia had slipped out into the warm pre-dawn breeze for a swim in the gulf.

"This is perfect," Lia had sighed, facing him as she tread water, her face exquisite in the pink glow of the rising sun despite a lack of sleep and the fact that her hair was completely soaked and slicked back.

Not many women looked that beautiful soaking wet, Marco thought appreciatively, reaching out to wipe a droplet of water from her cheek.

"I wish we could stay here forever," she said wistfully, leaning back in the water as though she were reclining in a cushy easy chair.

"We'd look like a couple of prunes before long," Marco had pointed out, grinning.

"Not in my perfect fantasy paradise. In my fantasy

paradise, we could float all day if we felt like it, and we'd never need to sleep."

"We haven't slept since we got here, remember?"

"But we're both tired, and you know that sooner or later we're going to have to sleep." She paddled lazily in the gently lapping water. "In my paradise, we would never be apart, not even for that."

"I like your paradise," he said softly, slowly swimming backward, facing her. "Tell me more about it."

"I wouldn't have to work for Victor, and you wouldn't have to do whatever it is you actually do, either. We would just lie around all day, relaxing and eating . . ."

"Wouldn't we get fat, doing that?"

"No, because making love would burn off hundreds of calories an hour." She splashed him playfully.

"I think the sex we had all night did that anyway," he said, splashing back.

"Then maybe we're actually living in my fantasy paradise right now."

"I think we are." He reached for her.

"We can't do anything in deep water, Marco," she had said, smiling. "We need our hands, or we'll drown."

"Not in paradise." He kissed her hungrily.

They both went under.

"Let's swim to shallow water," he suggested when they came up. "Now. I've never made love to you in the ocean."

"I don't think this is the time."

"Since when do you—oh," he said, spotting the elderly couple who had just emerged from a cottage on the beach. "We've got an audience."

"Maybe we should do it anyway. Give the sweet old seniors a thrill to jazz up their retirement years."

"A thrill? It would probably kill them. Come on," Marco said, resigned. "Let's swim back in and give ourselves a thrill in private."

"I'll take a rain check on that ocean lovemaking, okay?" Lia asked, swimming beside him.

"No problem. The next time we come to Sanibel."

She looked at him, startled, and he smiled.

"We're coming back to Sanibel?" she asked incredulously. "When?"

He shrugged, suddenly wishing he hadn't mentioned the future. They never did. "I don't know. Whenever."

"Oh."

They were silent for a moment, swimming toward shore, and his instincts told him she was on the verge of saying something . . . important. Something about the future . . . about making sure they would have one.

As he glanced at her face and saw her faraway expression, he was certain of it. She was finally going to open up, to let down part of her reserve. This was it. No more ice princess.

But his instincts, which until then had rarely been wrong, had misled him.

She didn't say another intimate word, not then, not later in bed, and not after they returned to Miami.

There were other times, after that episode on the beach, when he was certain he had gotten through to her, that she was going to let him into her private world. She never had.

And she never would, he thought now, looking back to see her sitting morosely on the dusty floor behind him, refusing to acknowledge his presence.

He thought he was so powerful, Lia thought, pretending she didn't see him looking at her.

He thought she was his meek little prisoner, that he was in complete control here, even as he stood with his back to her, tense, looking out of the shed.

Well, she had never allowed anyone, not even Marco,

to take charge of her life. Her whole life, she had been the boss—even when she was a child, when her parents were still alive.

They used to laugh about her strong will when they didn't realize she could hear them. Her father would tell her mother that little Lia was just like her, and her mother would proudly agree.

They laughed together often, her parents. That was one thing Lia remembered clearly about their relationship. They were always teasing each other.

Right up until the morning they were leaving for the airport on their way to Bimini.

Lia remembered sitting on their bed watching as her father tried to force her mother's suitcase to close.

"What do you have in here?" he had asked, bouncing on it. "Your entire wardrobe?"

"Just a few things for the weekend. You want me to look pretty, don't you, Jack?"

"You look most beautiful wearing nothing at all," he had murmured.

"Jack!" she said, glancing at Lia, who pretended not to have overheard.

Not that she knew what her father meant—not really. She had been too young then to understand the intimacy that could exist between a man and a woman.

Then, she had just thought it was sweet of her father to think that her mother would look nice without her clothes on.

"If you don't take something out of here, we're not going to be able to bring any of it," her father said giving up on trying to close the bag.

"All right, all right. I'll take something out." And her mother, laughing, had removed a pair of socks.

"Socks?" her father hollered in mock outrage. "You were bringing socks to Bimini? I suppose you have mittens in there, too. Let me look through that bag."

And he had gone through it, item by item, questioning her mother's reasoning for packing each thing. Lia and her mother had giggled at his antics, until he finally checked his watch and announced that if they didn't get the luggage into the car right now, they were going to miss the flight.

So her mother had hurriedly repacked, and they managed to zip the bag. And then her father was lugging it out to the car, complaining that they'd be lucky if the plane managed to stay in the air with such a heavy suitcase on board.

"What if the plane can't stay in the air, Mama?" Lia had asked worriedly after her mother had given instructions to the housekeeper, Rita, who would be staying with her while they were gone.

"Of course it will stay in the air, darling. Daddy was only joking. Now you be a good girl for Rita," her mother had said, bending to kiss her.

And then her father was kissing her too, and hugging her and telling her to be his good, big, brave girl while they were gone.

"Remember we love you, Lia," her mother had called over her shoulder before climbing into the car. "We'll be back before you know it."

But they were dead before she knew it—within an hour of that last goodbye. Their plane went down in the ocean, and their bodies were never found.

For a long time, Lia had thought that they weren't really dead—that maybe they had washed up on some island somewhere and were waiting to be rescued.

When she said as much to Uncle Bruce, he chuckled and said, "What do you think this is, Gilligan's Island?"

Tears had stung her eyes as she stared at his laughing face and heard the snickers of her cousins behind her.

Then his smile faded and he told her that her parents were gone for good—that they had died when the plane crashed, and their bodies had either been burned or eaten by sharks.

Uncle Bruce never was one to whitewash anything.

All Lia had left of Jack and Aurelia were her memories, their money, and her mother's jewelry, which she had inadvertently left behind on the bed when she repacked her bag that morning. Lia had discovered the red silk pouch shortly after they left the house, when, missing them already, she had gone back to their room while Rita washed the breakfast dishes.

She had asked Rita if they could call the airport and tell her mother she'd forgotten the jewelry, but Rita said it wasn't important, that her mother probably wouldn't even notice she didn't have it. Aurelia rarely wore jewelry, not even the sparkly rings her husband had given her for their engagement and wedding.

When Lia had asked her why not, she had said that it seemed wrong to wear such expensive jewels every day when her family was living in poverty back in Cuba.

But Lia had worn them every day, on a chain around her neck. Not because the gems were precious and beautiful, but because they represented the love her parents had had for each other—and for her.

Selling them had been the most difficult thing she had ever done.

But you traded them for your life, she reminded herself now, as she had hundreds of times since that day in the New Orleans pawnshop last September. Without the money the rings had brought, she would never have been able to start a new life.

But that had all been for nothing, she thought miserably, looking at Marco, who was again watching over the hills just outside the dingy little shed.

Chapter Eight

Marco hadn't expected the storm to let up, and it didn't, only seeming to grow more fierce as the night wore on. The small shed grew pitch black as darkness fell.

And it was silent as he and Lia huddled on the floor, sitting as far from each other as the cramped space allowed—which meant they were inches apart.

His wrist was still encircled by the handcuffs, but he hadn't fastened it around hers again. He could have; maybe he should have, but somehow he couldn't bring himself to do it.

She was silent and so was he, brooding in the dark, the fury of the storm outside punctuated occasionally by a muted scuffling sound inside the shed, not far from where they sat.

"What's that?" Lia had asked the first time they heard it.

"Mice," he had told her. "Or maybe squirrels."

She didn't reply.

He found himself disappointed that she didn't inch her way closer to him for protection from the invisible rodents that shared their quarters.

But then she never had been the type to cower from anything or anyone, he remembered. He knew she was deathly afraid of bugs, yet she would sooner face down a giant Florida grove spider or flying cockroach with a rolled newspaper than ask him to kill it for her.

He knew; it had happened more than once last summer.

Lia wasn't a woman who revealed or caved in to her weaknesses.

He admired her for it, and wondered if she considered her lust for him to be one of those weaknesses.

Lust for her was certainly the biggest of his, and he had been battling it for hours now—not so successfully, he acknowledged grimly, remembering the pivotal moment when his willpower had shattered.

When he'd kissed her earlier, he had found her desire as palpable as if she'd breathlessly told him she wanted him to make love to her.

She used to do just that, last summer . . .

Used to beg him, sometimes in heated Spanish, as he trailed his hot tongue slowly down her body.

"Please," she would moan, thrashing on her bed as his lips probed her most intimate crevices. "Please, Marco, please make love to me, please, now," she would gasp.

Still he would prolong her, taking his time to gently explore every sweet part of her with his hands and mouth until he could no longer hold back.

He inadvertently sighed at the memory, then tensed as soon as he realized the sound had escaped him. He listened for some response from Lia beside him.

She said nothing, and he realized, thankfully, that her breathing was deep and rhythmic. She had fallen asleep on the floor, leaning against an old wooden barrel.

"Lia?" he whispered, just to be sure.

She didn't reply.

After a few moments, he quietly got to his feet and made his way to the door of the shed.

Opening it on a storm-tossed landscape, he hesitated only for a moment before venturing out into the night. The rushing wind and pelting rain were no more savage than the torrent of emotions surging through him. Marco simply couldn't stay there another second, alone with Lia in the hushed shadows, aching for what could never be his . . .

What had never been his in the first place.

He jammed his hands deep into his pockets and walked into the gale, climbing the gentle rise behind the shed toward a grove of familiar trees he had spotted earlier.

As he walked, he thought of her sleeping back there, and he wondered if she was dreaming, and whether her dreams were of him, the way his own had so often been of her.

How many nights, of the past four hundred or so, had he finally drifted into a restless slumber, only to be teased and tormented by the woman he had lost.

The A.J. Sutton of his dreams had fittingly been an elusive temptress, seductively beckoning to him, making erotic promises in her throaty whisper, then vanishing—only to reappear momentarily, reaching out to him once again.

Those dreams had been a strange haven during the lonely, dark months without her, and he had welcomed sleep whenever it finally came, if only for a chance to see her again.

Had she felt the same way?

Was she dreaming of him even now?

Then reality jolted him, and he realized that if Lia's sleep was touched by images of him tonight, it wouldn't be in the form of dreams at all . . .

But nightmares.

His jaw set, he strode on toward the grove of trees, unfazed by the rain that soaked his hair and face and the wind that buffeted his body so that walking was no easy task.

When he reached the small orchard, he made his way among the creaking, swaying boughs, undaunted by the lightning that crackled in the sky almost directly above him. He reached up among the leaves and plucked an apple from a branch, biting into it with a savage appetite.

At least, he thought as he crunched the tart, juicy fruit, this was a hunger he could satisfy.

"Oh, A.J., you are the most exquisite woman I have ever seen," Marco murmured, his breath hot and his lips moist against her throat as he covered her naked body with his. She squirmed, feeling his taut, pulsing erection jabbing into the soft flesh just below her belly. Soon he would enter her. She wanted him now, but knew waiting until they were both beyond ready would make their lovemaking even more passionate. He had taught her that; had taught her a lot of things.

"How many have there been?" she asked, only half-teasing, tangling her fingers in his hair and lifting his head from her neck.

"Women? None who mattered," Marco said softly, brushing a strand of hair from her cheek.

But something in his blue eyes told her he was lying. Again.

Why did he have to lie?

"Marco . . ." She began, but he had lowered his head once more and was working his way down her body now, sucking gently on first one nipple and then the other, until they were both stiff with longing. He rained sweet kisses over her stomach and shifted his body to move lower still, parting her legs with his darting tongue.

Her thoughts were lost, then, replaced by ripples of sheer sensation as he moved his mouth over the most intimate part of her.

He had always been so incredibly good at this . . .

Good at everything.

So good . . .

A.J. closed her eyes as waves of pleasure swept through her. This was better than ever before.

She felt as though it had been such a long time since they had made love, and yet that was impossible. They had been together nearly every night since they met, driven by insatiable lust for each other.

"I want you all the time," she whispered, and moaned as Marco lifted his head, planted a wet kiss on her mouth, and then parted her legs once more, this time with his thigh.

"I want you, too . . ."

She moaned and so did he as he slid his hard, hot length into her.

"So good . . . you feel so good . . . don't ever leave me, Marco, please don't leave me . . ."

"I won't leave you," he said, thrusting slowly, his eyes locked on hers. "I love you."

"Oh, Marco . . ." Lia murmured in her sleep on the dusty floor of the shed as her erotic dream carried her further still from reality. "I love you, too."

"I know you don't want to hear this," Alberto said, as the car rolled slowly along the shoulder of the New York State Thruway heading west, retracing their earlier route, "but I think they're long gone. We should give up and try again tomorrow."

He saw Ramon and Hondo exchange a glance, then heard Ramon mutter, under his breath, *"Le patina el embrague a uno."*

Alberto considered telling them that he did *not* have a screw loose, that they were the crazy ones.

Instead he bit his tongue and tapped the gold rings that adorned his fingers so that they made a clacking sound on the window, mingling with the hollow tapping of the rain on the roof and the rhythmic slapping of the windshield wipers.

These two buffoons didn't know what the hell they were doing. Earlier they had insisted on repeatedly back-tracking ten miles or so toward Massachusetts, keeping an eye out for Marco's car approaching in the opposite direction.

Which was ridiculous, because if Marco had pulled off the road—which they all agreed was likely—he wasn't fool enough to pull back onto the road just a short time later.

No, he and A.J. Sutton were undoubtedly holed up somewhere, waiting for darkness. And even now that night had fallen, there was no guarantee that they would venture out. Especially in the furious storm that showed no sign of letting up.

Alberto had long since grown weary of this futile cat-and-mouse game. In fact, he was all for calling Victor and telling him they'd lost the trail, period.

Ramon and Hondo flatly refused to do that. It was Ramon who had decided, after they'd stopped to dump the driver's bloody body into a wooded ravine, that they should turn around again and drive along the shoulder, following the original path Marco's car had taken. They were ostensibly looking for signs, in the dense under-

growth lining the roadside, that a car had left the highway and gone into the woods.

But it was impossible to see much of anything, what
with the rain and wind, with only the car's headlights
to illuminate the scene ahead.

"What's that?" Hondo asked abruptly, lifting one
massive hand from the steering wheel to point ahead.

"What?" Ramon leaned forward and peered through
the windshield.

Alberto saw a gap in the dense undergrowth, almost
like a narrow road that led off through the trees. And
there were dark tire tracks burned into the pavement
along the shoulder that were faintly visible even in the
rain.

"The branches," Hondo announced, turning to
Alberto with a self-satisfied smile. "They're broken. And
the skid marks—they went through there."

"It might not have been them," Alberto protested,
for the sake of arguing.

Ramon mimicked, "It might not be them. What's the
matter with you? Who else would drive off the road fast
enough to knock branches off the trees and leave skid
marks?"

"Well? What are you waiting for? Get going," Alberto
commanded impatiently, as if it had been his idea all
along. "Let's drive down and see if they're there."

The car bumped over the edge of the road and down
a slight embankment. They passed between the trees
and into a narrow grassy pathway.

Alberto made a face and hollered, "Watch out for
the—"

There was a grinding sound as the tires spun beneath
them.

"Mud," Alberto finished, rolling his eyes. "We're
stuck. Now what?"

"Get out and push," Hondo ordered, turning around

with a gleam in his dark eyes that challenged Alberto to differ.

"You, too, Ramon," Alberto said, hesitating with his hand on the door handle.

"Why should we both get soaked and muddy?" Ramon asked lazily, crossing his right leg over his left knee. He was wearing black Gucci loafers. "And anyway, you're stronger than I am, Alberto. I'm just a little shrimp."

He and Hondo thought that was hilarious.

Alberto slammed the door on their laughter, stomping through the muck to the back of the car. He bent over and was about to start shoving against the trunk when a flash of lightning illuminated something shiny through the trees.

He frowned, then took a few steps to get a closer look. Was it . . . ?

"Hey," he shouted, squishing his way over to tap on the window of the driver's side of the car. "Hondo! Ramon! Look!"

He pointed toward his discovery, and through the rain-spattered window, saw them recognize the car hidden in the trees a few yards away.

Lia woke to the endless sound of the rain and wind, and it took a moment before she realized where she was.

"Marco?" she called tentatively, hopefully, thinking vaguely he might have gone.

"What?" came the gruff reply from right beside her, and she felt a sharp edge of disappointment.

"What time is it?"

A pause, and then she saw the flash of his illuminated watch face a few inches from her thigh.

"Two fifteen," he said curtly. "Are you hungry?"

"Am I hungry? Let's see, since the glass of orange juice I had before I left my house this morning, I've had . . . nothing. Why would I be hungry?"

He didn't reply.

"Anyway," she went on, "what's the difference if I am? What are you going to do, order in Chinese food?"

He snorted at that, and even she had to allow a wry smirk at the ridiculous scenario—a delivery man, perhaps on a bicycle, riding up to the shed with a brown, greasy paper bag laden with succulent ribs and dumplings and stir fry . . .

She heard him say, "Hold out your hand."

Great, she thought bitterly, *the handcuffs again.*

She thought of refusing, then wondered what would be the point of it.

Marco would do whatever he damn well felt like doing; that much had been proven since he'd whisked her away from Boston.

So she sighed audibly and grumbled, "Fine, here's my hand," as she shoved it toward him in the dark.

To her surprise, there was no brush of cold metal against her wrist.

Instead he clasped her fingers gently in his own, and placed something in them.

"What's this?" she asked, stroking something round and smooth. "It feels like—"

"An apple," he confirmed. "Taste it."

"Yeah, right. Let me guess . . . Gee, is it poisonous?"

"Who are you, Snow White? Eat the apple," he shot back. "Unless you want to starve."

When she didn't move, he made an impatient grunt and pulled her hand and the apple upward, toward him. She heard a crunching sound as he bit into it, and felt a spurt of juice over her fingers.

"There. Eat the rest of it," he growled.

She didn't have to be urged again, but tore into the

crisp fruit hungrily. She was half finished with it when she felt him press another one into her hand, brusquely saying, "Here. Take it. And there are more."

"Where did you get them? Out of your pocket?" she asked around a mouthful. "I didn't notice any bulges . . ."

She paused and winced as she realized what she'd said, and again heard him snort.

"Oh, really? I didn't realize you were looking for bulges," he said, almost . . . provocatively?

She could picture the look on his face. She had seen it often enough, whenever they engaged in the seductive banter and double entendres that had fueled so much of their early passion.

She cleared her throat now, said, "I obviously meant the apples."

"I picked them in the orchard up the hill," he told her, so huskily that she knew his thoughts had meandered, with hers, back over the long months to the hedonistic days before they'd been separated.

"In the dark? And the rain?" she asked dubiously.

"I knew you'd be hungry. And I was," he added quickly, as if to prove he would never have considered her needs if not driven by his own.

"Thank you," she said softly.

"You're welcome."

After a pause, she finished the first apple, and then another, and found that at least one hollow ache inside of her had somewhat subsided.

Too bad the other couldn't be eased by food, she thought wistfully.

She heard Marco yawn and asked, "Aren't you going to sleep?"

There was silence, and then, "I guess I should get some rest. Give me your hand."

She furrowed her brow but obeyed his terse command, this time knowing he wasn't going to offer her fruit.

She was right.

She felt the handcuffs clasped around her wrist, then heard the telltale click and found herself fastened, once again, to his side.

"You didn't have to do that," she told him.

"Yes, I did."

"Why? You left me here when you went out for the apples, and I didn't escape."

"You were asleep."

"But you took a chance. I could have woken and made a dash for the hills," she goaded him, wondering if she would have, had she found herself alone in the shed.

Somehow she wasn't so sure.

He didn't reply, only made a settling sound beside her as he leaned back against the wooden barrel behind them.

There was silence for a short time, and when she spoke, she wasn't certain she'd find him still awake.

"How did you find me?" she asked him.

He didn't respond right away, and she concluded, with regret, that he was sleeping.

Then she heard his voice. "You must know about your face being broadcast on television during the Red Sox–Yankees playoff game."

She nodded, then remembered he couldn't see her and said, "I know about it."

"I was watching," he said simply.

"I figured you might be. You loved baseball. The New York Yankees," she added, remembering. "I always thought it was strange for a California boy to love the Yankees."

He didn't respond to that.

She took a deep breath, and then a chance. "You

didn't grow up in California, did you, Marco? You grew up in New York."

For a moment, there was no response. This time she knew he wasn't asleep; she could feel him there, his body tense beside her. And she realized, even before he told her, that she was right.

"In the south Bronx," he said quietly. "Was that your only clue? That I like the Yankees?"

"Sometimes, when you forgot yourself, when we were arguing, or—" She broke off, unable to speak aloud of the passion they had known. After a moment, she resumed, "Anyway, I would sometimes hear a trace of an accent. A New York accent. But even if that hadn't happened, I knew you were lying about California. I knew you were lying about everything."

"All along?"

Had she known all along? She wasn't sure, now, when she had first realized he wasn't what he seemed.

"I don't know," she said honestly. "I just remember thinking that you weren't just some pal of Victor's who just popped in for a visit and stayed the entire summer and into the fall. When were you going to tell me what was really going on?"

Silence.

"You weren't ever going to tell me, were you?" she asked.

Silence.

And then, "Probably not."

She contemplated that.

Did it matter, now, after all these months?

It shouldn't, she told herself fiercely.

But it did.

"How did you find me?" she asked again, when she trusted her voice not to crack. "After you saw my face on television, I mean. How on earth did you track me down?"

"I called a friend in Boston who owed me a favor," he said, as though it were the most uncomplicated thing in the world.

"Okay," she said evenly, knowing better than to ask too many questions, "how did *he* find me?"

"The game went into overtime," he told her. "There was plenty of time for my friend to get over to Fenway and catch up with the crowd leaving the stadium after the game. All he had to do was keep an eye out for the people who were seated near you in the stands."

"How could he possibly do that?"

"By getting hold of the videotaped coverage of the ball hitting you."

"And you did that . . . how?"

"I have connections," was all he said.

"So," she continued after a minute, "you got a hold of this videotape—"

"My friend did," he interjected.

"And your friend, what? Played it in slow motion over and over so he could get a good look at the crowd around me?"

"Probably."

"And then he waylaid some unsuspecting spectator as he left the stands?"

"Exactly."

"And that's how he tracked me down to my house by the very next morning?" She shook her head incredulously. "That's impossible. No one sitting around me knew who I was, except my date."

"You were with a date?"

"Yes," she said, feeling irrationally pleased that he sounded jealous. She knew better than to tell him it had been a blind date that she had been tricked into, that she hadn't given a damn about poor Tony Lanzone.

"How did you track me down if no one in the stands even knew my name?" she asked Marco again.

"You're sure about that?"

"Of course I'm sure about that. They were all strangers."

"You'd be surprised at what you can reveal to a stranger without even meaning to," was his ambiguous reply.

"Okay," she said, "then how did you get to Boston from Florida in the blink of an eye?"

"I flew."

"On what? A magic carpet?"

"A chartered plane."

"Victor's chartered plane."

"No," he said firmly. "I told you. Victor and I aren't playing on the same team, Lia. We never were."

"Tell me another lie."

"I'll tell you more," he said, "but it isn't a lie. I've been looking for you ever since last September, trying everything I could think of to find you."

"I believe that," she said, her voice hardening. "Trying to find me so that you could kill me."

"Let me ask you something," he said, and an undercurrent of anger practically crackled in the air between them. "Are you dead right now?"

She shrugged. "In some ways, I am," she told him quietly. "In a lot of ways that matter."

He seemed to ponder that for a moment.

When he spoke, his voice was low and gritty. "Well, if it weren't for me, you'd be dead in the *only* way that really matters, Lia."

His words chilled her to the bone.

"Okay," she said, fighting to remain sardonic, "you're some wonderful superhero rescuing me from some arch-villain, I suppose. So where's your leotard?"

He didn't crack a smile at that.

Neither did she.

After a moment, she asked, "How, exactly, did you save me? And from what?"

"From Victor. He's vicious, Lia. And you've caused him a lot of trouble."

"But I didn't do anything to Victor. I could have come forward as a witness, but I'm not stupid. I knew the only thing to do was hide. I'd still be hiding right now if you hadn't—"

"When are you going to get it through your head, Lia?" His voice rose above the storm. "I saved your life. And Victor's right on my heels, determined to snatch you away from me."

"If that's true, then why don't you just take me to the police?"

"Because you're wanted for questioning in connection to the Trask case. You must know that. If we go to the police, you'll have to testify against Victor."

"I don't have anything on Victor. He wasn't even there the night of the kidnapping—but you were," she remembered. "If you aren't involved with his operation, then what were you doing hiding there, with a gun?"

"The same thing you were doing," he retorted. "Trying to save Karen and Tyler Trask."

She shook her head. "I don't believe you."

"I'm telling the truth."

"Why would I believe that now, after so many lies?"

"Okay," he said curtly, as if something had snapped inside him. "I'll tell you more of the truth. You were born Aurelia Jane Sutton in the heart of Miami—Little Havana, actually. Your parents were Jack Sutton and Aurelia Santiago Sutton. He was a naval officer, she was a Cuban refugee he rescued somewhere in the Atlantic off the coast of the Keys during Hurricane Kathy—"

"Hurricane Katie," she murmured, and shook her head. "How did you find all this? I never told you—"

"No, you never told me much, did you, Lia? Just like

I never told you much," he said harshly. "So, in a way, we were both living lies, weren't we?"

"I never lied. I just chose not to share certain details of my past."

"You chose not to share a lot of other things, too," he said, suddenly sounding not so much angry, as sad.

"What else did you discover?"

"Among other things, that your uncle Bruce remarried last spring, to a wealthy Palm Beach divorcee ten years older than he is. Did you know about that?"

"No, and I don't care," she muttered. "Figures."

"I also found Javier and Rosalita Santiago," he said, and paused significantly.

Lia froze at the mention of those names, names she hadn't heard or spoken in nearly twenty years.

When she finally found her voice, it sounded far more composed than she felt.

"You *found* them?" was all she could manage to get out.

She was glad he couldn't see the shock on her face, glad he didn't know how deeply he had shaken her.

Or did he?

"I found them," he repeated, with the air of a gambler who had just passed the queen of spades in a game of Hearts.

He went on after a beat. "I also found their son and two daughters. And a couple of in-laws. And grandchildren."

"How . . . ?" Flustered, she hesitated, began again. *"Where . . . ?"*

"I have connections," he said, an exact echo of his earlier statement.

Then it had been smug; now it was devoid of telltale sentiment.

"Are they . . . how are they?"

It seemed so trite—*how are they?*—yet it was all she

could think to ask; the only query she could pluck from the maelstrom and questions whirling in her mind.

His response was equally banal.

"They're fine."

And yet the tone of his voice told her he was fully aware of how deeply his news had unnerved her.

He knew, then—but how could he know?—that she had spent a lifetime wondering about her lost family, the way her mother had spent years wondering.

She had never mentioned it to him; it was one of her innermost secrets, one she clung to fiercely through all her days and nights with him. To have spoken about her past would have been to reveal her most vulnerable self.

She had never dared do that with him.

With anyone.

So how did he know?

"Did you . . . speak to them?" she asked Marco tentatively.

"Not directly."

She was impatient. "Well, can I?"

"They don't even know that you exist, Lia."

His words shattered the fragile, foolish shard of hope that had taken hold within her only moments before.

What had she been thinking?

Of course they didn't know she existed; she had realized that all along, her whole life.

Hadn't her mother told her wistfully how she longed to share her husband and child with the family she had left behind?

Hadn't her mother cried over the parents who didn't even know they had a little granddaughter?

Of course she had.

And of course Lia had known they weren't out there, weren't thinking of her, weren't searching for her.

It was just that when Marco had said he'd found them, a vision had darted into her mind . . .

An impossible vision of a warm, welcoming family that longed for her the way she had longed for them in all these years since her parents' death. A family that would embrace her, and keep her, and above all, give her a sense of belonging.

She had never, in all the years since she'd lost her mother and father, belonged anywhere.

Only in Marco's arms had she ever felt a glimmer of comfort—and that, it turned out, had only been an illusion.

"Where are they?" she asked again.

"I can't tell you."

Anger shot through her, and she glared at his invisible face in the dark. "Why the hell not?"

"Because it's my secret weapon," he told her in an infuriatingly straightforward way. "As long as I know where they are, and you don't, you have to stay with me and trust me."

"I'll never trust you again."

"You never did."

"Touché," she said with a flippancy she didn't feel. Then, "Why do you need me to stay with you?"

"Because if you don't, you'll stumble right into Victor's clutches."

"Oh, so you're my hero, protecting me from the evil Victor?"

"In a word, yes."

She glowered. "Why do I find that so hard to believe?"

"I keep wondering the same thing."

"Because you, Marco Estevez, are the last man on earth I want to spend time with. And the fact that you've supposedly found my long-lost relatives doesn't change that."

"I did find them—"

"Sure, you did. I don't know where you dug up my family history—then again, I'm sure it wasn't hard, what with all your 'connections.' But I'll tell you this, Marco. I don't believe a word you say."

"Then you're ignoring the truth."

"I doubt that," she said, fighting back a shred of misgiving. "You've never told the truth about anything in your life. At least not to me. Why would you start now?"

"Because I—"

He broke off, and she sensed he'd been about to make some big announcement, something important.

"Because you what?" she demanded, willing herself not to soften, not to cave in against the flurry of muddled emotions that reeled inside her.

"Never mind," he said with a weary sigh. "Just be quiet, will you, so I can get some sleep."

"Oh, sure, you poor thing. Of course I'll be quiet," she assured him.

"Good."

She allowed him a moment to get settled.

Then she began to sing.

Loudly.

Victor stood at the edge of the shimmering aquamarine water of Biscayne Bay, looking up at the vast home his money had built.

A mansion.

He had always said he would live in a mansion one day.

When he was a child in the cramped Bogota apartment where his mother struggled to singlehandedly raise him and his seven siblings, he would entertain her with descriptions of the palace he would build one day.

"Where will this palace be, Victor?" she would ask, smiling.

"In America, of course."

And Mama would nod and smile. "Of course."

Everyone knew that the best of everything was to be found in America.

If only Mama had lived to visit him here.

But she had died several years ago, of ovarian cancer, only two months after being diagnosed. There had been no opportunity to plan a trip to the States or show her the many beautiful things he had acquired with his enormous wealth.

She would have loved to see his Picasso paintings and the baby grand piano that nobody in the house, including Victor, knew how to play. He had bought it with his mother in mind, planning to surprise her with it when she came to visit.

She had once mentioned to him, when he was growing up, that she had wanted to take piano lessons as a child, but her parents hadn't had the money.

"Some day I'll buy you piano lessons, Mama," he had said. "Some day I'll even buy you a piano. I'm going to be the greatest baseball player who ever lived."

He sighed and began walking away from the water.

What would his life have been like if it hadn't been for that motorcycle accident that had robbed him of an athletic career? Would he be a celebrity, adored by thousands of American fans, remembered for generations to come?

Possibly.

But that wasn't what it was about for him. Victor had never needed fame.

Only wealth.

And the power that came with it.

He looked up again at his sprawling home. The boxy Mediterranean architecture was silhouetted against the darkening sky. Light spilled from the large windows and doors overlooking the water, casting a glow through the dusk like a lighthouse beckoning over the open sea. He could faintly hear Latin music coming from the stereo in the Florida room. Several of his men were gathered there, loyally standing by until he needed them.

He thought of Marco Estevez and frowned.

It hadn't been so long ago that he had been among Victor's associates.

Traitor.

Victor's lips curled at the very notion that he had foolishly trusted the man.

He should head back inside and wait by the telephone for word that Alberto and the others had captured Estevez and the girl. There was no question but that they would catch up with the fugitives sooner or later.

Victor smiled as he strode toward the stately mansion his money had built.

He always got what he wanted.

Always.

Marco came awake slowly, realizing that the air around him was still.

No thunder booming in the distance.

No raindrops plunking relentlessly on the leaky roof or dripping onto the floor by his feet.

No wind causing the rickety shed to sway perilously.

And, mercifully, no singing.

He sat up slightly and realized that not only was it silent, but he could see. A shaft of gray morning light filtered through the cracked windowpane.

Marco looked down and saw that Lia had fallen asleep on the dusty floor beside him, her dark, tousled head a mere fraction of an inch away from his thigh. It was as though she'd instinctively wanted to rest her head in his lap, but had stubbornly refused.

Oh, Lia, he thought, shaking his head and battling the urge to reach down and smooth her dyed hair.

Such a gentle gesture had been the last thing on his mind a few hours ago, when she'd assailed him with her vast repertoire of pop music. The worst had been an endless, off-key rendition of "Hey, Jude," that had erupted, of course, into the famous, repetitive finale . . .

"Bah-ba-ba, ba-da-da-dah . . . ba-da-da-dah . . . Hey, Jude."

Every time she paused to catch her breath—she *had* to be wearing out—he would close his eyes and hurriedly try to fall asleep. But just when he was drifting off, it would start up again . . .

"Bah-ba-ba, ba-da-da-dah . . . ba-da-da-dah . . . Hey, Jude."

God, she had a horrible voice. He used to tease her about it back when they were together in Florida.

Lia had told him—in one of the rare glimpses she'd provided into her past—that she had been brought up in a musical household, courtesy of her mother. Even as a child, she had loved to dance.

And she was good at it.

He had been so proud to take her to the glitzy South Beach clubs, where she would invariably begin moving to the Latin beat the moment they arrived.

She was one of those people who never seemed self-conscious or awkward on the dance floor, but moved with a fluid, sensual grace that riveted Marco. She had been so damned seductive on those hot summer nights, moving under the flashing colored lights—all bare, tanned skin and swinging blond hair and swaying hips. Even when she fell into step with the other dancers, doing the crowd-synchronized "Macarena" that was so new that summer, she stood apart from the others, distinctive in her own provocative interpretation of the choreographed movements.

Yes, she was a good dancer.

She had loved to sing, too.

She had been terrible at that.

And she knew it.

Whenever Marco teased her about her inability to carry a tune, she would, with characteristic aplomb, serenade him in her flat, loud singing voice.

And he would beg her to stop.

She would shake her head, grinning and singing until he captured her mouth with his own, ostensibly to silence her.

It had worked every time.

Now, glancing down at her peaceful, sleeping face, he wondered what would have happened if he'd used that tactic this time.

It had certainly crossed his mind as she tortured him last night.

But this time, unlike before, what he had wanted, needed desperately, was to go to sleep.

And if he had kissed her to get her to stop singing, falling asleep was the *last* thing he could have done as a follow-up.

Did she realize that?

Had her relentless singing been a seductive dare?

Had she been taunting him, trying to induce him into kissing her?

She couldn't have been, he told himself. *As far as she's concerned, I'm her enemy now.*

Not her lover.

No, she had merely been using her most effective weapon to torment him so that he would be unable to rest. She wanted him to be exhausted today so that he'd let down his guard, and the moment he did, she would slip away.

He scowled at the prospect of having her vanish again so soon, after so many months of trying to find her . . .

But then, who was he kidding?

He was about to lose her no matter what, if not in a matter of hours, then in a day, maybe two.

However long it took . . .

And anyway . . .

Hell, he didn't *have* her, except as his unwilling captive.

The sooner he was rid of her, the better.

Then he could finally go on with his life, finally make a fresh start, and forget her . . .

No.

How could he ever forget her?

Forget her . . .

Yes.

He had to.

Forget her . . .

He heard a rustling sound as she stirred.

He looked down and saw her eyelids flutter.

Then they were wide open, and she was staring sleepily up at him the way she had so many mornings, a smile creeping slowly over her lips . . .

Then with a start, she blinked, the smile vanished, and she jerked upright.

"What are you doing?" she demanded, her voice hoarse, from the dampness of the shed or from her interminable serenade, or both.

What was he doing?

What did he ever do, but think about her?

Not that he would admit it.

"I was about to wake you up," he said gruffly.

"Why? Is my breakfast omelet ready?" she asked without missing a beat.

Remarkable. After everything she'd been through, she still had that snappy sense of irony.

"Were you going to ask if I wanted jam or honey on my toast?" she continued, sitting up. "Because I think that today, I'll take both. And a side of hash browns. And don't forget the coffee. Steaming hot, and really strong."

She yawned and then abruptly arched her back and stretched, jerking his arm up with hers.

"Oops, sorry, Marco," she said in a mock apologetic tone. "I seem to have forgotten I'm shackled to you like some pathetic death-row inmate."

He grunted in reply.

"Pardon, what was that?" she asked pleasantly.

He rolled his eyes. "Come on, get up. We've got to get moving before someone spots us."

"What's on the agenda for today? A little sightseeing? Some shopping?"

"Not exactly." He shrugged. "For starters, I thought we'd steal a car."

"What are we, Bonnie and Clyde?" Lia asked when she found her voice. "We can't steal a car."

"We have to."

"No way."

"You don't seem to understand, Lia. We don't have a choice."

"Stealing is illegal."

He shrugged.

Infuriated with his cavalier attitude, she said, "I'm not getting myself arrested, Marco."

He sighed and said, with exaggerated patience, "Not stealing the car might mean getting yourself killed, Lia."

She waved him off with a flick of the wrist that wasn't attached to him with the handcuffs. "I'll take my chances."

"You don't have a choice," he said, touching her wrist that *was* attached to the handcuffs. "You're coming with me, and I'm stealing a car, so . . ."

She shook her head. "Where are you even going to find a car to steal? This looks like God's country to me, Marco. I haven't even seen a road since we left the highway miles ago."

"We'll find a car. Let's get going."

She stood her ground. "I don't like taking orders."

"And I don't like giving them."

"Yeah, right," she muttered.

"You don't know a thing about me, do you, Lia?" he asked suddenly. "You think I'm enjoying this."

"Enjoying what? Playing prison guard? Or wait—was it Superhero?"

"I'm not playing, and this isn't a game. We're both in serious danger."

She snorted. "Right now, the only danger I'm in . . ."

"Yes?" He leaned closer to her, studying her intently.

She cleared her throat, began again. "The only danger I'm in . . ."

She trailed off once more, unable to keep herself from looking into his blue eyes.

This, she thought, *is the danger.*

That he'll get to me somehow; that he'll work his way through all my defenses and make me forget that I hate him.

"Let's go steal a car," he said abruptly, shifting his weight, looking away.

"Fine. Let's go steal a car," she agreed.

Before you steal my heart.

Chapter Nine

Alberto's black dress shoes that had been so shiny just yesterday were thickly caked in mud, and his poor feet were killing him.

His shirt that had been soaked with perspiration was now saturated with the rain that had beaten against him as he and his companions combed the hilly, pitch-black forest through the stormy night.

Never before had he been so miserable, and filled with hatred.

Hatred for Victor, Hondo, and Ramon . . .

And for Marco Estevez . . .

And, most of all, for A.J. Sutton, the bitch who had started this whole thing.

If it weren't for her, Alberto would be warm and dry, basking in the Florida sunshine right now.

When he got his hands on her . . .

"There!" Hondo said, pointing ahead, as the trees opened onto a clearing overlooking acres of meadowland, a weathered farmhouse, and several outbuildings.

"You think they're down there?" Alberto frowned. "What makes you think that?"

"You're an imbecile," Ramon said disdainfully. "Where else would they be?"

Alberto shook his head, wondering—as he had countless times through the endless night—if he would ever be able to draw his pistol and fire two well-placed shots before they were able to react.

Several things had stopped him.

Enraged as he was at the way his companions treated him, he had no great desire to be left alone to find his way out of the forest. The closest he had ever gotten to the great outdoors had been years ago, back in Colombia, when he'd been forced to bury his victims in remote graves he dug and covered with lime and twigs and leaves.

Even then, he had loathed the damp, woodsy scent of the damp earth and decaying leaves. He had cringed every time he saw a fat snake slither under a rock or heard the ominous sound of animals rustling in the undergrowth.

No, he didn't want to be alone out here, even if the alternative was to be with Hondo and Ramon.

Anyway, just think what Victor would do to him if he discovered Alberto had annihilated two of the most prized members of his cartel. To put it mildly, he would hardly be pleased.

Besides, Alberto had no doubt that, quick and stealthy as he might be in launching his attack, Hondo's reflexes would be quicker, stealthier. The moment Alberto reached for his gun, he would be dead.

"Let's go," Ramon said, drawing his gun.

Hondo did the same.

After a moment's hesitation, Alberto followed suit. As he drew the weapon from his pocket, he again contemplated firing two quick shots and doing away with Hondo and Ramon.

Then Hondo looked at him with those lethal black eyes. "If I were you," he said in his distinct Jamaican patois, "I would be very careful with that weapon."

Alberto clenched his jaw. He got the message, loud and clear.

"Come on! We'll start down there," Ramon said impatiently, gesturing with his pistol at the smallest structure on the property—the shed.

"Come on . . . down there," Marco said, pointing.

Lia saw an old farmer walking toward his barn, stooped as if against a strong wind. But there was no wind; only cold, and a thick blanket of fog.

"No," Lia said, standing her ground on the hill above the barn. She would have folded her arms resolutely against her chest if she hadn't been shackled to him.

He looked exasperated. "What do you mean, no?"

"You aren't going to hurt that poor old man."

He stared at her. "Who said I was? We're only going to steal his car."

"How do you know he has one?"

"He must. You can't live way out here in the middle of nowhere without some kind of vehicle."

"What if . . . what if his wife is out driving it?"

"At this hour?"

"She might be."

"Right. Come on, Lia. Let's go while he's busy in the barn doing his chores. He doesn't even have to see us."

"Well, what if he does? What if he calls the police."

"From the barn?"

"There could be a phone there. This *is* the nineties."

"By the looks of this farm, it's the *eighteen*-nineties," Marco pointed out wryly.

"You don't know that. Maybe he's more cutting edge than he looks. Maybe he has a cell phone in his pocket, and he's already spotted us, and he's calling the police as we speak," she said, knowing she was being preposterous, yet unable to help herself.

Marco smirked. "I promise you don't have to do any of the dirty work. Come on."

"Wait." She held back again when he started to walk.

"What is it now?"

"How are you planning to steal a car even if you do find one? I mean, have you thought about your technique?"

"Let me handle it."

"Believe me, I plan to. I'm not exactly a pro at hot-wiring vehicles."

"No . . . really?"

He started walking again, and she had no choice but to move alongside him.

They were almost down to the barn when she tripped over a tree root that was sticking out of the ground. She found herself falling forward . . .

Until a pair of strong arms grabbed her.

Her hands gripped his broad shoulders and her head landed against his massive chest as he steadied her, and their bodies were aligned front to front. She could feel his muscles tense against her, as though he were suddenly coming alive, as though their abrupt physical contact had stirred the same buried instinct in him as it had in her.

She could feel her heart leap and her stomach quiver as they stood there, breathless, holding each other.

For a moment neither of them spoke or moved.

Then Marco asked, "Are you all right?"

His voice was gruff, not gentle.

Had she actually been expecting gentle?

Of course she hadn't.

Not from him. Not now.

The impatience in his tone jarred her into motion, and she pulled back, refusing to look up at him.

"I'm fine," she told his shoes.

"Are you sure? Because it looked like your ankle twisted, and—"

"I'm fine," she repeated through clenched teeth.

He shrugged, shook his head, and they resumed walking.

On cold, foggy mornings like this, Charlie Lima regretted that he hadn't listened to his oldest daughter, Mary Lou, and sold the farm when Mabel died back in '91.

If he had, he would probably be relaxing by the ocean right about now, reading the morning paper on the balcony of some retirement condo in sunny Boca Raton. Better yet, he might still be sound asleep.

Instead here he was, sloshing through the heavy gray Sunday dawn, facing the same morning chores he had faced for the past seventy-odd years, since he'd been a boy growing up on this very farm in the Adirondack foothills just east of Albany.

It was just as well he hadn't retired and gone south, he thought as he unlatched the door to the barn. He probably wouldn't be able to snooze all morning, even if he could.

In the long years since he'd lost Mabel, it was hard enough for him to fall asleep at night, let alone stay asleep until five. Not when he felt so lost in the big old bed they'd shared for over fifty years.

Besides, he couldn't bring himself to sell the only home he'd ever known. He had been born in the sprawling front bedroom of the house, and he suspected that he would die there one day soon. His ticker had never been strong, not since his heart attack back in '79, and lately, tingling pains in his chest and arms had warned him that his days were numbered.

Just as well. As Mama had always said, it was best to leave a party before it was over.

He grabbed a pitchfork and began cleaning the nearest stall, where the old blind mare, Lucy, stood patiently to one side. Sometimes he marveled that Lucy, like him, was still alive and kicking. She looked as tired as he felt, and he had a feeling she, too, was biding her time.

He suspected the grandkids would miss him and the farm, though. They loved visiting, especially at Christmas, when he would hitch the old sled to his tractor and drive them over the snow-covered hills. Then again, they were teenagers now—getting too old for the tradition.

And so, as his daughters liked to remind him, was he.

Sometimes he found it difficult to recognize the two gray-haired women who called him "Dad" and who complained about the rigors of country life every time they visited.

Had there really been a time when Mary Lou and Paula planned to get married and live on the farm with him and Mabel? "We'll be one big happy family, Daddy," they used to say, just the way it had been with Charlie's own folks before they passed on years ago.

But then his girls had grown up, and those plans had been lost along the way, and the busy years had taken his daughters far from home, just as they'd cruelly snatched Mabel away in their twilight years, when he needed her most.

Now he was alone on the farm, struggling to keep the old place running, knowing the kids would sell the place anyway, the minute he was gone.

The end of the line.

The phrase had been running through his mind for

days now, as the pains in his chest grew more persistent. He supposed he should give Doc Taunton a call, but the way he figured it, why fight the inevitable?

He had to go sometime, and lately he figured the sooner, the better. He almost welcomed it.

He just knew Mabel was up there somewhere, waiting for him, along with Charlie Junior, who had been still-born back in the forties, and his ma and pa, and the rest of the old clan.

The end of the line . . .

No more Lima boys to carry on the name and the family farm, the way Charlie had, and his father before him, and his grandfather before that, and . . .

Charlie froze, hearing a sound outside the barn.

It sounded like a car door slamming . . .

And then another.

Frowning, he straightened and turned toward the barn door. He'd closed it against the chill. Now he shuffled toward it, wishing he could move as quickly as he once had. He used his pitchfork to pull him along like a walking stick, anticipation dogging his slow, short steps.

Could it be that one of the kids had flown up back east and dropped in for a surprise visit?

Seemed unlikely, particularly at this hour of the day. The girls never rose before nine, and the grandkids, God love 'em, were just as lazy.

But maybe widowed Susan Willis from down the road had brought him another coffee cake. Or maybe old Arty Jones was dropping by for a game of cards. He hadn't done that in months.

Charlie opened the door and peered into the mist-shrouded morning. The barn yard was empty.

"Who's there?" he called, scowling when he saw no vehicle other than his old, faded green pickup truck parked over by the back porch.

The only reply was a chugging sound, then a distinct roar as the truck's engine turned over.

"What the . . . ?" Charlie stared as his truck disappeared down the driveway toward the road that led to town.

"How did you know the keys would be in the ignition?" Lia asked Marco, still shocked at the ease with which they'd managed to steal the pickup truck.

"I didn't know," he replied over the rattling motor, steering around a rut in the road.

"Then how were we going to steal it?"

"I would have gotten it started." He shrugged.

"You mean by hot-wiring it?"

He ignored her question and posed one of his own. "Why didn't you scream for help when that old farmer came out of the barn back there?"

She had been wondering the same thing herself. In the split second that she had seen the elderly man, before they were driving away, she had realized it might be her chance to be rescued.

From Marco.

Rescued from Marco.

That was what she wanted, wasn't it?

He *was* the enemy, wasn't he?

He couldn't be telling the truth about saving her. Why would he start telling the truth now, when he hadn't back when he'd cared about her?

At least he'd seemed to care . . .

But then, that was probably a lie, too.

"Lia?"

"What?" she asked sharply, irritated by his prod.

"Why didn't you yell?"

"Because I figured if I did, you'd shoot the old man. And me," she tacked on for good measure.

There was a pause. She snuck a peek at Marco and saw that he was staring straight ahead, through the windshield. After a moment he asked, "Did you really think I'd shoot him?"

"Yes," she lied.

"And you?"

"Wouldn't you have?" She watched him.

He frowned, then turned to look over his shoulder, distracted. "Did you see that sign?"

"What sign?"

"The one we just passed on the curve. There were some branches in front of it, and I'm not sure what it said."

Lia looked back at the road behind them. "Oh. No, I didn't see it." *I was too busy waiting to hear if you're capable of killing me.*

"Damn. There's a fork up ahead, and I need to know which way to go. We want to head northwest."

"Why northwest?"

"Why not?" He jerked the wheel to the right at the fork, and the pavement was smoother. "This must lead toward town."

"What town?"

"The nearest town," he said, as if she should have known. "That's where we need to go."

"Why?"

"The gas tank on this thing is almost on empty. Are you going to keep asking questions?"

"Does it bother you?"

"Frankly, yeah."

"Why's that?"

She saw a muscle clench in his jaw, and smiled to herself. Why did she get so much pleasure out of rankling him?

For that matter, how could anything about him give her pleasure, after what he'd put her through?

For a brief moment, she had just found herself almost *enjoying* the early morning drive through the rugged autumn countryside.

How could she enjoy it, when she should be panicking about where he was taking her?

After all, she didn't believe that bull he'd handed her, did she? About his being some kind of savior, out to rescue her from the dark, evil Victor.

She honestly didn't buy that crap about his being on her side, did she?

No.

Because if he were on her side, he wouldn't have treated her the way he had. He wouldn't have pulled a gun on her, and abducted her . . .

Or would he?

He *had* pointed out that he knew the only way he could get her to go with him was by force.

And he was sure as hell right about that. She wouldn't willingly accompany him anywhere these days.

Although . . .

There *had* been a time when she would have gone to the ends of the earth with him, for him—if he had so much as asked.

Which he hadn't.

There had been a time when she was dreading the day they would say goodbye, though neither of them ever mentioned that it was inevitable. She had sensed all along, that summer, that sooner or later, what they had would come to an end.

She had known Marco would leave Victor's home, and Florida, and somehow she had known that he wouldn't ask her to go with him.

No, she had never truly entertained the possibility that they might last forever, not even during those languid moments when they would lie naked in each other's arms, sated and sleepy, fantasizing about sailing away together to some remote spot where the real world could never intrude.

Now here they were, alone together in some twisted variation of their fantasy, moving farther from the real world with every passing moment.

But this wasn't paradise. Far from it.

This was hell, she informed herself firmly, and it was hell because Marco wasn't the man she had fallen in love with.

She, too, was utterly different from the woman she had been then.

And yet . . .

There was still some part of her that was drawn to some part of him.

She could only hope fervently that he wouldn't dare kiss her again . . .

And that whatever the day ahead brought, it wouldn't end with them spending another night together in close quarters.

At least she had stopped asking questions, Marco thought, glancing at Lia. For the past twenty minutes, she had been staring morosely out the windshield at the road ahead.

But for some reason, he suddenly found himself missing the pseudo-aura of companionship, missed the sound of her voice even if he didn't miss her endless questions.

It was just that he couldn't provide answers.

He couldn't even start trying now.

How would he explain to her—in more detail than he had already provided—exactly who he was, what they were doing, where they were going.

She might not even believe him.

And even if she did . . .

He wasn't ready to expose so much of himself to a woman who already knew too much. Not his real identity, or what his past had been like, but the important things.

Like how to find his weakest spot, and exploit it, and wound him more deeply than anyone else ever had . . .

Not an easy feat in his world, where pain and loss had dogged him from the cradle and probably would to the grave.

If he looked back over his life, trying to pinpoint a single, pivotal moment that defined who he was, what he would become, he couldn't find it.

Was it the day, when he was only two months old, when his father was killed by two junkies who robbed the family's Westchester Avenue produce store? Marco had been there, lying in his bassinet behind the register. So had his mother, and his sister and two brothers.

Thankfully it was impossible for Marco to remember the bullet that shattered his father's skull, or the one that ripped into his oldest brother, Eduardo, when he tried to save his father. He couldn't remember his mother passing out when she ran out of the back room after hearing the shots, or the terrified screams of his other brother, Chico, and his sister, Jacinta.

But he had no doubt the horror of that day had somehow been imprinted on his infant brain so that he would never feel safe again. Photos of him as a toddler and young boy showed him clinging to his mother's leg, peering out at the camera with haunted blue eyes.

He didn't remember, either, the day his mother had remarried, only a year later. Juan Ramirez, a twice-divorced cabbie with an eye for beautiful women, lived down the hall from their cramped two-bedroom apartment.

Marco's mother, Anna, was beautiful.

So was his sister, who was only eight when Juan had married their mother.

Marco recalled, with sickening clarity, the day he had come home early from school and found Juan naked on top of a weeping Jacinta, doing terrible things to her. He remembered the rage that had filled him in that moment, and the way he had leapt on his stepfather, beating on his fat, bare ass.

But then Juan had done what Juan always did when he was drunk and angry—he had started slamming his fists into the nearest human target. Marco had blacked out, only to awaken the next morning in his bed, with his mother crying over him. She wanted to know why he had angered poor Juan, and when he told her what Juan had done to Jacinta, his mother had slapped him across his still-aching face.

After that, his mother stopped loving him.

At least that was how Marco interpreted her emotional retreat.

And after that, Juan beat him over every little thing.

Meanwhile, Chico, who had once been fun-loving and affectionate, was never home, having joined a street gang and turned to drugs. Even Jacinta closed herself off from him, having descended into some private world he later recognized as pain and denial.

Only Eduardo, confined to a wheelchair ever since the robbers' gunshots had rendered him a paraplegic at age ten, was there for Marco. He was the only member of the household that Juan never laid a hand on, but tears filled his big brown eyes every time Marco came to him with black eyes and swollen lips.

It was Eduardo, as the oldest child, who tried, on and off through the years, to persuade their mother to leave Juan. But as he reported to Marco, she wouldn't do it. Juan supported them; without him, where would they be?

"If I wasn't in this damn wheelchair," Eduardo used to say to Marco, "I would go out and get a job. I would take care of Mama, and all of you, so that we could get rid of Juan."

Marco was eight years old, and sound asleep with the rest of the family, when Eduardo hoisted himself onto the kitchen windowsill of the fifteenth-floor apartment building in the wee hours of a steamy August morning.

Marco had often sat in the same window in the years that followed, wondering if his brother had been frightened as his lame body hurtled toward the concrete courtyard below, and whether he'd felt any doubts over what he had done.

There were no answers in the note Eduardo had left. It simply said that he was ending his suffering at last, and that he loved his mother, brothers, and sister.

With Eduardo gone, Marco had no one to turn to. His mother was more silent and grim than ever before. Her doctor prescribed tranquilizers to help her through her grief; she clung ferociously to them in the years that followed.

Jacinta started hanging with a rough crowd, dropped out of school and disappeared for days at a time. At sixteen she became pregnant by a neighborhood lowlife, and moved out to live with him and raise their baby girl on welfare.

Chico left home in anger one night after a violent fight with Juan. He rarely came back to visit after that; when he did, it was to beg, borrow, or steal any money their mother had. His once lively expression was vacant and his once sturdy young body almost skeletal, with telltale tracks on his skinny brown arms.

Juan's anger and drinking escalated, and Marco bore the brunt of his rage.

Meanwhile the streets outside their shabby apartment seemed to disintegrate daily. Marco found himself dodging solicitations from hookers and drug dealers on his way home from school, stepping over smelly, drunken bums on the sidewalk in front of their building.

As a child, Marco used to dream of the day when they would finally flee the city, all of them—except of course for Juan. They would go someplace bright and warm and sunny, someplace with green grass and trees instead of brick and concrete, with real, cozy houses instead of drab boxy buildings filled with noise and roaches and strangers.

The older he got, the more he resigned himself to the fact that only *he* would escape someday. His mother and sister and brother were already lost to him now, firmly entrenched in the bleak world he wanted to leave behind.

And he *would*.

He studied hard in high school, hoping to eventually win scholarships, and he worked as a stockboy at D'Agastino's to save for college. Of course he dutifully gave his mother most of the money from his meager weekly check, and he never told his family he wanted to get a real education. He knew they would scoff at his impossible dream, or find some other use for the small sum in his secret savings account.

As a teenager, his only pleasure was the New York Yankees. He collected their baseball cards, and he listened to every game on his cheap transistor radio. Whenever he managed to save a few extra dollars, he would splurge on a ticket to a game. Those warm summer nights he spent at the historic stadium, beneath the wide-open sky, brought him the few moments of joy he had ever known.

Until he met Carla . . .

"Look."

The single word from Lia in the passenger's seat

yanked Marco back to the present, intruding on his memories like an abruptly slammed door.

Startled, he glanced at her, and then back at the road ahead, and realized they were approaching a town. There was a reduced speed limit ahead, and an intersection with an old-fashioned traffic light. It was red.

He slowed the truck, then told Lia, "Don't even think about jumping out."

She didn't reply, and he wondered if he should have once again handcuffed her to his arm, or to the truck. There hadn't been time before, but he could have stopped along the way.

He would have, if he hadn't been so lost in memories he usually managed to hold at bay.

The town was small and rundown, with most of the old-fashioned buildings boarded up. There was a small supermarket, a bank, and a liquor store, all of them closed at this hour of a Sunday morning. The streets were deserted, and the few houses they passed were dark.

"Are you going to stop for gas?" Lia asked as the light turned green and they coasted through it.

He looked at the gauge and nodded. He had no choice. It was on Empty.

A block ahead, he could see a lit sign for a self-serve station with a minimart attached.

He headed toward it, wondering how he was going to manage to keep Lia from escaping as he filled the tank and bought food, maybe even coffee.

There was only one way, but he hated to resort to it again.

Still he had no choice.

Just as he'd had no choice yesterday.

He pulled into the station, turned off the truck, and reached into his jacket.

"You're coming in with me," he said, making his

voice cold and hard. "I'll have this in my hand, inside
my pocket." He allowed her a fleeting glimpse of his
gun. "If you make one wrong move, or say anything to
anyone, you know what'll happen."

"You'll blow my brains out," she said dispassionately,
eyeing the gun and then him.

He didn't reply.

A sign on the concrete service island advised custom-
ers to pay before pumping.

He opened his door, then went around to open hers.
She stepped out into the chilly morning air, shivered,
and seemed to sway for a moment.

Marco reached for her arm, and she looked sharply
up at him.

"Don't touch me," she said curtly.

"I was just—" He cut himself off, clamping his mouth
shut resolutely. "Let's go. And remember, not a word."

"Not one? Not even 'help'?" she asked defiantly, and
he saw a familiar, stubborn glimmer in her dark eyes.

He forced back a twinge of admiration for her relentless spunk, hating himself for it as he led the way to the
store. Why couldn't he turn off his emotions with her,
the way he had so many times in his life?

He opened the door, and they both stepped into
the warm, brightly lit store. An overweight, long-haired
teenaged boy sat behind the register, his gaze fixed on a
small portable television behind the counter. He barely
murmured a greeting and didn't bother to glance up
at them.

Grateful, Marco moved toward the counter where full
pots of coffee sat on upper and lower burners. He pulled
two large foam cups from a stack nearby, filled them
both, and put cream and sugar in one.

The other he left black, with only a dash of sugar.

"You remembered," she murmured, as if she'd forgotten his orders not to speak.

He flinched at the sound of her voice, first because he feared she was about to alert the clerk to her plight, and then because the meaning of her words struck him.

You remembered.

Was she surprised that he hadn't forgotten how she liked her coffee? Would she be shocked to know that he hadn't forgotten how she liked . . . other things?

Stop it, he commanded himself. *Stay focused.*

He snapped two lids on the cups, grabbed a couple of packages of Hostess cakes from a display nearby, and handed everything to her.

"Take this stuff," he muttered, half expecting her to protest. She would know he needed his hands free— one to pay the clerk, the other to clutch the cold steel in his pocket.

Lia said nothing, just followed him to the register.

"Morning," said the clerk, his eyes still on the television, which was showing an old Road Runner cartoon.

"How's it going?" Marco gestured for Lia to put the coffee and Hostess cakes down on the counter. She did, with resounding plunks that again spoke of her defiance.

Marco shot her a warning look.

"This be all?" mumbled the boy.

Marco told him they needed gas, too, and pulled out the wad of bills stashed in his pocket—not the one where he kept the gun. The clerk rang up his sale, pushed some buttons on a device that controlled the pumps, and briefly said, "Go ahead," before turning his attention back to the cartoon.

"Thanks." Marco opened the door for Lia, relieved that it was over. Now they could get back into the truck, get on the road, and . . .

He frowned as he saw an old, rusty Buick pulling into the parking lot. The driver, a round-faced, middle-aged man wearing a brimmed hat, did a double take at the green pickup parked by the pumps, then at Marco and Lia.

Marco cursed under his breath and said to Lia, "Don't say a word."

"You already told me—"

"Shhh."

The door of the Buick was opening, and the man stepped out. "Morning," he called. "That Charlie Lima's truck?"

"This?" Marco shrugged. "We bought it a few days ago from a farmer who lives out that way." He pointed at the road they'd just traveled into town.

"Old Charlie sold the truck? Never thought I'd see the day. He going to sell the farm, too?"

"You'd have to ask him," Marco said, pasting a casual grin on his mouth. "All we were interested in was the truck."

"Geez, why?" He shook his head. "Old thing'd be better off in a junkyard."

"We're planning on using it for parts," Marco improvised, then added with a wave, "Well, have a good day."

His hands shook as he pulled the nozzle from its hook and thrust it into the hole beneath the license plate. Lia stood silently beside him as he filled the tank, and when he looked up, he saw her watching the man who had walked into the store.

"Can I speak now?" she asked Marco.

He grunted, and she apparently took it as permission.

"He's telling the clerk about the truck. They both keep looking out here. See?"

He followed her gaze toward the plate glass window near the register and saw that she was right. Both the clerk and the customer were watching them, wearing tentative expressions.

"We'd better get out of here," Marco said. "Get into the truck."

"What if I tell you I won't?" Lia asked, standing her ground and looking him in the eye. "What if I march back into that store and tell them that the truck is stolen, and that I'm your hostage?"

"I told you what would happen," Marco growled, conscious of the two strangers watching from the window of the store. "Get into the truck."

"No, Marco, you didn't *tell* me. You showed me a gun. But somehow, I think you *can't* bring yourself to say you'll shoot me with it, because you're not sure you'd be able to do it."

"You're taking a big chance here, Lia. Get into the truck, *now!*"

She stared at him for a moment longer, her chin raised and her arms folded across her chest, one hand clutching the bag from the minimart.

"You're right," she said finally, smugly, moving toward the truck. "I was taking a chance. And it paid off, because now I've found out what I wanted to know."

He got into the driver's seat and started the engine, pulling out onto the road with a savage jerk of the wheel.

So.

Now she knew.

Marco had no intention of hurting her.

Had she ever doubted that?

She stole a glance at his profile as he headed the old truck out of the small town, careful not to exceed the posted speed limit.

Yes, she thought, noticing the steely glint in his eyes and the set of his granite jaw. She had doubted it, somewhere in the back of her mind.

She really *had* feared Marco, as much for how she thought he might harm her physically as emotionally.

After all, if she had been callous enough to live a lie

all those months they were together, with utter disregard for her feelings, then who knew what he was capable of doing?

Okay, maybe murder was pushing it . . .

But he *had* abducted her. And threatened her, she thought stubbornly.

And now he was taking her . . . where?

More importantly, what was going to happen when they reached their destination?

"Can you at least tell me where we're headed?" she asked him.

"Not yet."

"Well, when are you planning to tell me?"

"I don't know."

"What, are you going to wait until we get there?"

"Whenever I feel like telling you, I'll tell you, okay, A.J.?"

A.J. Hearing her old name on his lips did curious things to her heart.

Trying to ignore that, she said again, "Tell me where we're going."

He struck the steering wheel with his palm and shook his head. "Damn, you always were persistent."

"Damn, I always was," she echoed, glaring at him. "And there was a time when you didn't think that was such a bad quality, Marco."

Oh, Lord.

Why had she gone and brought *that* up?

Well, maybe the word "persistent" hadn't triggered the same memory in him as it had in her. Maybe he had no idea what she was talking about . . .

"We can't do it here," he had whispered that day in the laundry room at Victor's mansion, when she finished tossing a load into the washer and turned her attention to him. "Victor and the others are right out in the kitchen, sitting around the table. Somebody might walk in."

"We'll do it fast," she had whispered to him, kissing his neck.

"We *never* do it fast."

"Sure we do. We just never do it *once.*"

"We can't do this, A.J. This isn't a good idea . . ." He moaned softly as her fingers slid into the front of his baggy drawstring khaki shorts.

"But you want me so badly . . . I can feel it . . ."

"Hell, A.J., I *always* want you."

"So, take me. I'm all yours."

"Later . . ."

"Now," she had insisted, hopping onto the washing machine and hiking the skirt of her uniform around her hips.

He gasped. "You're not wearing . . ."

"No, I'm not. Not today. I figured, why wear panties when I'd just have to take them off? It would waste valuable time."

"You planned on seducing me this morning?"

She grinned and nodded, shifting impatiently as the washer's rhythmic vibrations beneath her enhanced her arousal.

"I'm waiting, Marco," she purred, straddling her legs and pulling him to her. "I'm ready for you now."

"Did anyone ever tell you you're the most persistent woman on earth?"

"Only you," she said, "and I take it as a compliment."

"Good, because I meant it as one," he said raggedly, running his hands over her bare bottom.

And she had closed her eyes and let out a little gasp as he swiftly dropped his shorts and plunged into her.

Now, remembering those stolen sensual moments, she shifted uncomfortably on her seat, and saw Marco do the same.

So he did remember.

She swallowed and looked away, out the window.

She would rather think he had forgotten all the intimate, erotic details of their relationship. Knowing he, too, had stored them in his memory made it all the more difficult to tell herself that there was nothing between them now but anger and loathing.

Alberto, standing in the doorway of the shed, scraped his right shoe along the raised threshold, trying to dislodge a clump of dried mud.

"They were here."

At Ramon's terse proclamation, Alberto looked up and saw that Hondo was nudging several brown apple cores along the dusty floor with the pointed toe of his sleek black boot.

"How do you know it was them?" Alberto asked, frowning.

The other two men ignored him.

"They haven't been gone long," Ramon said, after bending and poking at a muddy imprint on the floor just inside the door. He held up his finger, and Alberto saw that it was smeared with mud. "This is still damp," Ramon announced. "They can't be very far."

"Let's go down to the house," Hondo told him, already moving for the door.

He shoved Alberto aside as he was balancing on one foot, cleaning his shoe.

Alberto went sprawling into the muddy yard just outside the doorway.

"You shouldn't be so clumsy, Alberto," Hondo chided, as Alberto cursed under his breath. "You're going to hurt someone."

"I'm going to hurt someone, all right," Alberto muttered.

"What was that?" Ramon pounced, turning on him with a dangerous gleam in his eye.

"Nothing."

"I heard something," Hondo announced.

"It was nothing." Alberto got up and tried to brush the mud from his slacks, succeeding only in smearing it into the already damp fabric.

"Watch your step, Alberto, eh, Alberto?" Ramon said in his heavily accented English.

Hondo said nothing, just flashed a dark look that warned Alberto he was on shaky ground.

The three of them picked their way down the marshy slope toward the house and barn. The place appeared deserted.

"What are we going to do? Knock on the door?" Alberto asked, his thoughts muddled from the most recent confrontation with these two bozos. The first chance he got, he would pull his gun and get rid of them both. Just as soon as they turned their backs on him . . .

Which they never did.

"Shh," Ramon hissed, stopping short at the edge of the barnyard.

Alberto saw that someone was standing just outside the barn. It was an old man in faded coveralls and an old cap, and he was leaning against a pitchfork. Just standing there, motionless, with his back to them.

Hondo raised a hand, and Alberto saw that he had drawn his gun. Ramon was following suit, and Alberto reached into his pocket for his own pistol. If he could bring up the rear as they approached the old farmer, he might be able to take out both Hondo and Ramon before the old man got his turn.

But Hondo motioned him to approach first, and he found himself stealthily leading the way into the barnyard, wary of the two armed men behind him. He won-

dered if either of them was considering shooting him
n the back, and the skin at the back of his neck prickled.

Finally, when they were within a few feet of the old
man, he seemed to sense their presence and turned
his head slowly. Alberto saw that his wrinkled face was
ghostly pale and contorted, as if he were in agony. The
surprise that flickered in his eyes when he saw the three
gun-toting strangers didn't erase the vestiges of pain.

And Alberto noticed that there seemed to be no fear
about the man, which seemed odd. Was he some kind
of nutcase?

"Drop the pitchfork," Ramon ordered him. "Now."

The old man gasped, then said, "I . . . can't . . . "

Alberto realized then that the pitchfork was holding
him up. The old man clung to the handle so tightly
that his knuckles were white and the handle shook with
the tremors of his body. He appeared to be having some
kind of seizure, or maybe . . . had he been shot?

He swiftly looked for traces of blood on the man's
baggy clothing, but found none.

"Drop the pitchfork," Hondo echoed Ramon, his
voice low and menacing.

The old man obliged, weakly releasing the handle so
that it toppled to the ground. He moaned and sank
slowly to his knees, clutching his chest.

"What the hell is wrong with you?" Ramon asked,
kicking the man's knee.

"My . . . heart . . . "

"Yeah, that's it. Something must have scared him so
badly he's having a heart attack," Alberto said, pleased
with his own ingenious deduction. "Something like
Marco Estevez and A.J. Sutton showing up out of
nowhere."

"Stole . . . my . . . truck," the old man gasped.

"They stole your truck?" Ramon crouched beside
him, hovering and clutching his shirt to lift him partly

off the ground and speak into his face. "What kind of truck?"

"Green . . . pickup . . . "

"Which way did they go?" Alberto could barely conceal his excitement.

The old man didn't speak; it seemed that he couldn't. He jerked his head slightly toward the road that ran west in front of the house.

"Is there a town that way?" Ramon asked impatiently.

The man didn't reply, only made a gasping sound.

"Finish him off," Ramon said abruptly to Hondo, as he rose and gave the old man another kick.

"He's almost finished off now," Alberto protested.

"So? Put him out of his misery." Ramon straightened his jacket and looked restlessly at the road.

"Why waste a bullet and my time?" Hondo argued. "Let him suffer. Let's go."

Alberto glanced down at the man who lay dying at his feet. His eyes were losing focus, his breathing growing loud and ragged. He managed to gasp several words.

"What was that?" Ramon asked, turning back. "Did he say something else about the truck?"

"Nah." Alberto put his gun away and followed Ramon and Hondo away from the barn, toward the road. "I think he said, 'end of the line.'"

Chapter Ten

"What makes you think no one's going to miss this car?" Lia asked, as Marco steered the white Hyundai Excel out of the shopping mall parking lot. "It's ten after twelve. The mall just opened. And it's parked in the employees' parking area," Marco said. "Whoever owns it just started a shift, and chances are, it's going to last until the place closes at five this afternoon. By then we'll be—"

She frowned when he broke off abruptly. "We'll be what? Or where?"

"Out of the country," he told her, steering the car onto the Thruway ramp heading west.

Out of the country?

"Are we going to the airport?" Lia asked incredulously. "Because if we are, we passed that turnoff about an hour ago, in Albany."

"We're not going to the airport. I was talking about Canada."

"We're going to Canada? Why? Wait, let me guess—you have connections there."

He shrugged and slowed the car as they approached a toll booth. "Don't say a word," he cautioned her.

She rolled her eyes.

He slowed only long enough to grab the ticket the clerk handed him, then sped along the ramp and merged into the smattering of Sunday afternoon traffic.

Lia stared out the window for a few moments, then turned to Marco. "What about the old man's truck?"

"What about it?"

They had left it parked in the mall parking lot with the gas tank almost on empty again, after the several hours it had taken them to drive this far on back roads.

"How's he going to get it back?" she asked Marco in an accusatory tone. "He's so old, and he was so upset that we were taking it. Don't you feel the least bit sorry about it?"

"What do you take me for, Lia—a cold, uncaring son of a bitch?"

Yes, she wanted to shout at him. *What else would I take you for?*

But something stopped her. Because maybe she just wasn't so sure now as she had been yesterday that this man was someone to loathe.

"Of course I feel sorry," he went on. "But our lives depended on stealing a car. And he'll get it back. I'm sure that by now he's reported it missing, and the police will find it."

She shook her head doubtfully, and her eye fell on the graduation cap tassel that dangled from the Hyundai's rearview mirror. The car was littered with candy bar wrappers, diet soda cans, and tattered fashion magazines. A can of hairspray rolled from the seat beneath her feet as they flew around a curve in the road.

"Well, what about this Hyundai?" Lia asked Marco,

kicking the hairspray back under so she wouldn't have to look at it and feel guilty, imagining its owner.

Not that it was *her* fault the car had been stolen.

"What about it?" Marco asked, sounding exasperated.

"It probably belongs to some poor hardworking teenager who has a part-time job at the Gap and saved up all her money to buy the car. What's she going to do when she comes out and sees that it's missing?"

"She's going to report it stolen, and she'll either get a nice, new car, or maybe the Canadian police will return it to her when we're through with it."

"Gee, you've thought of everything, Marco," Lia said dryly. "It's all running like clockwork so that no one will get hurt, huh?"

"Not if I can help it."

"No one except me."

"I haven't hurt you."

She didn't respond.

She felt him looking at her.

"How did I hurt you?" he demanded. "You're fine. I've treated you very well. Christ, Lia, I even got you coffee and breakfast this morning."

"I hate Twinkies."

The statement sounded so ridiculous, even to her own ears, that she almost cracked a smile. She fought against it, carefully keeping her expression sullen as she watched the passing traffic. She didn't want him to mistakenly think she was enjoying herself, did she?

Because she wasn't.

She hated every minute she was forced to spend imprisoned with Marco Estevez.

She hated *him*.

She really did.

"After you take me out of the country," she said after

a few moments, "then what? Our madcap adventure is over?"

Again, sarcasm had crept into her voice like a shield, protecting her from Marco, so that he wouldn't sense her vulnerability. That, she knew, was the key to surviving this little drama.

It had always been the key to survival, for her.

"I'm afraid it's not over then, no," he said. "Our madcap adventure is only beginning."

"Oh, really? What have you got in store for us next? Are we going to drive to the ocean and sail away together to some tropical paradise?"

She saw him glance sharply at her, and for the briefest moment, she was struck by the wild notion that she might have guessed his plan.

Then common sense took over, and she realized that was ridiculous. That plan had existed in another time and place, for two different people who had long since vanished.

But why had he looked so keenly at her when she'd said it?

Was it because he remembered, as she did, those faraway, dreamy days when they would imagine an idyllic future? Just the two of them, in paradise . . .

"What, Marco?" she asked wryly, watching his expression. "You thought I had forgotten our big plan? Or maybe you thought I wouldn't dare to bring it up now, after everything that's changed between us? Or maybe you actually forgot all about it, and what I just said reminded you—"

"I never forgot," he interrupted quietly. "I never forgot anything, Lia."

"Neither did I," she heard herself say, her voice suddenly taking on a soft tone that matched his.

She looked up at him and their eyes collided. She was struck by the urge to move closer to him, to slip into his arms and rest her head on his big chest, the way she used to do. She suddenly longed for him to hold her, not in the steely grip he'd used yesterday, but with strong, gentle arms that sheltered . . .

Rather than imprisoned.

Then he looked back at the road, and she looked down at her lap.

Him, and Lia, and a bunch of healthy, happy, chubby-cheeked kids.

That had been Marco's idea of paradise.

But only secretly, of course.

The whole thing set against a gorgeous tropical island backdrop would have made it perfect, but he wouldn't have minded if they had to live in a hut in Siberia as long as they were together.

A family.

The kind of family he'd been fortunate enough to have many years ago, if only for the merest fraction of his life, long before he was old enough to remember.

A family in which none of the roles were vacant. Doting father, loving mother, wholesome, happy children.

Children who were allowed the innocent, carefree days every child deserved. Children who did whatever it was that children enjoyed.

Like spending sunny days giggling and frolicking, playing games and making friends in an untroubled world.

Not that Marco knew a thing about children.

Not anymore.

They were foreigners, where he was concerned—miniature, big-eyed beings with whom he had nothing in common, other than the fact that he had once, in another lifetime, been a child himself.

Hardly innocent or carefree. Fate had robbed him of his childhood not once, but over and over again.

Maybe that was why he made it a point these days to keep his distance from children, and had all of his adult life—the part that mattered, anyway. The part that came after he had lost just about everything he could lose . . . or believed he had, anyway.

That was before he had found, and then lost, A.J. Sutton.

Lia Haskin.

Whatever the hell her name was.

It didn't matter.

A.J., Lia, whoever she was, he had never gotten her out of his system.

And from the moment he'd first taken her into his arms and felt her heart beating swiftly against his own, he had found himself, in some remote, irrational corner of his brain, longing to go for it with her, the whole cliché—marriage, kids, growing old together . . .

All the things a man like Marco Estevez yearned to believe he didn't want, or need. He had spent years, anyway, trying to convince himself of just that.

Somehow, though, the thought of this particular woman carrying his baby in her belly had seemed incredibly erotic. Once in awhile, as he and A.J. were making love, he would imagine that there was a purpose to their coupling, beyond mere carnal pleasure. He would pretend that they were creating a child—that somewhere deep inside of her, a minuscule part of him was irrevocably joining with a minuscule part of her.

During those moments they were together, he had even wondered, fleetingly, what would happen if she accidentally got pregnant.

Had maybe secretly *longed* for it, even as he prayed that it wouldn't happen.

After all, what would they do? They couldn't get *mar-*

ried. Which meant she probably wouldn't keep it—if she even decided to have it.

No.

Of course she would have it.

The thought of her destroying that was something so profoundly a part of them disturbed him even more than the thought of her giving it away.

And yet, what choice would she have?

Logically, he knew he couldn't settle down and raise a family. Not in his line of work. It wouldn't be fair. Children and violence didn't mix.

Christ, no one knew that better than he did.

But he couldn't help fantasizing about the idea of creating a living testimony to their relationship—something that would live on even if they were wrenched from each other, as he had always suspected they would be.

Anyway, A.J. hadn't gotten pregnant, so none of it mattered. Not now.

She would never have his child. He would never be a father . . . because if A.J. couldn't bear his children, no woman could. He couldn't fathom that.

He wondered if she had ever shared his thoughts— if, with all her talk of a fantasy paradise the two of them would share, her visions had ever included marriage, or children.

He looked at her and their eyes collided.

He found himself biting his tongue, now, to keep from blurting a question he would regret. A question that would break the illusion that they were enemies. A question that would render him vulnerable.

He couldn't afford vulnerability.

Especially not now.

He broke the gaze, looking back at the road ahead. From the corner of his eye, he saw her turn her head to look out the window.

No, he couldn't start talking to her now about what might have been.

He needed every ounce of concentration, every ounce of strength, if he was going to stay focused on his objective and pull this off.

He sure as hell couldn't go back to dreaming silly little dreams about a wife, and children, and a future that could never be his.

The phone call Victor awaited had finally come through just as he was unfolding the morning edition of the *Miami Herald* on his terrace overlooking Biscayne Bay. Calypso music was piped over the stereo speakers, and his traditional Sunday brunch—a plate piled with huevos rancheros and a steaming cup of true Colombian coffee—waited on the glass-topped table in front of him.

By the time he hung up, the eggs had congealed into an unappetizing mass on his plate and his coffee had grown lukewarm, even under the blazing Florida sun.

Victor tossed the paper aside and paced across the terrace to the railing facing the bay. The water that lapped gently below was a clear, calm aquamarine pool, and he realized it had caught him by surprise.

He had irrationally expected to see an angry, storm-tossed sea . . .

To match the mood that had rapidly descended over him with every word the caller had spoken.

So.

Now he knew who Marco Estevez really was.

Why hadn't he bothered to investigate the man a year ago, when he'd let him go?

How could he have been such a fool?

Al mejor mono se le cae el zapote, protested a little voice in my mind.

Yes, everyone made mistakes . . .

But yours could have been prevented.

You grew careless, he scolded himself, staring vacantly at the crisp white outline of a sailboat heading toward the open sea.

You were distracted, upset by the botched Trask abduction, and you didn't cover yourself as meticulously as you should have.

Never again would he make that mistake.

He could only hope it wasn't too late to make up for it.

He spun abruptly, strode back to the table, and grabbed his cellular phone again.

"Where are you?" he barked, when Ramon answered on the other end.

"Still on their trail. We left the car behind, though, and we had to get another one."

"What? Why?"

"We tracked them through the woods to the spot where they spent the night," Ramon said, sounding pleased with himself. "Then they stole a pickup truck from a farm not far from Albany. We flagged down a car on a road near the farm, and Hondo convinced the driver that it would be in his best interest to let us take his car."

"What about Estevez and Sutton?" Victor asked impatiently.

"We think they're heading west."

"You *think* they're heading west?" Victor echoed, fury coursing through his slight frame.

"We're pretty sure," Ramon hurriedly amended. "We've questioned a few people in a few towns, and—"

"Pura quasa!" Victor cut in, fed up.

"No, Victor, I'm telling the truth, we—"

"Listen to me. Marco Estevez owns a fishing cabin on a lake up in Ontario. They're heading up there."

There was a pause.

Then Ramon asked, "But Victor, how do you know that's where they're going?"

"Instinct," Victor said thoughtfully, his dark eyes flashing. "Now listen carefully."

"So, what's in Canada?"

Marco glanced at her, and she was pleased to see that her voice had startled him. He had probably assumed that she would just shut up and sit sedately for the remainder of the trip. Well, he was wrong.

She had just spent the last few hours trying to plot an escape when they got to the border. Marco would have to stop and talk to the Customs officials, wouldn't he? Of course he would. You didn't just drive into another country with having any human contact.

The trouble was, she couldn't figure out exactly how to use that moment to escape him. She didn't want to fall into the hands of the authorities, and that was, ultimately, what would happen if she made a scene at the border.

"Have you ever been to Canada before?" He answered her question with a question, his tone surprisingly mild.

"No. Have you?"

He seemed to hesitate, then nodded.

"Where in Canada are we going?"

He shrugged and looked back at the road.

She fell silent again.

Funny. This was what she had always wanted—to sail off somewhere exotic with Marco, just the two of them.

Now here they were, off on an adventure together.

Only they weren't sailing.

And Canada wasn't what she'd had in mind when she'd thought exotic.

Being transported at gunpoint wasn't, either, she thought wryly.

A little over a year ago, if she'd had to picture this scenario—that Marco would become her captor, abducting her at gunpoint and keeping her in shackles—she would have said it was impossible. That their relationship, imperfect as it was, could never dissolve into what felt like a scene from an absurd Movie of the Week. That the mere idea was ludicrous.

So, here they were.

Living a farce.

And the biggest joke of all was that they were still wildly attracted to each other. They still couldn't keep their hands and lips off each other. And every time their eyes happened to meet, undeniable passion smoldered.

She had to get away from him, before . . .

Before he killed her.

What a joke. That's not what you were thinking. That's not why you need to escape him.

Before something happened between them, something that had been building from the moment he first laid a hand on her back in Boston. It didn't matter that his initial reason for touching her had been to force her into accompanying him on this bizarre journey.

What mattered was that after so many months apart, she could once again see him, and touch him, and feel the emotion he refused to voice.

And if he touched her again, even slightly, she knew she would lose all her hard-won reserve.

She had to get away from him.

She absently glanced at a green and silver sign at the side of the highway announcing that Canada wasn't far off.

And that was when it struck her.

He was transporting her to Canada.

She would be a fool to stop him from doing that. If

he got her out of the country without incident, the American authorities couldn't touch her. She would be free of her past forever.

She still had to get away from Marco, of course . . . but not, she vowed, until after they had crossed the border.

They reached the Peace Bridge in downtown Buffalo just before four in the afternoon. There were considerably long lines of cars waiting to cross over into Canada, something Marco had been counting on.

He had pondered taking the more sparsely traveled Whirlpool Bridge several miles up the Niagara River, but discarded the idea. The busier the bridge, the busier the Customs agents would be, and the less likely that they'd devote unnecessary attention to Marco and Lia.

He had already warned Lia that he expected her to cooperate with the agent's questions. She had smirked and remained silent, as she had been all afternoon.

Marco's heart pounded as he inched the white Excel over the bridge suspended high above the foaming river. He stole a glance at Lia and saw that she was staring out the window, brooding.

All she had to do was open her mouth and tell the Customs agent that she was being abducted, that the car was stolen, that he had a weapon in his coat . . .

It would be all over.

He had to believe that she wouldn't do it, though.

That she was intelligent enough to know what it would mean to her. Surely she didn't still believe he was in cahoots with Victor, delivering her to her death.

Or did she?

If she did, then she would give him away, he thought, as the car passed by the American and Canadian flags that marked the border in the center of the bridge.

They were in Canada now, and the Customs booths were just ahead.

This was her chance, if she thought he was the enemy.

But she had to be aware that in giving him away, she would be giving herself away as well.

She would be brought back to Florida for questioning in the Trask murder and kidnapping case. She would once again become A.J. Sutton, forced to testify against the most powerful drug lord in the country.

A sitting duck for Victor's lethal Jamaican posse, who would never let her live long enough to speak out and destroy the empire they had built.

She *had* to be aware of all that, Marco thought as he steered the car into one of the lines waiting for Customs.

She *had* to believe that her only chance for survival was to trust him.

Blindly.

He hadn't given her any reason to trust him.

And if she decided to, he knew it would be because some deep, strong instinct told her to do it.

He lifted his foot from the brake to let the car roll forward another length as the line moved on.

He clenched the wheel and inhaled, then let the breath out slowly, noisily through pursed lips.

He looked at Lia and found that she hadn't moved, that her head was still turned away, facing out the window.

Another vehicle moved ahead through Customs, and he inched closer. Now the car in front of them had its turn, with the unsmiling, uniformed Customs agent leaning in to question the passengers.

"I would die before I would ever hurt you," Marco told Lia hoarsely. "I want you to know that."

She didn't move, didn't even flinch.

He sighed and looked back out the windshield to see the brake lights disappear on the car in front of them.

It was pulling away, cleared to enter the country, and now it was their turn.

This is it.

Marco eased the car forward, fighting the wild, sudden impulse to slam his foot down on the gas pedal and tear through the booth in a mad dash for freedom.

But he knew that would be insane. They would never make it. He would get them both killed trying.

So he stepped on the brake, and the car rolled to a stop in front of the agent. It was a woman, her dark hair severely pulled back from her cosmetic-free face, tucked beneath the austere uniform cap.

Marco knew better than to turn on the charisma that had helped him out of many a sticky spot in the past. Female Customs officials couldn't be bought or bribed through flirtation.

"Citizenship?" she asked, leaning toward Marco, her eyes perusing the contents of the car.

Too late, he realized that the graduation tassel and fashion magazines were incongruous with a pair of adults. He struggled against a renewed surge of anxiety.

"United States," he answered the agent, and was shocked when his voice betrayed no hint of his inner alarm.

"Citizenship?" The agent addressed Lia, who had turned to face her.

"United States," Lia replied, sounding utterly serene.

Marco exulted.

"Why are you coming to Canada?"

"To spend a few hours sightseeing at the Falls," Marco replied smoothly.

The agent nodded, and he thought she was going to let him go. Then, her eyes once again flicking over the contents of the car, she asked him, "What are you bringing into the country?"

What was he bringing into the country?

A woman I abducted.

A stolen car.

A gun.

"Nothing," Marco said easily. "We're just here for the day."

"All right, then," the Customs official said with a nod, and waved them on.

Marco smiled calmly and accelerated toward the QEW, overwhelmed by the urge to shout, to rejoice, to grab Lia and kiss her, tell her how right she was to trust him.

But he did none of those things, just resumed driving, headed for his fishing cabin two hundred kilometers north.

Lia gradually came awake to the vague sensation that something had changed.

As awareness crept over her, she realized that the motion had stopped, and she no longer heard incessant humming of the car cruising along the highway.

She opened her eyes.

They had come to a stop, and she was alone in the front seat.

Startled, she put her hand on the door handle, sure that Marco would appear and stop her.

He didn't, and she found herself oddly torn between hope . . .

Maybe he was gone, and she was alone.

. . . and dread.

Maybe he was gone, and she was alone.

She opened the door, looking around as she stepped out of the car on wobbly legs.

The Hyundai was parked in a grassy clearing in front of a low log cabin. The place was decidedly rustic, but did have a couple of Adirondack chairs on the small porch. There were a few windows, and a rough-hewn door that stood ajar.

A shadowy forest loomed beyond the cabin on three sides, broken only by a narrow dirt lane. A few feet from the porch steps was a narrow, grassy bank sloping down to a lake that seemed to be surrounded by nothing but trees on the distant shore.

It's breathtaking, Lia thought, allowing herself a moment to take in the landscape. The sun was just setting on the horizon, tinting the sky and the still water in its glowing, pinkish-red path.

"Beautiful, isn't it?"

Marco's voice behind her made her jump, and she spun to see him standing on the porch of the cabin.

Lia shrugged, turning back toward the water. It would have been so easy to forget, just for a fleeting minute or two, that she was here against her will.

Marco walked down the steps and came to stand beside her.

For a long time they were silent, staring out over the dusky lake.

Lia became aware of the calling birds and chirping crickets, and a gentle breeze rustling the trees overhead.

"I found this place and bought the land years ago," Marco told her unexpectedly, as if answering a question she hadn't posed.

His voice sounded reverent as he added, "I built the cabin myself, from trees I cleared from the land."

"You must be proud." Her comment sounded trite, but she could think of nothing else to say, and he seemed to have been waiting for an acknowledgment.

He shrugged. "I've never brought anyone here."

"Why not?"

He hesitated, and when he spoke again, it was with another shrug, but she was startled to hear a melancholy note in his voice. "There was no one to bring."

You could have brought me, she thought. *You could have shared it with me. We could have shared so much . . .*

"Come inside," Marco said brusquely.

She wondered if it was an invitation or an order. For the first time, she couldn't tell.

She looked up and caught his gaze.

Something about him seemed to have changed in the last few hours while she'd been asleep, Lia realized.

There was a wistful aura about him, and his blue eyes revealed that he was keeping some troubling secret.

"Marco, what is it?" she found herself asking, laying a hand on the sleeve of his jacket.

"It's . . . "

He paused.

She waited, holding her breath.

"It's nothing," he told her.

The breath escaped her in an audible sigh of disappointment.

He had been on the brink of opening up to her; she was certain of it. Why hadn't he?

"Let's go into the cabin," he said, turning away from the lake, and from her. He headed toward the porch steps, his hands shoved deep in the front pockets of his jeans, his shoulders hunched as though he were heading into a bitter wind.

He didn't turn to see if she was following, and she knew that if she wanted to, she could make a break for it now, running into the woods.

Another chance to flee.

Another chance she let slip away.

The opportunities seemed to come and go with increasing ease, Lia told herself as she followed Marco onto the porch. She had felt little regret when they'd left the Customs agent behind this afternoon.

It wasn't that she trusted Marco—not entirely, anyway.

But, she figured, what did she have to lose by letting

him transport her into Canada? She had entertained that very notion a year ago, when she'd disappeared and changed her identity. Then she'd been too skittish to risk crossing the border.

Now the decision had been made for her.

And now that she was here, she had only to make a break from Marco so that she could start over yet again.

And she would, she promised herself, turning to look back over the lake.

She'd soon have another opportunity to go; she was sure of it. But for now, night was rapidly falling over the forest, and she wasn't particularly anxious to be out there alone. After all, who knew what wild animals and poisonous snakes lurked in the Canadian wilderness?

Marco pushed the door open and stepped back, gesturing for her to enter the cabin.

Too late, she realized that perhaps a more formidable hazard lay *within* the cabin than outside its long-hewn walls.

If you walk over that threshold, you'll spend another night alone with Marco . . .

The one thing you swore you wouldn't do.

"Go ahead," Marco said impatiently.

She hesitated, glanced over her shoulder.

The light had dimmed considerably already, casting the woodland in ominous shadows. The waters of the lake no longer glowed in fiery remnants of the sun, but lay murky and still, reflecting the vast, dark sky.

"Thinking of running?" Marco asked quietly.

She looked slowly back at him, unwilling to convey her apprehension.

"I wouldn't, if I were you. We're miles from the nearest town. And I guarantee that these woods are full of bears and wildcats. And rattlesnakes. Not to mention the biggest, nastiest bugs you ever saw."

Still she said nothing, holding back a shudder as his words sank in.

"You'll be safe in here, with me," Marco told her then. "I won't let anything happen to you, Lia. Just like I promised before, in the car. I know you believed me then. Don't change your mind now."

"Who said I believed you?"

"You did," he told her. "By saying nothing to that Customs official, you told me everything I needed to know."

"You don't know anything."

"I do."

He stepped closer to her, one hand still stretched behind him, holding the door open. But the other hand reached out, slipped beneath her chin, tilted her face up toward his.

For an instant, she thought he was going to bend his head and kiss her.

When he didn't, she fought not to let her potent disappointment show.

"I can see everything I need to know in your eyes," he commented.

"Good. Then you know that I don't trust you, and I can't stand you."

He laughed softly. "That's not what I see."

Again she found herself bracing for his kiss, almost letting her eyelids flutter closed in anticipation.

But he removed his hand from her chin and turned away.

"After you," he said, motioning her toward the cabin door.

Marco hadn't been to the cabin since July, but it was just as he'd left it.

He often worried, in the long stretches of time that

he was away, that he would return to find that the place had been broken into and ransacked by stray hikers, or at the very least, disturbed by rodents or insect infestation.

That had never happened in the fifteen years since he'd built the cabin. Today it looked the same as always.

Clean. Cozy. Welcoming.

When he had left Lia sleeping in the car earlier, the first thing he had done inside was open the windows to air the place out. That should have been the second priority, but he wanted to procrastinate the phone call.

The one that would set the final stage of his plan into motion.

After making a brief inspection of the cabin, he had picked up his cellular phone and reluctantly dialed.

"We made it," he had told the familiar voice on the other end. "We're at the cabin."

"Good. Listen carefully."

And as he had listened to the instructions, he had wondered if maybe, just maybe, there was some way to back out of the plans he had engineered himself.

But he knew that was impossible.

Tomorrow it would be over, and Lia would be gone. But they still had tonight to get through.

He allowed Lia to hover in the doorway of the cabin, just inside the large living area, as he moved to the low table beneath the large double front window to light an ancient oil lamp he kept there.

The light flickered and cast a mellow glow over the single room that made up the cabin, except for a small enclosed storage area and a no-frills bathroom.

Marco glanced around, trying to see it as Lia must be seeing it.

Did she notice the massive hand-hewn rafters overhead, the painstaking moldings he'd carved around the windows, the smooth, sanded grain of the plank floorboards beneath their feet?

Did she notice the stone fireplace with its hearth of antique tiles, and the heavy mantel shelf above, lined with candles?

The long, low bookcase he'd fashioned from pine boards and old red bricks, lined with rows of well-worn classics he'd discovered in those long-ago high school English classes?

The scarred, antique table he'd lugged from a flea market outside Hamilton; the pair of red rockers beside the fireplace, the braided rag rug on the floor?

He saw her head turn to one side, toward the narrow nook that served as a kitchen.

There he had built a wall of open shelves that were stocked, as always, with the bare essentials—canned goods, powdered milk and bottled water, along with tightly sealed jars of staples like rice and macaroni. There was a sink with cold running water, and a pile of wood waited beside the ancient black iron cookstove.

His gaze turned from the kitchen back to Lia's face.

He caught her eye, saw her redden, and realized he'd caught her staring at the centerpiece of the main room.

The bed.

It was a massive oak four-poster, its pencil posts etched with scrolling vines and leaves. Two plump pillows rested against the headboard, and the mattress was covered in a quilt he'd found in a thrift shop years ago.

The old woman who owned the shop had told him the quilt was in remarkable condition for being almost a hundred years old—"Just like me," she'd added with a wink.

Then she'd asked him if he knew what the quilt's circular pattern was called.

He'd laughed and said that he didn't; he wasn't exactly up on American folk crafts.

"Then I'd better warn you about the quilt, seeing as you're a bachelor."

Not for long, he'd thought, and asked her, "How do you know that?"

"No ring. And besides, you've got that bachelor way about you. But I guarantee some woman's going to change that."

"Maybe sooner than you think," he'd said contentedly, thinking of Carla. "What's the quilt called?"

"The 'wedding ring' pattern," the woman had said with a knowing gleam in her eye as she lovingly ran her wizened fingers over the narrow, circular patches that decorated the ivory background.

The wedding ring pattern.

It had seemed so fitting, then.

He had bought it, of course, and brought it home, and spread it lovingly over the feather bed so that it would be ready and waiting . . .

"It's really nice."

Lia's voice shattered the memory that had been about to intrude, and he looked up at her, grateful for the interruption.

"The bed?" he asked her.

"Uh, I meant the cabin." She stiffly avoided looking at the bed, as did he.

"Thank you."

"Did you read any of these books?" she asked, moving to the shelves beside the fireplace.

"All of them," he said proudly. "Most of them more than once. There's not much to do up here, alone."

She nodded.

He wondered if she was thinking what he was.

That this time, he wasn't up here alone.

And right now, staring at Lia, with her tousled mane and her big dark eyes and those womanly curves, Marco decided that reading was the farthest thing from his mind.

Suddenly he was breathless, consumed by a hunger that literally made him ache.

Reality faded, and all he could think of was being alone here with her—forgetting, for the moment, why they were here, and how he had forced her to come. Forgetting, too, that he had built this cabin for another woman, an elusive woman who, like Lia, had slipped from his grasp, lost to him forever.

He stared at Lia, needing desperately to stride across the few feet of floor between them, to take her in his arms and kiss her fiercely, to lead her to the bed where he would lay her gently and slide his hands beneath that prim blouse of hers, over silken skin and hot, eager flesh.

What he saw in her eyes as he watched her gave him the initiative to speak the truth at last.

"Lia," he began abruptly, wondering vaguely if his voice sounded as hoarse to her ears as it did to his. He cleared his throat, tried again. "Lia, I've felt so empty for so long. And it's been so damn long since we—"

"I know," she interrupted. "I'm hungry, too."

For a split second he stared, shocked by her unexpectedly wanton agreement.

Then he realized what she meant. That she was *hungry,* hungry.

For food.

Not for him.

He reddened, fumbled, managed to mumble, before turning away from her, "I'll see what there is in the kitchen."

*   *   *

Victor sat on a wicker chair in the shadowy Florida room, looking out at the magnificent grounds of his estate.

Strategically placed spotlights illuminated the winding paths and the pool complex, and the water of the bay sparkled in the darkness just beyond.

He had propped the door open so that warm, humid, evening air drifted in. He did that, sometimes—let the tropical night indoors. It reminded him of the old days, in his childhood, when air conditioning had been an unimaginable luxury and he spent many stifling nights lying awake, restless.

Never in his life had he been more restless, though, than he was this evening.

For the first time, a glimmer of true doubt had worked its way into Victor's mind.

What if he didn't succeed?

What if A.J. Sutton and Marco Estevez evaded him?

What if they managed to bring his entire world down, crumbling at his feet?

They had the power to destroy him, and they knew it.

He couldn't rest.

Not until they were his, squirming before him as they realized they were doomed . . .

He smiled faintly at the image that slid into his mind. How he would enjoy that exhilarating moment. How he would make it last, and last . . .

He lifted his head as a faint sound reached his ears.

A rustling.

It was coming a spot over near the open door, where the hanging leaves of a vast potted plant brushed onto the tile floor.

Standing, Victor peered in that direction, seeing nothing at first.

Then he spotted movement along the floor.

A long, black snake, its skin glistening in the dim light from a nearby lamp, slithered beneath a chaise lounge several feet away from him.

There were some drawbacks to leaving the door wide open in southern Florida, Victor acknowledged with an inner sigh.

He moved swiftly and silently across the room until he was standing beside the chair.

Then he waited.

Long minutes passed.

Patiently, Victor continued to wait, knowing his prey would emerge sooner or later. When it did, he would be ready to strike.

Finally, he heard the slightest stirring from beneath the chair.

Then the snake's head emerged, its sharp tongue darting rapidly from its mouth as it slithered out into the open.

Victor pounced, grasping the creature just behind its open jaws and squeezing and pulling with his strong, bare hands until the head was severed from the flailing body.

Lia sat in the rocker before the big stone fireplace, idly moving it back and forth with her toe, staring at the empty hearth as though mesmerized by a blazing fire.

She could hear Marco moving about the kitchen area behind her, and a delicious aroma wafted from the old stove. He'd stoked it an hour ago, then busied himself opening cans and jars, stirring something in a big old iron skillet over the flame.

They hadn't spoken, not since he'd started to tell her that he felt empty, and she had deliberately misunderstood his intent.

He felt empty.

It had been so long . . .

Hell, who did he think he was, looking at her with that hot, provocative blue gaze that practically seared her flesh, and telling her *he* felt empty?

She was empty; she had been since the day her parents had been killed.

Only once in her life had the hollow ache subsided somewhat—back in Florida, last summer, with Marco.

What a fool she had been then, to believe one man— a man like Marco, no less!—could make up for the long years of emptiness she'd suffered, for everything she had lost and for everything she had never had.

She rocked and she stared into space and she listened to Marco's movements . . .

And she found herself yearning for another interlude of contentment like the one she had so briefly discovered in his arms and in his bed so long ago.

She couldn't help wanting it again; the craving was there, and it had been building all day.

She wanted Marco to kiss her, to caress her, to take her.

Even if her eyes were wide open this time . . .

Even if she knew it wasn't real, that it couldn't, wouldn't last . . .

How sweet it would be to let someone hold her, to let someone love her, to drift to sleep in someone's arms . . .

Not just anyone.

If all she needed was a warm body in bed with her, she knew she could find it somewhere out there, could have found it anywhere, anytime.

No, she needed *him*.

Marco.

Only him.

She wanted to fear him; she wanted to loathe him.

Yet at this point, she was capable only of *wanting* him.

On her terms.

Just for tonight.

But what you want is impossible, she told herself, rocking more forcefully in the creaky old chair. *What you want is to forget, for a little while, that he is your captor and you are his prisoner.*

What you want is his attention, his affection, his body . . .

Without the emotional entanglement.

Without the love . . .

Love.

But there had never been love, she reminded herself. Only a passionate charade that had almost fooled her into believing she *had* fallen in love, like the heroine of one of those novels she read, about people who lived happily ever after.

That didn't happen in real life.

Not to people like her.

She was only thankful she had never given herself to him completely; never allowed him to see the lost little girl still buried deep inside of her.

She never let him know how desperately she had needed him, then.

Well, she didn't anymore. Not like that.

Things had changed over the past year. She had learned to take care of herself, to rely on herself. And she had survived.

Alone.

And now she knew that needing and wanting were two different things.

She turned her head slightly so she could see Marco from the corner of her eye.

He stood at the stove, swiftly stirring whatever was in

the skillet, yet he was staring at the wall, as if he were lost in thought.

There was something desolate about his posture, about the way his blond head was bent slightly.

And yet it didn't betray a weakness in any sense. Nothing about Marco was weak.

Just as nothing about Lia was weak.

Not anymore.

She and Marco were so much alike, she thought reluctantly. They met on so many levels, intellectually, physically, spiritually.

Except the most important.

Emotionally.

But one thing was certain: Marco wanted her the way she wanted him.

Yes, he wanted her so badly that earlier, when he stood tensed before her, she had actually felt the desire pulsating from his body. Its power had frightened her so that she had to react; she couldn't let him say whatever he had started to say.

She had been so afraid of where he was leading.

I feel so empty . . .

It's been so long . . .

She didn't want to hear anything that would change the way she felt about him now. She didn't want to lose herself to him again, to begin caring about him again.

No, if she allowed herself a fleeting moment or two of pleasure, it would be on *her* terms, not his.

I need him to hold me, to touch me.

Just one last time, she promised herself. *One last night.*

Tonight.

Yes.

If he made the slightest move toward her, she would take the lead.

No, not *if.*

When.

She was certain the moment would come, sooner or later, when Marco's lust would get the best of him; when his willpower—which had already crumbled, little by little—would finally shatter completely.

So she would let him make love to her.

And then, in the morning, the first chance she got, she would run.

And she wouldn't look back.

Rice, he thought absently, finding a tightly sealed jar on the shelf and peering inside to find it half full. *Rice is good.*

I like rice.

She likes rice.

He remembered that about her.

"I could eat rice every day, even plain, with no salt, no butter, nothing," she had said once, as they feasted on Chinese food at her condo. She had grabbed the carton of pork-fried rice and was deftly shovelling it into her mouth with chopsticks as he watched, amused.

He loved a woman who wasn't afraid to exhibit a voracious appetite—for food and for other things.

He had met few females like that in his life. Most of the ones he dated, he had found, ate like birds when he took them out to dinner, picking on salads or steamed vegetables and refusing dessert.

A.J. Sutton, by contrast, wasn't afraid to order a steak if she felt like it, with mushrooms sautéed in butter and a baked potato with sour cream on the side. She had done just that on one of their first dates, telling him she was famished because she had skipped lunch.

"How do you eat like that and stay so slim?" he had asked her as she gobbled every bite of her dinner.

"I burn off a lot of energy doing other things."

"Like what?"

And she had shrugged and given him a wicked grin.

Later, as they lay back, panting and exhausted after a particularly strenuous lovemaking session, he had said, "I see what you mean. You probably just burned off every calorie you ate at dinner."

And she had rolled over to straddle him again, smiling and saying, "Now let's work on getting rid of the fettucini alfredo I had for lunch."

"I thought you said you skipped lunch."

She had tossed her hair and stroked his chest lightly with her fingertips. "Oh, gee. You caught me. I did skip lunch. Oh, well. Let's work off the fettucini alfredo I'm going to eat tomorrow for lunch."

Marco shook his head to rid himself of the disturbing memory, and turned his attention back to the cupboard.

He picked up a can of artichoke hearts, considered it, and then put it aside.

Only if he couldn't find anything else to use, he told himself firmly.

"Did you know artichoke hearts are an aphrodisiac, Marco?" she had asked once, with her fork poised in front of her mouth.

"I thought you said that about strawberries. And chocolate."

"Those, too."

"How do you know so much about aphrodisiacs?" he had asked, popping another marinated artichoke into his mouth.

"I just do."

"I think it's just you," he told her. "I think everything turns you on."

"Only when I'm with you,"

Stop it, Marco commanded himself, shoving the canned artichokes to the back of the shelf. *Stop thinking about the past, with her. Why are you torturing yourself?*

Because the more time he spent in her company, the more frustrated he grew.

The more everything, every tiny thing, reminded him of her, he thought soberly. Of the way they had once been, together.

He continued to peruse the pantry stock.

Continued to force memories from his mind.

But the jar of half sour pickles reminded him of the picnic they'd had in a Miami waterfront park one glorious August afternoon.

The Campbell's chicken noodle soup triggered a memory of the summer cold she'd caught, when he'd nursed her back to health as she lay in bed at her condo, tenderly seeing that her every need was met.

The small container of chocolate sprinkles—what were they doing here, anyway?—brought back images of eating ice cream sundaes with her after a movie one night, of how aroused he had been just seeing her tongue hungrily licking the creamy confection.

After this was over, he told himself, grabbing a can of kidney beans—mostly because it was the one thing he didn't connect to their past—he would take a long vacation.

Go someplace far away, alone; someplace that wouldn't remind him of her.

Europe, he thought idly, opening the can of beans. He could go to Paris . . .

But Paris was a city for lovers.

"Damn," he cursed aloud, draining the liquid from the beans into the drain.

There had to be some escape from the torture of thinking of A.J. Sutton—Lia Haskin—every moment, for the rest of his life.

Unless . . .

Was there any way they could somehow come away from this . . . together?

Could they salvage the love they had shared from the shambles their relationship had become?

Could his dream of a future with her—making her his wife, having children together—somehow come true?

He wanted to think that it couldn't—because that was easier. It was what he had trained himself to think, what he had drilled into his mind from the moment he met her.

Marriage, a family . . .

Not him.

He had had that chance once, and it had been violently snatched from him. Just being back here, in this cabin, should remind him that some things were never meant to be.

That no matter how badly you wanted something—*someone*—there could never be guarantees.

He measured the rice into a battered old kettle, another memory forcing its way into his weary mind.

This time, thought, it didn't involve the woman sitting by the fire.

It was another woman, a long-ago woman who, like Lia, had worked her way into his very soul, making him forget everything but how he felt when he was with her.

She, too, had been beautiful.

She, too, had inspired visions of marriage and children.

But with her, Marco had been naive enough to take a chance. He would have made her his wife . . .

Had been so close to doing just that . . .

When tragedy had struck.

No, there were no guarantees, he thought, vigorously stirring water into the rice.

And that was why it was best to forget about dreams.

It was best to be alone.

Chapter Eleven

"What is this, exactly?" Lia asked Marco, peering at the contents of her heaping plate.

He shrugged. "Rice. And beans. And a little of this, a little of that. Taste it."

He half-expected her to shove the plate away and shake her head, but she surprised him by scooping up a forkful and popping it into her mouth.

"It's good. Spicy," she said after she'd swallowed, and reached for her water glass.

He nodded, picking up his own fork and beginning to eat.

"You always did like spicy food."

Again she surprised him. He acknowledged her comment with another nod and told her, "My mother made everything hot and spicy. Even cookies."

She smiled at that. "My mother did, too," she told him. "But not cookies. She used to make delicious sugar cut-outs at Christmas and let me decorate them with colored sprinkles and those red cinnamon candies."

"You remember her that well?"

"Of course." She shrugged and went back to scooping rice onto her fork, but continued, "I was nine when my parents died. She loved to cook and bake, and I always got to help her. My father loved to eat."

"I don't remember my father."

She glanced up sharply at his flat statement, and he wondered why he'd said it. He had never discussed his family with her. He didn't particularly want to now. But it was too late.

"He died when you were young?" Lia asked, and her voice was startlingly tender.

Marco barely nodded, not wanting this to happen. Just a few more hours to get through, and she would be gone forever. He didn't want to connect with her one last time, and be left aching for her the way he had before.

He was aware, suddenly, that the wind had picked up outside, rustling the trees and rattling the windows. The cabin had grown chilly now that the fire in the cookstove had died down, and he vaguely thought of laying wood at the hearth.

"What happened to your father?" Lia's soft voice brought him back.

"I don't—it was a long time ago. I was just a baby." He tried to shrug it off, but she wouldn't let him.

"Don't you know what happened to him then?"

"Of course I know. He was murdered."

She gasped softly.

And he found himself telling her the story, in a matter-of-fact tone that belied the anguish he felt inside.

He told her not just about his father and the robbery, but about Eduardo, and how brave he had been, and how he had done his best to look out for their mother, for all of them.

"Are you still close to him now?" Lia asked.

And so he'd told her the rest, about Eduardo's suicide, and about how it had destroyed what was left of his family.

"Did your mother ever get over it?" Lia asked.

Marco shoved his empty plate away and shook his head. "No, she didn't. She died when I was in college, and I think it was of a broken heart. She wasn't even fifty."

"Do you ever see your stepfather?"

He felt his jaw clench, and he said, "No, and if I ever run into him . . . "

"He sounds about as charming as my uncle."

"But your uncle didn't abuse you."

"How do you know?"

He wanted to tell her that he knew everything about her; all the things she had never trusted him enough to confide.

Instead he said, "You don't flinch whenever someone reaches out to touch you."

Not the way Carla had . . .

"You do that," she told him. "I mean, you used to. When we were . . . together."

He shrugged.

Lia stared at him for a moment, then looked away, at the flickering oil lamp in the center of the table.

He thought he saw her shiver and asked, "Are you cold?"

She shook her head, but he knew that she was. He rose and went to the tall cupboard he had built into a corner beyond the bed, and opened it.

"Here," he said, reaching inside and pulling out a large woolen sweater, a pair of thermal long johns, and thick cotton socks. "Put these on."

"Whose are they?"

"Mine—whose did you think?"

She shrugged. "I don't need them."

"It's cold in here."

"I'm fine," she said stubbornly.

He sighed and tossed the clothing onto one of the rocking chairs, hoping, as he returned to the table, that she had forgotten what they were discussing.

She hadn't.

"Anyway," she went on as though the conversation had never lagged, "what about the rest of your family— your sister and brother?"

"Jacinta lives in the projects in New York, and she's an alcoholic," he said evenly. "She's also a grandmother already. Her daughter got pregnant when she was eleven."

"That's a shame. Do you see them?"

He shook his head. "Jacinta doesn't want anything to do with me."

But she sure as hell cashed the checks he had sent monthly for the past ten years, he thought bitterly. He used to hope that maybe she spent at least some small part of the money on food for the kids, but he knew better now.

"People don't change. Not for the better, anyway," he muttered, almost to himself.

"How about your brother?"

He brought his attention reluctantly back to Lia's question. "Chico?" He tried to keep the harsh edge from his voice, but couldn't. "As far as I'm concerned, he's dead."

"What happened?"

He waved his hand, as if to dismiss the topic, and he took a long drink from his water glass.

He could feel Lia's eyes on him, could feel her waiting for him to tell her.

And then suddenly, he *wanted* to tell her. All of it.

"When I was seventeen," he began, staring off into space, "I met a girl named Carla."

She had been a slender Italian beauty with big, haunted black eyes and a sweet, sad smile, and from the first moment he saw her approaching on the street, Marco had been struck by the profound need to reach out and protect her. From what, he didn't know then, but he had been moved enough to stop her, to introduce himself, to fall into step with her when she tried to walk on.

He had fallen helplessly in love with her in those first few moments.

He didn't tell Lia any of that, of course.

He got up from the table and moved restlessly to the fireplace, where he worked methodically, removing logs from the pile stacked beside the hearth.

As he stacked them in the fireplace, he told Lia only that he and Carla had been high school sweethearts, that she lived on his block but somehow he had never met her before that spring day, and that she had an old-fashioned, overprotective father who beat her whenever he had a bad day. He rarely had a good day.

"After we graduated, I went to Baruch College on a scholarship, and Carla went to secretarial school," Marco went on, remembering how they used to steal time together wherever they could, precious few tender, passionate moments that were filled with wistful dreams of the future.

They had talked of getting married, though Marco knew her father had long ago decreed that his only daughter would marry an Italian, someone he hand-picked. He had banned Carla from seeing Marco when they first met, but that hadn't stopped them from sneaking around.

Maybe that was part of what made it so exciting, Marco had speculated countless times since. The lure of forbidden ecstasy, the thrill of danger—because he knew what Carla's father would do to him if they ever got caught.

Other times, Marco believed that those days with Carla were so good because he was truly in love.

He didn't say that to Lia, either.

He only told her, as he lit the kindling and returned to the table, that he and Carla got engaged when they were juniors in college—secretly engaged, because she was still living at home. As soon as they graduated they were going to leave the city, make a life together in some small country town someplace far from New York and their families.

"I never knew you were married," Lia mused softly, a strange expression on his face.

"I wasn't," Marco said simply.

She said nothing, and he couldn't look at her.

Instead he stared into the flickering lamplight as he told her the rest of the story.

How his brother, Chico, had resurfaced sometime shortly before he graduated, claiming to have struck it rich by winning the lottery, and what a joke that was.

"I knew he was dealing." Marco's voice was tight with fury. "The way I always knew he was an addict. I knew, and you know what? I didn't give a damn."

"Why not?"

"Because he gave me a huge amount of cash as a graduation present. He said, 'Take it, little brother, because I'm really proud of you.' I thought it was my ticket to heaven. It turned out to be a one-way ticket, nonstop, to hell."

He cleared his throat.

She was silent.

"So I took the money," he continued after a moment, "and I went away with Carla for a month that May after we graduated. We drove and drove, up into Canada, and I bought this land with the money Chico gave me."

He looked at Lia, to see her reaction. She was motionless, her eyes intent on his face. He glanced away.

"I stumbled into a really high-paying job in New York that summer, doing construction. I wanted to make enough to live on for a while once we were married, because I wouldn't have a permit to work in Canada."

"Were you going to get a permit?"

"I didn't know," Marco told Lia. "I wasn't thinking that far ahead. It didn't seem important. I guess I was thinking we'd go up there, and we'd live off the land for a while, I don't know. Anyway, we started making plans for our wedding."

"What about her Carla's father?"

"He had found out, and he had kicked her out of the house, but my mother was dead by then and my stepfather was long gone. So she stayed with me in our apartment. With me and Chico. All summer. I worked fifteen-hour days, and Carla tried to find temp jobs, but she didn't have much luck. She got waitress work for the weekends, but I was gone most weekends, up here, working on the cabin."

"What about Chico?"

"He was home," Marco said darkly, narrowing his eyes at the memory. "I thought it was nice that the two of them got along so well. She was an only child, and said Chico was like the big brother she never had. I never knew that on the weekends I was 2gone, he was taking Carla out to clubs when her waitress shifts ended."

"Were they . . . ?"

"Not at first," Marco told Lia. "At least that's what they told me. They were just friends. He was going to be best man at the wedding. That was Carla's idea, and of course I agreed. Who else did I have to ask?"

He stopped, thinking back over the years, wondering, as he always did, how he could have been such a trusting fool.

"They were sleeping together behind your back,

then?" Lia asked when he had been quiet for a while, lost in thought.

"Sleeping together?" He laughed an acrid laugh. "If it had just been that, I might have been able to deal with it."

Lia frowned. "But what could be worse than that?"

"He had gotten Carla into drugs," Marco said flatly, marveling that his voice didn't begin to reflect the horror of what had happened.

How the sweet, beautiful woman he loved had transformed, seemingly overnight, into a pale, shrill, miserable human being.

How he hadn't wanted to face it, how he refused to face it, until the night he came home from work and found her passed out on the living room floor with Chico huddled over her, bewildered and apologizing all over the place.

"I don't know what happened to her, man," he kept protesting as Marco, in a panic when he failed to find her pulse, called 9–1–1.

The paramedics revived her, informing him, in the ambulance as they raced to the hospital, that she had apparently overdosed on crack cocaine.

"Not Carla," Marco had protested, tears streaming down his face, denial thick in his throat.

But he had known it was true, and that his brother was responsible for what had happened to her.

That day he threw Chico out of the apartment.

He waited until he brought Carla home from the hospital to tell her that he knew, and that Chico was gone, and that the two of them were going to get through her problem, together.

Carla had been strangely silent.

"I figured she was scared," Marco told Lia, still bemused by the fact that he had misread Carla so easily.

He had seen only what he wanted to see, even then, after all that had happened.

"Did she get over it?" Lia asked.

Marco ignored her question. "The cabin was almost built," he said, "and I came up here for a week that September, when my construction job ended, to finish it. While I was gone, Carla and Chico—well, you can figure it out."

She nodded, her eyes fastened on his face.

"When I came back from Canada," he went on slowly, "the wedding was two weeks away. And Carla told me she didn't want to marry me, that she was in love with Chico. She was using again; I could tell. She and Chico threw me out of the apartment."

"That's awful," Lia said, her voice a whisper.

"I stayed in my truck that night, parked out front of the building. It was so cold—like winter. But somehow I managed to fall asleep. The sound of an ambulance siren woke me up. It's not like you never hear that sound in the city, though, you know?"

He stared at the lantern, but he was no longer in the quiet cabin. He was back there, on the dark city street, on that terrible endless night that had changed him forever.

"But for some reason, that night the siren got to me. I wake up, and I'm lying there on the seat, shivering and looking around, and I hear the siren coming closer, and then the light in the truck gets all eerie and red, and I realize the ambulance is stopping right in front of the building."

"Carla overdosed again?" Lia asked softly.

He nodded, struggling to find his voice. "This time, they couldn't bring her back."

"Oh, Marco . . . "

He was vaguely aware of Lia's hand on his forearm, stroking him, but he was lost in the past.

"I saw them wheeling her out with her face covered, but there were strands of long, dark hair poking out from under the sheet. Oh, God . . . "

His voice broke, and he swallowed hard, fighting back a sob. It had been so long ago, and yet . . .

"It's all right," Lia was murmuring, and he realized that she was no longer seated across the table from him.

She had come to stand beside him, and she was cradling him in her arms, and stroking his hair.

He turned toward her, trying to find his voice, to tell her that it was all right, that he was over it.

But he couldn't find his voice or the words; he could only lean against her, letting her comfort him, slowly coming to realize that he wanted more than that from her.

"Lia," he finally whispered, looking up into her warm brown eyes. "It was a long time ago, but . . . "

"It's okay, Marco."

"I know . . . "

"I'm here . . . "

"You're here," he echoed. "You're here."

He captured her hand in his, brought it to his lips. He kissed her fingers gently.

"No, Marco." She pulled her hand away. "Please don't . . . I'm not Carla."

"I know you aren't Carla," he returned, his voice strong at last. "I don't want you to be. I never did."

She shrugged.

He reached again for her hand, encouraged when she let him take it. "I want *you*, Lia. See?" He placed her palm over his wildly pounding heart, then brought it down to graze the front of his jeans, stiff with the throbbing pressure of his need.

"Marco, please don't . . . "

"And you want me." He lifted his other hand toward her, letting it rest against the warm silk of her blouse.

He could feel her heartbeat thumping in time with his own, and his hand trembled against the swell of her breast.

"I do want you, Marco," she acknowledged, her gaze not wavering from his.

Then she slipped her fingers from his, and began unbuttoning the blouse, slowly, seductively.

Marco exhaled with a shudder as she slid the soft fabric from her shoulders, revealing pale shoulders and white cotton bra.

He smiled. "You used to wear black lace," he whispered.

"That wasn't me," she told him, her voice husky in his ear. "That was some naughty young girl who didn't know any better than to seduce you."

"It was you," he countered, expertly reaching behind her to unfasten the bra, then back around to cup her breasts.

They were fuller than they had been before, round and heavy in his hands, and when he moved his thumbs over her nipples, she moaned softly.

She looked down at him stroking her flesh, then back at him with smoky eyes, silently asking him for more.

"Do you want me to put my mouth on you?" he asked in a low voice, feeling his manhood thrust violently against the confining zipper of his jeans at the mere suggestion.

"Yes," she urged him, tilting her head back and closing her eyes.

He heard her let out a high little gasp when he closed his mouth over one sensitive bud, and he felt her nipple shrivel and grow hard as he swirled his tongue over the warm surface. He licked and sucked, then moved to the other side and settled his mouth over her again.

She had her hands entangled in his hair, and when

he finally lifted his head to look at her, he saw that her head was still thrown back, her eyes closed.

He trailed hot kisses up the curve of her neck and buried his mouth in the sensitive hollow behind her earlobe, breathing her clean, musky essence deeply, gratefully.

"God, how I've missed you," he murmured, sweeping her against him so that their bodies were pressed together length to length.

He caught his breath, realizing that she used to be more angular. Now she was all soft curves, and he sighed with pleasure as he rested his hands against her rounded hips and moved his swollen, masculine flesh provocatively against the soft hollow at the apex of her legs.

But some things hadn't changed. He smiled roguishly when he felt her squirm against him, the way she always had.

"You feel how much I want you?" he asked raggedly, looking down at her.

"I feel it."

He searched her expression for the sign that she wanted him to keep going—the helpless desire, the wanton abandonment he had seen there so many times before.

What he saw instead shook him to the core.

It wasn't that she didn't want him. Far from it.

But this wasn't a naive girl surrendering to mindless passion.

It was a woman fully in control, a seductive woman thoroughly aware of what she was doing to him with every slight, deliberate movement of her hips.

For a moment, he faltered.

Then she lifted her lips and swept his mouth into a deep, brazen kiss.

And he knew he was past the point of no return.

* * *

It was Lia who moved toward the bed first, breaking the kiss she had initiated and leading Marco by the hand across the room. She stopped him with his back to the bed, then with a small smile, planted her two hands in the center of his solid chest and gave a little push.

He went willingly; she could never have budged him if he didn't want to. He lay back against the quilt, propped on his elbows, and watched as she kicked off her shoes and slipped out of the hated blue slacks that were part of her Boston existence. The plain white cotton panties were next, and she took her time with those, easing them inch by inch over her hips and down her smooth thighs, finally tossing them onto the floor and glancing at Marco's face.

She could just make out his appreciative expression in the flickering firelight. His smoldering eyes roamed over her newly womanly body, and he started to sit up and reach for her.

"No," she said, stepping up to the bed, between his straddled legs. "Not yet."

He raised an eyebrow at her, and she reached for his shirt, sliding the tails out of his jeans and deftly unfastening the buttons. She shoved it from his shoulders and felt something quiver deep in her stomach as she examined his powerful upper body, first with her eyes, then with her fingertips.

She felt him quake, heard him murmur her name as she lightly, slowly stroked his bare, smooth, sculpted chest and down along his flat, rippling abs, where a faint line of dark hair disappeared alluringly into the waistband of his jeans.

He wore button-front Levis; he always had, and she took her time releasing each straining button. He groaned and raised his hips so she could pull the jeans down over his muscular thighs.

He kicked them off impatiently, then looked back at her, as though daring her to keep going.

He wore only a pair of white boxer shorts.

She began to peel them down over his hips, holding her breath as she revealed the rest of him, inch by tantalizing inch. His manhood sprang eagerly from the cotton boxers and she fought the urge to take him in her hand, or in her mouth.

She would.

But not yet.

First she tossed the boxers on the floor behind her, then bent to kiss his knees, ever so lightly, letting her long hair trail over his erection.

"Aaah," he breathed, and thrashed on the bed.

She continued to tease him erotically, working her tongue and lips up his body, avoiding his most sensitive, urgent appendage except to graze it, almost by accident, with her hair.

Repeatedly she skimmed him with the silken strands, delighting in the way he shivered and groaned and helplessly reached for her, only to have her slip from his grasp.

She could feel pressure building in her core, and knew that soon she would have to have him inside her, or she would start writhing against the ache of her savage desire.

"What do you want, Marco?" she asked finally, lifting her head to look into his blue eyes.

She was startled at what she saw there; startled that it wasn't just carnal need.

She nearly pulled away, so thrown was she by the raw emotion that glimmered in his eyes.

Then he spoke, and she was lost in the growl of his voice, in her own fierce craving.

"I want to be inside of you."

At his words, she sank onto the bed beside him, allowing him to capture her upper arms, to flip her gently so that she was lying on her back beneath him.

He braced himself on either side of her head with his strong forearms, and he dipped his head and kissed her thoroughly. His expert hands reached down her body to stroke her damp, tingling skin, and then his fingers probed the intimate folds between her legs, sending ripples of almost unbearable pleasure through her body.

Now it was his turn to tease her, first with his hot, thrusting tongue and then with the rigid tip of his erection, brushing it against her sensitive nub, then pulling away, laughing softly in her ear when she wriggled beneath him.

"Now?" he finally asked her, just when she was certain she would have to abandon her self-control and beg him to plunge into her.

"No . . . " she somehow managed to say, then slid out from under him, laughing softly at the surprised dismay on his face.

She pushed him back against the bed again and swiftly threw a long leg over to straddle his thighs, poised above him for one titillating instant.

"Now," she breathed at last, and lowered herself onto the glistening length of him.

She let out a guttural moan as he filled her; heard him groan with pleasure beneath her. She stayed that way for a moment, until he opened his eyes and looked up at her. Their gazes locked, and she rested her palms on his chest and felt his hands on her hips.

Then she lifted herself with tantalizing restraint until his tip just grazed her once again. He gasped, and she sank onto him with a little squirm that sent shimmers of bliss rocketing through her.

She rode him slowly at first, then more urgently as the ache in her core became more and more persistent. She bent forward without breaking the rhythm, resting her face against his broad shoulder as she approached release. They were both silent except for their furious panting as they worked toward release.

Then, with a cry, she was swept into sparkling waves of rapture as he exploded into her.

She collapsed against his chest and his strong arms held her. He was still deep inside her, moving with the last little shudders of her climax.

Exhausted, she lay still at last, listening to his racing heart beneath her ear.

She stared at the fire blazing on the hearth across the room as she drifted slowly back to earth . . .

And to the shattering reality.

One last time.

It was all she had wanted, earlier, when she had set out to seduce him.

Now, though, she realized that this one exquisite interlude would never last her through the long, lonely years that lay ahead.

Once wouldn't be enough . . .

Nor would a hundred thousand times.

She would never get enough of Marco, she thought drowsily.

And then sleep stole in to prolong, for a blessed little while, the inevitable.

Chapter Twelve

The cabin was cold and dark when Marco awoke.

His eyes flickered shut again and he rolled over and burrowed into the quilt, remembering how he had pulled it up around himself and Lia as they slept. He reached out to stroke her hair, frowning when his fingers touched only the pillow beside his head.

His eyes flew open and he saw that the pillow was empty.

The other side of the bed was empty.

"Lia?" he called urgently, sitting up and looking around, even though he knew she was gone.

Knew it when he jumped up to search the room as though it were remotely possible that she might be hiding behind a rocker or beneath the old pine table.

Knew it when he yanked open the door to the bathroom, found it empty, then tried the storage room and found it empty, too.

Knew it when he raced, still naked, to the door, threw it open, and bellowed her name into the wilderness.

She was gone.

"Damn," he cursed, slamming his fist against the rough log wall beside the door.

How could she have left?

He simply refused to believe she had walked out of here.

For a wild, irrational moment, he thought that Victor might have snuck into the cabin while they were sleeping and spirited Lia away.

But he knew that hadn't happened. Victor would never have left Marco behind, alive. There was no telling what the drug lord knew about him at this point, but even if Marco's deepest secret was intact, the fact remained that Marco had lied to Victor about killing Lia. And Victor would make him pay.

So she *had* left the cabin on her own . . .

Even after what they had shared.

He stared up at the sky, saw the faint pink smears at the horizon, and knew she wasn't long gone. He had seen her expression yesterday when he warned her about the animals and reptiles in the woods. He realized that, gutsy as she was, she wouldn't strike out on her own, in the dark.

Had she lain awake in his arms, then, waiting for first light as he slumbered, unsuspecting, beside her?

Her ruthless betrayal stabbed ferociously into him, and he was filled with sharp regret for what had happened between them last night.

Yet he knew, even as he cursed the passion that had caused him to let his guard down, that if he had it to do over again, he would do nothing different.

He *could* do nothing different . . .

Because *he* hadn't been in control, perhaps for the first time in his life.

Last night all the power had belonged to Lia, a fact that obviously hadn't escaped her.

No, she had used it, had used *him*.

He wondered angrily just when she had decided to stage her erotic little seduction, and how she knew he would go along with it. Then he remembered kissing her, unable to help himself. She must have known how fiercely he still desired her physically.

Still it was the emotional need that had been his ultimate downfall. He had made himself vulnerable to her, and in doing so, he had enabled her to take control.

She had pounced at the opportunity.

And yet . . .

She couldn't have known he would open up to her about his past, and Carla. That had been spontaneous. He remembered how genuine she had seemed when she'd consoled him in his renewed grief, how he had let himself be soothed by her gentle touch and comforting words.

Had it been an act?

Somehow he didn't feel inclined to believe that . . .

And yet what else could he think?

Marco cursed again, a single, vile word that echoed over the still lake. Then, suddenly shivering in the pre-dawn chill, he turned and strode back into the cabin.

She couldn't have gotten very far, he thought as he snatched up his cellular phone and punched out a familiar number.

Lia shivered despite the thick woolen sweater and thermals, and she hugged herself as she pushed on along the rutted path through the forest. She didn't want to remember how she had slipped out of bed and left Marco gently snoring, yet it was all she could think of.

She went over it repeatedly as she hurried through

the shadowy woods, moving swiftly despite the fact that she wore only Marco's thick cotton socks on her feet.

Earlier, as she moved stealthily about the cabin preparing to leave, she had considered slipping into the low-heeled pumps that were still lying where she had left them after her impromptu striptease. But she was afraid her footsteps in the shoes would awaken him, and she didn't know what she would do if that happened.

What would she say?

"Thanks for everything . . . see you later?"

She didn't like to imagine the fury—or even worse, somehow, the hurt—that might cross his features if he realized what she was doing.

Would he resume the bizarre captor-captive scenario and try to stop her? After what they had shared, it hardly seemed likely that he would pull out the handcuffs again . . .

At least not for practical use.

But if she was suddenly free to leave, she had to wonder whether she really *wanted* to.

So then . . .

Why was she doing it?

She had asked herself that question as she fled the quiet cabin, forcing herself out the door into the cold and dark when all she wanted was to steal back inside and snuggle into Marco's sturdy arms.

If only they hadn't made love, she kept thinking.

But would it have been any easier to leave him if they hadn't?

She almost believed it was the fact that they *had* made love that spurred her to walk away in the end.

When she had awakened an hour ago to find herself lying against his bare chest, listening to his rhythmic breathing, she had felt a growing sense of panic.

Maybe it was the sense of familiarity that frightened her . . .

How many nights had they slept that way, naked and entangled in each other's arms?

Only, back then, it had been Marco who would get up before dawn and steal away, leaving her to awaken and find that she was alone in her bed.

Whenever that had happened, she would experience a keen pang of loss, as acute as if it were the first time she had found herself abandoned by him; by anyone.

She would lie there in her lonely bed and think about her enigmatic lover, speculating about his secrets and wondering why she couldn't have fallen for a man who would be *there*, forever.

Marco Estevez never had been that kind of man, and he never would be.

People don't change; not for the better.

Hadn't Marco himself uttered those very words only hours ago?

Lia rounded a bend in the road and noticed that the sky had grown light behind her. That was east, then, and she was heading west. West toward . . . what?

As far as she knew she had covered a few miles; she had yet to come to a main road. If only she hadn't been asleep as they drove up here yesterday . . .

But then, if she hadn't slept, she would have been exhausted last night, and Marco might have awakened before she could make her escape.

She wondered if he was sleeping still, back at the cabin, and whether he was dreaming.

She had dreamed, in those few welcome hours of sleep last night.

It was a familiar dream, a nightmare, really; one she hadn't had in over a year, not since last summer.

In it, she was living in her Florida condo, and she received a letter that said her parents hadn't died after all. They were alive, and they would be flying in shortly.

She hadn't questioned the letter or wondered where

they had been for all those years. No, she had simply accepted it in that strange, unassuming way that one tends to accept the senseless circumstances of dreams.

She recalled the joy that had surged through the dream-Lia, and the way she bustled around her condo, preparing for their visit. She was nervously pacing her living room, waiting for her parents, when she heard a terrible crashing sound outside. She rushed out to find a plane wreck on the condo's lawn, and Marco was standing beside it, shaking his head.

"They almost made it this time, Lia," he had said, then turned and walked away without another word.

She had started screaming for her parents, then screaming Marco's name, but he kept walking, toward the ocean, as though he didn't hear her.

She stopped walking and closed her eyes briefly, rattled by the nightmarish memory even now.

And as she stood still in the forest path, she heard a distant sound. It was the engine of a car, and it was up ahead somewhere.

Lia impulsively broke into a run, heading toward it.

If someone would just give her a ride to the nearest town, she could . . .

You can what? a mocking inner voice asked. *You have no money, no identification, not even a pair of shoes. You're alone in a foreign country, and if what Marco says is true, you're on Victor Caval's hit list.*

She kept running, frantically, as if trying to escape the truth even as she headed toward the phantom car ahead.

Maybe you should just turn yourself in, she considered.

But the thought of the inevitable publicity terrified her. Not to mention the fact that if she testified against Victor's men in the Trask murder case, it would be all over for her. She would be as good as dead.

But what other option did she have?

You can vanish, the way you did before.

But then she had at least been prepared—she'd had a considerable amount of money with her, enough to travel and get settled somewhere new.

Now she had nothing.

Besides, she wasn't sure she was capable of doing it all again—changing her identity, finding a place to settle, telling constant lies, always looking over her shoulder . . .

So that was it, then.

She could either turn herself in, and take her chances . . .

Or she could go back to Marco.

He'd claimed he was trying to help her escape Victor, but did she really believe him?

Why else would he have done what he had?

Surely Marco hadn't intended to harm her.

Well then, why are you running from him now?

Because I'm afraid of how he'll hurt me, she admitted mentally, *but not physically.*

Emotionally.

Somewhere, somehow, during the past forty-eight hours, her motives for escaping Marco had changed.

Panting from exertion, she slowed and looked back over her shoulder. The sky was bright behind her, and the rising sun cast a rosy glow over the winding road through the trees.

It's a sign, Lia thought wildly. *A sign that I should go back to Marco.*

Don't be ridiculous! an inner voice scoffed. *You should keep going, turn yourself in . . .*

She glanced up ahead, where the road straightened, and saw that a car was approaching. It slowed momentarily, as if the driver had spotted her, then seemed to pick up speed.

Lia was rooted to the spot, torn.

Should she turn and go back to Marco?

Or should she flag down the approaching car?

She thought of what Marco had told her, about his traumatic childhood, and how he, like she, had lost everyone he loved.

And in the fleeting moments before the car slowed in front of her, she realized that they were soul mates, she and Marco. And she had suddenly forgiven his lies and the secrets he had kept from her when they were together.

He had his reasons for holding back . . .

Just as she did.

He was terrified of being vulnerable, of getting hurt, of being abandoned again . . .

Just as she was.

Oh, Marco, she thought, *I'm so sorry I never realized until now.*

Her mind made up, she turned around to head back toward the cabin, hoping only that he hadn't yet awakened to discover her gone.

A ray of morning sunlight captured something glinting through the trees. She heard a car engine, and realized it was Marco in the stolen Hyundai. He must have found her missing and come out to look for her.

She stood in the road and raised her arms toward him, then realized the other car, the one that had been coming from the opposite direction, had stopped.

She looked over her shoulder and saw that the doors were opening, and then several men stepped out into the road.

Confused, Lia looked at them, then back at Marco, just visible in the driver's seat of the Hyundai as it sped closer.

"FBI," called one of the men standing in the road. "Are you all right, ma'am?"

"I'm fine," Lia returned hesitantly.

This was it.

Her choices had melded into a single option.

She would turn herself in, with Marco by her side.

The three men were approaching briskly now, grim-faced and official. One was tall and dark-skinned, one short and fat, the third slightly built. They all wore dark glasses, and Lia felt unnerved by that. The trees that loomed overhead cast the men in murky shadows, so that she couldn't make out their features.

"Lia, no!"

Marco's voice shattered the stillness of the forest. He was leaning out the car window, steering right for them.

"It's okay, Marco," she called. "It's the FBI, and I'm going to turn myself in."

"No! Lia, it's not the FBI." She saw that he was aiming a gun out the window at a target behind her.

She turned in confusion and saw that the three agents had also pulled weapons.

"Don't shoot him!" she shrieked, hurtling herself toward Marco's car. "He's just trying to protect me!"

"Shut up," ordered the tall black man, capturing her in steely arms.

"No!" Lia screeched, flailing blindly at him.

Then she felt cold, hard metal poking into her cheek.

"Shut up," he commanded again.

She gasped incredulously, alarm and disbelief slicing through her as she realized he had a gun to her head.

Marco stopped the car a few yards away. She could see his expression through the windshield. His jaw was set, and his icy eyes glared into the face of the man who held her.

"Throw your gun out of the car, Estevez," called the slightly built man in a Hispanic accent. "Now."

The moment she heard his voice, Lia recognized it.

Oh, God, Marco was right.

These were no FBI agents. The voice belonged to

Ramon, one of Victor's henchmen. She couldn't see the face of the man who was holding a gun to her head, but the nervous, pacing fat one was Victor's cousin, Alberto. How could she not have realized it right away?

Dread ripped through Lia, and she fought back the panic that threatened to overwhelm her. She knew that if she moved or cried out, she'd be dead.

"Drop the gun, Estevez," Ramon commanded again, "or Hondo blows her head off."

Marco's eyes locked on Lia's as he tossed something out the open window of the car.

"Get it," Ramon ordered Alberto, who huffed and grumbled as he bent to retrieve the weapon.

"Get out of the car, Estevez," Ramon directed. "Hands above your head."

He turned to Hondo as Marco opened the door. "Do you want the honor, or can I? Or maybe we should count to three and both start shooting."

Lia trembled and fought back a whimper. She felt the large man strengthen his hold on her as Marco emerged from the car, his hands clasped over his head.

"What do you say, Hondo?" Ramon asked, chuckling, cocking his weapon. "Let's go. One . . . two . . . "

"You can't do that!" Alberto protested. "Victor wants him alive. Her, too."

Ramon scowled at him, but hesitated. "Victor can't argue if we had to take Estevez out while he was trying to escape."

"He isn't trying to escape," Alberto pointed out.

"He's right," came the booming voice behind Lia. "Victor wants him alive. Get him."

Ramon glowered, but moved forward toward Marco. He hurled something at Alberto in derisive Spanish, and Victor's cousin opened the trunk of the car, then scurried to help Ramon.

Lia watched in despair as the two of them propelled

a grim-faced Marco to the car and forced him to climb into the trunk at gunpoint.

"What about her?" Ramon asked, slamming it closed and turning back to gesture at Lia.

"She rides with us," Alberto said, lifting his sunglasses to stare at Lia.

Something in his intent expression made her skin crawl.

"Come on, let's go." Her monstrous captor moved the gun away from her cheek, but a moment later she felt it against her back, nudging it against her spine as he escorted her to the car.

"We've got them both."

Victor let out a sigh of relief at Ramon's smug words. He grasped the phone to his ear and closed his eyes briefly, thankfully.

Then he got hold of himself and asked, "Where are you?"

"Heading away from the cabin. We should be back at the airfield in forty-five minutes."

"A plane will be waiting," Victor replied. "Just see that you bring them both here alive, Ramon."

"Of course, Victor. What else would we do?"

What else, indeed? Victor knew Ramon and Hondo were like bloodthirsty sharks, instinctively needing to be rewarded with blood at the end of a hunt.

And then there was Alberto.

A smile curled Victor's lips.

"Ramon," he said, "I want you to keep Estevez and the girl separated on the plane. I want you to have Alberto ride with her in the back cargo compartment. You and Hondo keep watch over him in the front."

"Are you sure about that?" Ramon asked dubiously. "Alberto isn't exactly the most trustworthy—"

"I'm sure," Victor barked. "Just remind him that if she isn't delivered to me alive, he'll pay."

He hung up and chuckled softly to himself. When his sick cousin was through with her, A.J. Sutton would *wish* she was dead.

But only Victor would decide when she died. First, he would force her to watch her precious lover slowly tortured and then exterminated before her eyes.

And when the time came, *he* would personally kill her, seeing that she suffered the most excruciating death imaginable.

Chapter Thirteen

"Time to wake up, sleepyhead."

Marco blinked into the glaring sun as the trunk was thrown open. He saw Ramon looming over him, sneering.

"Get out of there," the smaller man snarled, brandishing a gun. "Nice and easy."

Marco gulped the fresh air that hit his face as he sat up. He looked around for Lia. The moment he had seen her in trouble earlier, he had forgotten his anger over her leaving. It seemed insignificant when her life was in grave danger. All he had been able to think about, as he fought to stay conscious in the cramped, airless trunk, was whether she was all right.

He climbed out of the trunk, his legs wobbly and disoriented.

He spotted Lia by the car, but his relief was short-lived when he saw that she was once again in the grasp of the enormous black man Ramon had called Hondo.

Marco heard her stifle a whimper as her captor jerked her away from the car.

Her eyes met Marco's, and something twisted in his gut. He wanted to call out to her, to tell her it was going to be all right.

But it *wasn't* going to be all right.

He glanced around and saw that they were at a makeshift airstrip in the middle of a vast, overgrown field, surrounded by forest on three sides and a stream on the fourth. A small propeller plane sat ready nearby, and Marco recognized the man who stood waiting beside it—Victor Caval's best pilot, Caesar, who was responsible for transporting the bulk of the cartel's cocaine from Colombia to Jamaica.

The pilot beckoned impatiently.

"Walk," Ramon barked, and wrenched Marco's arm behind him—rather, he tried. But the little man was no match for Marco's strength, and Marco easily shook him off.

"I wouldn't do that if I were you." Hostility flashed in Ramon's eyes as he grabbed Marco again. "Remember, I'm the one who has the gun."

Marco thought of pointing out that he knew damn well that Ramon wouldn't use it. He had clearly heard Alberto's earlier admonishment about Victor wanting him and Lia delivered to him alive.

Still . . .

"Marco, don't take any chances," Lia begged.

He grudgingly allowed Ramon to take his arm and roughly usher him toward the plane, followed by Hondo with Lia, and Alberto trailing behind, panting from the exertion.

Once they were on board, Ramon directed Alberto to take Lia through the narrow, low doorway to the small compartment in the rear.

Marco saw that the stout son of a bitch practically drooled and rubbed his hands together. Alberto closed the door behind them with a resounding slam.

Marco caught Hondo and Ramon exchanging a knowing glance.

There was no one who worked for Victor who didn't find out, sooner or later, about his cousin's twisted, violent, criminal past.

He felt sick inside at the thought of what Alberto might do to Lia, but he was powerless to stop him. He had never felt so helpless in his life.

Ramon shoved him into one of the four seats behind the pilot. Ramon sat across from him, Hondo in front.

"Let's go," Ramon ordered the pilot, strapping his seat belt around his hips and folding a stick of gum into his mouth.

The engine hummed, and Marco saw the propellers begin to twirl outside the small oval window.

He thought of the phone call he had made just before leaving the cabin. They had only one chance for survival, but not until they reached Florida. In the meantime, they had to get through the flight.

Marco glanced over his shoulder at the closed door separating the cabin from the tail section.

"What's eating you?" Ramon asked, seeing him. "Worried about what that fat pig might be doing to your little sweetie back there? I'd be worried, too," he added with a snicker. "When she starts screaming, just cover your ears."

Marco swallowed hard and resolutely faced forward again as the plane taxied over the bumpy runway.

Please, Lia, he prayed silently, *don't let him lay a hand on you. I don't know how you're going to stop him, but if anyone can, it's you.*

* * *

The tail section must once have been part of the
plane's cabin, because it had an emergency exit door,
several small windows, and grooves in the floor where
seats must have been. Now there were only two jump
seats against the dividing wall.

Strapped into one of them, Lia looked out the small
window as the plane's engines roared to life.

Maybe we'll crash on takeoff, she found herself hoping
irrationally, *and Marco and I will survive, but the others
won't. We'll run away together, and . . .*

And what? a shrewd voice countered in her head. *Live
happily ever after in some island paradise? Not any more likely
than the plane crashing.*

The plane rushed along the ground, then lifted off
gently.

See?

Lia glanced at Alberto and saw that he was gripping
the edges of his seat beneath his plump thighs, his eyes
squeezed tightly shut. His heavy body trembled from
head to toe.

Lia stared. What was wrong with him?

Then she realized.

"What's the matter, Alberto?" she couldn't resist asking in mock concern. "Are you afraid to fly?"

His eyes snapped open and he frowned at her. "Of
course not. I'm not afraid of anything," he said valiantly,
though his white knuckles betrayed the truth.

"Are you sure?"

"Of course I'm—"

He broke off and his gaze flew to the window as the
plane lurched, gaining altitude.

"I think you're afraid," she said, chuckling softly and
shaking her head.

Her laughter seemed to rile him, and he glared at

her. She could see the fine film of sweat on his face as he leaned toward her.

"Maybe I need something to take my mind off of it, then, eh?" he asked.

Even across the few feet separating them, her nostrils were assaulted by the stench of his stale breath and the pungent odor of perspiration. She grimaced and turned her head away.

"What's the matter?" Alberto asked, a menacing undercurrent in his voice. "You think you're too good for me? Is that it? You think you're a little princess?"

Uneasiness settled over Lia when she heard a loud click as he unbuckled his seat belt. Then she felt a sweaty hand on her thigh.

"Get your hand off me," she said, reaching down to brush off his vile touch.

He caught her fingers and squeezed them so painfully she cried out.

"Let go of me, you beast!" she yelled, trying to pull her hand away. She saw that he was grinning, and there was a sinister gleam in his beady eyes as they left her face and traveled down over the length of her body.

"Such a shame that you've decided to hide that beautiful figure of yours underneath a baggy sweater like that," he said, shaking his head as if in regret. Then he snapped tersely, "Take it off."

"You're out of your mind." She darted a glance at the closed door, wondering if there was any chance the other two bozos would come to her rescue. She hadn't missed the animosity they had for Alberto.

"Take off the sweater," he said again, a snarl in his voice.

She opened her mouth to scream, but he was out of his seat and on top of her before she could utter a sound, clamping a smelly hand over her lips.

"No!" she tried to protest, but he slapped her across the face, leaving her stung and terrified.

"Shut up, bitch," he growled. His weight pressed her painfully into the seat, and she tried to squirm out from under him, but couldn't.

Livid and filled with disgust, she opened her mouth to yell at him.

The plane hit a patch of turbulence just then.

Lia didn't miss the trepidation in Alberto's expression as his head jerked toward the window.

He was still afraid, she realized. He was on the attack, but he wasn't in control. The knowledge buoyed her determination to fight him off.

Feeding off his raw fear, she asked in a low voice, "What's your story, then, Alberto? Are you planning to force yourself on me?"

He seemed startled by the direct question, but bared his yellow teeth again, chuckling. "That's my story. Take off the sweater."

"Oh, come on. Let me do it the right way." She forced a seductive note into her voice. "I'll take everything off while you watch."

He seemed to tremble with excitement, watching her face. Then, as if wrenching himself back to reality, he said, "Who are you kidding? You think I'm stupid?"

"You think *I'm* stupid?" she shot back. "I'm stuck in the back of this plane, alone with you for the next couple of hours. I'm not an idiot, Alberto. I know you're going to have me one way or another. I'd rather make it easier on both of us."

He seemed to consider that.

"Get off me," she said, grunting under his weight. She managed to add, "Please?"

He actually moved, perching expectantly on the edge of his own seat again.

She rose gingerly, a plan forming in her mind. It wasn't at all appealing. But she would do what she had to, to survive.

"Okay," she said in a teasing voice, fighting back her apprehension. "Watch this."

Holding her breath, she began to edge the oversized sweater up, above her hips and waist, pulling it over her head and tossing it aside. Beneath it she wore the thermal top to Marco's long johns.

She heard a hiss of disappointment escape Alberto.

"That, too," he ordered, his voice tense, his eyes darting over her body. "Take the shirt off. Now."

She took a step backward, away from him. "Why don't you do it for me?" she invited.

He hesitated only a moment before standing and moving toward her. He reached out for her, and in the instant before his hands would make contact, she lurched away.

Startled, he cried out in rage.

Her hands were already on the handle to the emergency exit door. She yanked it up and threw the door open before he could stop her.

A mighty rush of icy wind swept into the plane, and terror shot through Lia. She nearly lost her balance and reached out to steady herself against the wall.

Caught off guard by what she had done, Alberto wavered at the edge of the threshold, his eyes wide with fear.

Lia reached out and shoved his hefty body with all her strength.

"You little—" He stumbled, clawing at the air as he fell through the door.

A snatch of petrified shrieking reached her ears as he plummeted to earth behind the plane.

* * *

An alarm sounding in the cockpit yanked Marco from his muddled thoughts. He looked up at the pilot and saw him examining the control panel.

"What is it?" Ramon asked nervously, leaning forward in his seat. "Is something wrong?"

"It's the rear emergency exit. The alarm means it's open."

"The exit's open? What the hell?" Ramon leapt up and hurried toward the door at the back of the cabin, with Hondo right behind him.

Marco twisted in his seat, his heart pitching at the thought that something might have happened to Lia. Jesus, had the bastard thrown her out of the plane?

Ramon opened the door between the cabin and the cargo hold, and Marco heard him curse.

"Where's Alberto?" Hondo demanded in disbelief.

"Alberto?" Lia's voice echoed, as though she had forgotten all about him. "Um, he left."

Good girl, Lia! Marco exulted, wondering how on earth she had managed to pull it off. He'd known she was a feisty little thing, but this . . .

"Alberto *left?*" Ramon stepped into the cargo hold, followed by Hondo.

"Yeah. He forgot to shut the door behind him," Lia was saying, "so I just did it myself."

There was silence for a moment.

Marco braced himself for their reaction, for the fury they were sure to unleash on Lia. His only hope was that they would remember Victor's orders and wouldn't kill her. He clenched his fists in his lap, waiting.

The sound that reached his ears was the last thing he expected to hear.

Laughter.

"You pushed the fat son of a bitch out of the plane?"
Ramon asked, mirth and admiration infusing his voice.

"God, of course I didn't push him," Lia said innocently. "He sort of . . . fell out."

Even Hondo sounded amused when he commented
he hadn't known Alberto would fit through the door.

Relief coursed over Marco, and he leaned his head
back in the seat in closed his eyes briefly. She was safe.

For now.

"You're a clever little bitch, aren't you?" Ramon
asked then, a malignant note creeping back into his
voice. "You'd like to toss me out of the plane, wouldn't
you? And Hondo, here, too?"

"Not particularly," Lia responded. "You two are gen-
tlemen. Poor Alberto wasn't."

"Well, don't get any ideas," Ramon warned her. "You
pull one more thing like this, and you'll regret it."

"I promise I'll behave," Lia said almost meekly, but
Marco heard the mocking edge in her voice.

"Sit," Hondo commanded her. "And don't move.
I'll keep an eye on her for the rest of the trip," he
informed Ramon.

Marco watched as Ramon returned to the front of
the plane, conferring briefly with the pilot in Spanish.
Caesar looked startled, then shook his head as if in
disbelief.

Hondo had left the door to the rear compartment
standing open.

Marco slowly turned his head to look over his shoulder. He glimpsed Lia strapped into one of the jump
seats just inside the door. Catching her eye, he offered
her a thumbs-up.

She nodded slightly as if to acknowledge it.

But he didn't miss the flicker of fear in her eyes.
She knew, just as Marco did, that despite her fleeting
moment of victory, they were heading for their doom.

* * *

"What are we going to do?" Lia whispered to Marco as soon as they were alone in the dark, locked in a small storage closet at Victor's Miami estate.

"What else can we do? Nothing but wait," Marco told her gruffly.

She sank to the floor and heard a rustling as he came down beside her. "Wait for what?" she asked. "For them to come back with Victor, and kill us?"

He didn't reply.

One thing was certain. Lia was thankful Victor hadn't been there to greet them when they'd arrived. Ramon and Hondo had been told to escort the prisoners to a safe place in the mansion and await his return.

The two henchmen seemed to have had their fill of playing prison guard, because they decided, after a hasty conference, to lock Marco and Lia in the closet rather than watch over them.

Lia had noticed that they looked haggard, as though they hadn't slept or eaten in days, and she realized that was probably the case.

She knew now that Marco had been telling the truth when he'd said they were being followed by Victor's men on Saturday.

He had been telling the truth about a lot of things.

"Marco?"

"What?"

She hesitated, then blurted, "I'm so sorry."

She waited for him to reply, but he didn't.

Not at first.

She expected him to ask what she was sorry about, or maybe for him to tell her that it was all right, that she didn't have to apologize after what they'd just been through.

She wished she could see his face so she would know whether to continue or to leave it at that.

When he finally spoke, he said only, "I'm sorry, too."

Caught off guard, she blurted, "For what?"

"For not using the handcuffs on you last night when we went to sleep after—"

"For *what*?" Enraged, she faced him in the dark, thankful now that his face wasn't visible. She wouldn't want to see that smug expression he always wore whenever he thought he had the upper hand.

"I should have known you couldn't be trusted," he went on, his voice maddeningly calm. "I should have known you'd take off and run the minute my guard was down. But then you say you're sorry you did it, so you must realize—"

"I'm not sorry for *that*," she retorted. "I'm sorry I forgot what an arrogant jerk you can be, and I'm sorry I slept with you last night."

"Well, that makes two of us then," he shot back. "I never should have let you seduce me."

"Oh, please. You seduced *me.*"

"That's a laugh."

"You kissed me. Remember? Long before last night at the cabin."

"So you're saying what happened between us last night was all my fault."

"You got it."

"You're saying you weren't totally in control last night, Lia. That you didn't know exactly what you were doing when you . . . "

He trailed off, and she felt her face grow hot, wondering if he was remembering their steamy encounter.

She was, and she hated herself for it, but she felt aroused at the mere memory.

"This is crazy," she told Marco, squirming on the hard floor. "I can't believe our lives are at stake, here, and we're arguing over whose idea it was to sleep together. Maybe we were both to blame."

He seemed to consider that, then said, "I knew I shouldn't be doing it the whole time, but I couldn't help myself. I never could, where you were concerned."

"I know what you mean."

"It's a good thing we never ended up together then, isn't it?"

"Definitely."

She took a deep breath; let it out slowly.

"What was that?"

"What?"

"That sigh," he said. "It sounded wistful."

"Well, it wasn't," she told him sharply. She couldn't let him think she wished things had worked out differently between them. They didn't belong together. And yet . . .

"We're going to die, aren't we?" she asked him quietly. "Soon."

Some part of her expected him to deny it, or at least to give her some hope.

But he said only, "It looks that way."

A wave of sadness came over her, but ebbed swiftly, replaced by anger. Raw, pure anger that took hold in her gut.

"It isn't fair," she told Marco. "How can this be happening? I didn't do anything to Victor, I don't know anything about his business, and here I am, about to be slaughtered for no reason. And you—"

"And I'm going to be slaughtered for a very good reason," Marco interrupted.

"What are you talking about?"

"Lia, I was with the DEA. I had gone undercover to infiltrate Marco's operation. That's what I was doing at the compound last summer."

Her jaw dropped.

Marco was with the DEA?

She vaguely supposed that she shouldn't be surprised by his revelation.

Her common sense had told her all along that he was lying about being a friend of Victor's.

And her heart had told her, these past few days, that he really was one of the good guys.

But . . .

Marco?

Working for the government?

He seemed too rash, too reckless.

She fought to voice one of the questions that tumbled through her mind, but all she could come up with was, "Why?"

"Why?" He gave a bitter laugh. "I told you my story, Lia. Last night. Do you really have to ask?"

"What do you mean?"

"My father was killed by a couple of junkies. My brother was an addict and a dealer. My fiancée died of an overdose. Drugs, Lia. They're at the root of every goddamned rotten thing that ever happened to me." His voice was ragged with conviction. "So I decided to do something about it."

"So . . . you're with the DEA." She couldn't help repeating it incredulously. "That's what you meant when you said you had connections. That's why you came after me—"

"No," he cut in. "I left the agency last fall, after the Trask fiasco. Victor had already caught on, I think, that I was up to something, anyway. And after what happened to Gordon's wife . . . I didn't want to play the game anymore."

"But if you left, then . . . "

"My coming after you had nothing to do with my work, Lia," he said. "I did it on my own. I had been looking for you since you left that night. I knew Victor

wanted you dead, and I had told him that you were. I
told him I killed you.''

She was silent.

''But Victor's a shrewd man. I knew he might not believe
me, and that if he ever found you before I did . . .''

''So you came after me on your own?'' She tried to
make sense of it. ''But you said you had connections—''

''I did. I still do. There's a network of people I used
when I was working, and I can still rely on them when
I need a favor. I called on a friend in Boston the other
night when I saw you on television. He used to work
for the CIA. He's good at sniffing around. All he had
to do was show up at Fenway Park, question the guy
who sat next to you in the stands, and he had enough
information to track you down.''

''I didn't even talk to that guy next to me.''

''Apparently that doesn't matter.''

''That's really scary.''

''What's scary is that I almost didn't get to you before
Victor did.'' He paused. ''Not that it matters now. Look
where we've landed.''

She swallowed hard over the lump that had risen in
her throat, her thoughts whirling madly.

''Why did you wait so long to tell me the truth,
Marco?'' she asked him softly. ''Why didn't you just
tell me at the beginning, when you showed up at my
apartment?''

''Because I saw the look in your eyes the night you
ran away from me in Florida, Lia. I knew you were
terrified of me, that you didn't trust me. I couldn't take
a chance. There was no time to waste. I knew the only
way to keep you safe was to force you to come with me.''

''At gunpoint,'' she said flatly.

''It wasn't loaded.''

''It wasn't?''

"I didn't want to risk having it go off by accident."

"God, Marco." She shook her head. "We wasted so much time. Both of us. If only I had known last summer—"

"No," he said, "you couldn't have known. I couldn't have told you then. A lot of people's lives depended on my staying undercover. I couldn't trust anyone."

"Not even me?"

"Not even you." He sighed. "But Lia, it wasn't just me. You didn't trust me with your secrets, either. You never opened up to me about your past, or how you felt about anything, or what you wanted for your future. There was always a barrier between us."

She thought about that. Of course he was right.

But had she shut herself off emotionally because she sensed he wasn't being open with her?

Or was it because she hadn't been ready to bare her soul to anyone—to give anyone the chance to love her, and then abandon her.

"Maybe that was partly my fault," she agreed at last. "But I had so much to lose. I was afraid ... "

"Of me?"

"Of letting you in. Of trusting you."

"Are you still afraid?"

He was close, so close to her. She could feel his breath stirring, could smell his masculine scent.

"What does it matter, Marco?"

"I want to know."

"But why? It's too late for us now, even if—"

Her words were cut off by his lips crushing her own. Marco swept her against his chest and kissed her deeply, desperately. She opened her mouth beneath his; clung to him, a sob in her throat as he deepened the kiss with his tongue.

"Lia," he murmured, tearing his lips from hers at last. "I want to make love to you, one last time."

She gasped. "We can't," she protested, though her body ached with ardent need. "What if someone—"

"They're going to kill us anyway," Marco told her, his hands sliding beneath her sweater, beneath the thermal shirt, encountering her hot, bare skin.

"Oh, God . . . "

"Lia, I need you."

"I know." She gasped and threw her head back, feeling his wet mouth on her breast. "I need you, too. Now."

"There's only now . . . " he murmured.

As those words sank in, she let go, let everything go, every last bit of hesitation.

"Yes, Marco . . . yes . . . "

There was an urgency in his movements as he suckled her. She moaned and held him against her, running her fingers through his flowing hair. Her breasts tingled with intense pleasure, and she could feel a familiar tickle mounting between her legs. She shifted, wriggling against his thigh.

She felt him pulling her thermal leggings down, over her hips, and then his tongue sizzled an electric trail down her belly. He spread her legs gently and explored her with his fingers, then with his mouth, until she was wet and moaning and riding the crest of release.

"Now?" he finally lifted his head to ask, his voice hoarse with desire.

There's only now . . .

"Yes, now," she begged. "Now."

He swiftly unzipped his jeans and plunged his hard, hot length into her, thrusting just once before she felt her body quaking with exquisite sensation.

Sated, she sighed, continued moving languidly beneath him until she felt him shudder, heard a telltale groan. His thrusts grew deeper, frenzied, and she grasped his muscular, bare buttocks as he spilled into her, crying out her name.

Then he collapsed and lay panting against her breasts. She slid her hands beneath his shirt to stroke his sweat-dampened skin, and she tried valiantly to swallow the words that threatened to spill from her lips.

I love you, Marco.

She simply couldn't tell him.

Not when he hadn't said it first.

Still she was so close to taking a chance and letting it out anyway. It was the truth.

She no longer just desired him, wanted him, needed him.

She loved him.

Truly and deeply.

She wondered if she always had.

She knew that she always would.

Till death do us part, she thought, and the irony wasn't lost on her.

"What are you thinking?" Marco asked, stirring on top of her as though he'd sensed her inner turmoil.

"That it's so hard to believe we're going to die," she told him, and as she uttered the words, the reality of the situation hit home. Hot tears sprang to her eyes.

He said nothing, just lifted his head and stroked her face tenderly as she struggled not to break down.

"Isn't there some way out?" she asked desperately, reaching up to swipe at the tears spilling down her cheeks.

Then she froze, hearing footsteps on the other side of the door.

"Someone's coming," Marco hissed, sitting up and fastening his pants again.

Lia swiftly pulled on her leggings, and Marco pulled her to her feet as they heard a key fitting into the lock.

She felt faint, but took a deep breath, willing herself

to stay strong. She refused to go to her death a coward, weeping and pleading for mercy. She wouldn't let Victor Caval get the best of her.

Yet her body was overcome by violent trembling, and she felt panic spinning through her.

As though he sensed her distress, Marco's arms went around her, and he whispered, "I'm here, Lia. We'll do this together."

Then with an ominous click the door swung open.

Chapter Fourteen

"Well, if it isn't Marco Estevez." Victor Caval chuckled softly. "And . . . my goodness, is that A.J. Sutton, too? But I thought you were dead. I seem to have . . . Hmm. Didn't you tell me she was dead, Marco? Or am I mistaken?"

Marco was silent, looking his nemesis in the eye.

Victor shrugged. "In any case, you can't imagine how happy I am to see you. Both of you."

Marco tightened his arms around Lia as Victor stood in the doorway, looking them over. He wore a black double-breasted tuxedo, and thick gold rings adorned his long, carefully manicured fingers. His dark hair was slicked back from his face, revealing a malevolent leer.

"You may think I dressed up for the occasion of greeting you after all this time," Victor commented, gesturing at his evening wear. "But you're wrong. I've been at a charity dinner, a black-tie fund-raiser event at the new modern art museum. I'm one of the generous benefactors, you know. I like to do good with my fortune. It's a shame people like the two of you think they can stand in my way."

"You make me sick, Caval," Marco bit out. "You're no swanky philanthropist."

"Oh?" Victor took a menacing step closer.

"You're just a sleazy criminal," Marco told him, shaking with rage, "and sooner or later, you're going to hit a dead end."

"Is that so?" Victor asked serenely. "I beg to differ, Estevez. I'd say it's you—and our delightful Ms. Sutton—who have reached a dead end. And trust me, I do mean *dead*."

He turned to bark an order over his shoulder in rapid-fire Spanish. Instantly three figures stepped forward from the shadows. Marco recognized them as members of the Jamaican posse. All of them were armed.

"Why don't we go to my private quarters," Marco suggested, turning again to Marco and Lia. "I'll personally escort Ms. Sutton."

He reached out and yanked Lia toward him. She didn't make a sound as he stood behind her and closed his hands tightly around her upper arms, propelling her along the back hall. His polished wing tips tapped along the terra-cotta floor as he moved briskly to the stairway.

Marco, following along behind, flanked by the three armed posse members, kept his eyes peeled for any possible chance to escape. But he knew it was hopeless. What he needed was—

"Enrique. There you are," he heard Victor say as he mounted the stairs. "I've been wondering where you've been these past few days. I'm glad you got my message to meet me here."

"I needed some time off, Victor," Enrique responded.

"Well, I need you here, now. It's a good thing you came. Look who dropped in."

As Marco reached the top of the stairs, he saw that Victor was still holding Lia like some prized kill.

Enrique's dark, expressionless eyes flicked over her, then toward Marco.

"I think you'll be surprised to discover, as I was, that our friend here wasn't who he claimed to be," Victor told Enrique. "He's with the DEA. He was undercover, trying to infiltrate my business."

Enrique's eyebrows shot up, and he cursed softly in Spanish. "What about her?" he asked, tilting his dark head toward Lia, who stood rigid in Victor's grasp, her chin held high.

"She's exactly who she said she was. Just a maid," Victor said in a tone of dismissal. "I've been checking into her past, and that's all I can come up with. But that doesn't mean she's innocent. For all I know, Estevez had her poking around, trying to come up with evidence against me."

"He did not!" Lia protested hotly. "He never—"

"Quiet!" Victor's hand lashed out, smacking her across the mouth.

She turned her head and closed her eyes briefly, as if in pain, and Marco struggled against the urge to leap on the bastard. He knew that if he made a move, he would be dead in a matter of seconds.

He couldn't do anything foolish. Not now, when their only chance to stay alive depended on playing it cool.

"As I was saying," Victor went on, "I suspect she did some snooping around while she was working for me. I have no idea what she knows. But it doesn't matter now, anyway."

"What are you planning to do?" Enrique asked, folding his arms and leaning against the stucco wall.

"What do you think?" Victor returned. "They have to be terminated immediately. Let's go."

He spun and headed down the hall toward the master bedroom suite, jerking Lia along beside him.

"Move," one of the guards growled at Marco, jabbing him with the butt of an assault weapon.

He followed, aware of Enrique moving swiftly along the corridor, a few steps ahead. The bodyguard was all-business—not that Marco was surprised. Enrique always had been a pro when it came to hiding his emotions.

At the door to the suite, Victor turned to the posse members. "This is as far as you go," he announced. "I'll take it from here."

They stepped back, their expressions blank and movements mechanical. Silently they retreated down the hall and back to the first floor.

"I need you to come with me," Victor told Enrique when they had gone, and nudged his head toward Marco and Lia. "There are two of them, and I can't take any chances. Cover me while I open the door."

Enrique nodded and drew his weapon, an automatic assault rifle. He stood watching Marco and Lia, his eyes warning them not to dare move.

Victor removed a set of keys from his jacket pocket and inserted them, one at a time, into the three locks on the bleached wood door. Then he dismantled an alarm by punching several numbers into an electronic pad. Finally he opened the door and stepped aside with a grand gesture and a smirk.

"Welcome to my inner sanctum. Please come in."

Lia wavered on the threshold, knowing that her next few steps might be her last. Did Victor plan to kill her and Marco as soon as the door closed behind him? Or would he order Enrique to do it for him?

She eyed the deadly weapon in the bodyguard's hands, then glanced up at his face, hoping to see some sign of compassion. Surely if he had really cared about Marco, he would be dismayed at this turn of events, she thought. He might even decide to help them somehow . . .

But Enrique's demeanor was aloof; his face indifferent. He just stood there, holding the gun, obeying Victor's orders like a robot.

Damn you, Lia cursed him. *Can't you see what's going to happen here? Don't you care?*

She glanced at Marco. He stood stiffly to the side, tense and still, as if waiting for something. Lia thought she sensed a subtle change in his demeanor. There seemed to be an almost defiant air about him, as though he had no intention of going down without a fight.

Lia prayed he wouldn't do something reckless. She knew there was no way out of their predicament, unless, of course, there was a miracle.

But maybe some infinitesimal part of her soul believed in miracles, because she couldn't help clinging to a shred of hope. As long as they were both alive, they had a glimmer of a chance.

Please, Marco, she beamed a silent message. *Don't get yourself killed.*

"Move!" Victor thundered at her, and Lia forced her feet into motion, crossing the threshold into the largest, most beautiful room she had ever seen. It looked like something out of a fine European castle. The muted color scheme showcased the dazzling view outside the French doors, where the tranquil bay shimmered beyond in dusky shades of purple and rose.

The walls of the room were covered in a rich, pale brocade with gilt accents; the floors in silvery embroidered carpets; the round bed in white satin.

Lia took it all in silently, grimly, knowing the lovely

room was intended to become a grisly chamber of horrors for her and for Marco.

"This," Victor said to Enrique, "is my private world. What do you think?"

"It's nice," Enrique said dispassionately.

"Only a few trusted friends have been invited here, Enrique," Victor said. "Don't take my invitation lightly."

"I don't, Victor," Enrique responded hastily. "It's my privilege."

Your privilege, Lia thought bleakly, *as a witness to the execution.*

She glanced at Marco, who stood a few feet away, so close she could almost reach out and touch him. His jaw was set and his eyes were icy, but when they collided with hers, they softened.

She ached to go to him, to lean against him, but she knew that if she moved, it would be all over.

Not that they had a chance either way, she realized, apprehension bubbling up inside her as Victor closed the door after them and locked the bolts.

This was it.

They were his prisoners.

There was no way out.

"It's time to share with you, Enrique, the secrets of my empire," Victor said, walking briskly toward the closet door on the far wall perpendicular to the balcony.

"And time to show both of you," he addressed Marco and Lia smugly, "what you tried so hard, but failed to find."

Instead of reaching for the closet door, he slid a hand along the molding that framed it. Moments later there was a soft click, and Lia saw grooves in the wall where none had been before.

She realized she was looking at a hidden panel, cleverly concealed by the wallpaper pattern and some kind of spring mechanism that had caused it to jump forward.

Victor pulled and the panel slid to the side, revealing some kind of passageway.

"After you," he said gallantly, motioning the three of them to go through the low door.

Enrique took her arm firmly and led her across the room to the opening. It was only a few feet high, and narrow. Lia had to stoop to follow Enrique through. She wondered if Marco's massive frame would fit, and how Victor would react if it didn't.

She was able to stand on the other side, and found herself in a small room with low ceilings. The walls were lined with filing cabinets, and there were charts and maps tacked everywhere. The only furniture was a desk littered with papers and a telephone. Two large heavy-duty steel safes stood on either side of the small entryway.

"Well, here it is," Victor said behind her, stepping into the hidden room.

Lia saw that he was holding a small revolver, and her stomach lurched at the sight.

"This is the nerve center of my operation—at least the part that's based in the United States. I only keep what I have to keep here."

He lifted a hand, gave a sweeping gesture. "Now do you see why you could find nothing through the rest of the compound to use against me? It's all in here, and only in here. Very few people have ever had access to this room. Only a trusted few." He glanced meaningfully at Enrique, then added to Marco, "So you see, your DEA, with all their intelligence and technology and manpower, is no match for my own clever brain."

"I wouldn't be so sure of myself if I were you, Victor."

Lia turned and saw that Marco had made it through the doorway. In the cramped space, he appeared to be a giant, broad-shouldered and towering over both Victor and Enrique.

Yet they were armed, and he wasn't.

Don't do anything stupid, Marco, Lia begged silently, willing him to look at her, to read her thoughts.

His gaze was focused on Victor. There was a challenging gleam in his deep blue eyes.

"Really, now," Victor said, glancing at Marco with an amused expression. "You don't think my little setup is clever?"

"It's clever," Marco allowed. "I'll grant you that. But you're nothing, Victor. You're no match for the DEA."

"Then tell me," Victor said, "why you never managed to find the evidence you needed while you were here, living among my associates, posing as my ally?"

"If you'll recall, Victor, my stay here was cut short. Given the time, I'm sure I would have found what I needed."

"No, you wouldn't have," Victor countered. "Because very few people know this hidden chamber exists. And you would not have been one of those who do. I realized long ago that you were not to be trusted, though I'll admit I wasn't aware of the extent of your disloyalty. You're lucky I allowed you to live when you left, Estevez. I wouldn't have, had I known then what I know now."

Marco shrugged. "Now that you've gloated over your secret, you plan to kill me and Lia; is that the plan?"

God, Lia thought, what the hell was he doing? His attitude was almost cocky.

She wanted to scream at him to shut up, to stop taunting their captor, but she knew better than to open her mouth.

"The plan," Victor said with a self-satisfied smile curling his lips, "is to take care of you first, while she watches."

A shiver slithered down Lia's spine as he voiced the

inevitable horror in a cunning, matter-of-fact tone. She fought back a scream.

"Then," Victor continued, almost thoughtfully, "I think I'll keep our young maid around awhile longer. This little room is soundproof, which will come in handy."

"A regular torture chamber, is that what you have in mind?" Marco asked grimly.

Victor nodded. "It's exactly what I have in mind. I'll make her *long* for death, to finally put an end to her torment."

"You son of a—" Marco vaulted forward in a sudden, swift movement.

As Lia gasped in shock and horror, he and Victor toppled to the floor.

"Marco, no!" she shrieked, bracing herself for Enrique to open fire.

"Enrique!" Victor grunted beneath Marco's bulky weight, his hand holding the revolver over his head as Marco grasped his arm, reaching for it.

Lia's gaze flew to the bodyguard. He stood over the scuffle, taking aim with his weapon.

"No!" Lia screeched. Without thinking, she threw herself on Enrique, kicking and clawing.

"What the—" He tried to shake her off, cursing.

She continued, desperate to somehow save Marco . . .

And then she heard the shot.

It had come from Victor's pistol, which he'd managed to wrestle from Marco's grasp.

A pitiful wail escaped Lia's lips as she realized what had happened. She wilted at the horrifying sight before her.

"No," she sobbed. Her legs gave way and she crumpled to the floor.

"Such a shame," Victor murmured.

Through the tears that already blurred her vision, she

saw a flash of amusement in Victor's sadistic black eyes.
Then she realized Enrique had regained his balance
and was raising his weapon.

"No! What are you doing?" Victor hollered.

Lia heard a deafening report from the automatic rifle.

Her eyes flew shut and she waited for a burning flash
of agony to sear her flesh.

There was none.

Bewildered, she glanced up and gasped.

Enrique had fired not, incredibly, at her . . .

But at Victor.

The drug lord's bullet-riddled, bloody body lay on
the floor, utterly still.

And beside him, in a slowly seeping pool of red that
streamed from the gaping wound Victor's bullet had
torn in his side moments before, lay Marco.

"Marco . . . I've been waiting . . ."

Her voice came to him over a great distance, lilting,
sweet, young . . .

Who was she?

Someone close to him, someone he had loved . . .

But not Lia.

No, her screams, the shrieks that had assailed him
for endless, excruciating seconds, had faded.

Now the pain was gone.

And everything around him was hushed, except for
the voice.

"Marco . . . it's time . . . I've been waiting . . ."

No.

It's not time.

Lia . . .

He struggled to find his way back to Lia again, but
couldn't seem to life the shroud of darkness and silence
that had enveloped him.

Then the voice returned, growing louder, more persistent.

"Come with me, Marco . . ."

Who was she?

He should know.

He should remember.

"Marco . . ."

Somebody he had loved, a long time ago . . .

Carla.

He suddenly saw her face, a distant vision surrounded
by shimmering white light.

He smiled with recognition. She was young and beautiful again, the way he remembered her, before her face
and body had grown ravaged as she moved along the
path of destruction.

She was smiling back at him now, beckoning.

"It's time, Marco. I've been waiting. We've all been
waiting."

And there, beyond her, were the others.

His mother.

And . . .

Oh, Lord.

There, at her side . . .

It was his father, the father he had never known.

Yet now, Marco's heart remembered.

"Dad . . . Mom . . ."

"Marco, we've been waiting . . ."

He was coming home, at last.

"Marco . . . it's time . . ."

Their voices joined Carla's, and they were soothing,
so soothing . . .

He moved toward the sound, toward their welcoming
arms, toward the comforting, bright light . . . then hesitated.

Something was holding him back.

And now he saw other faces in the distance, heard other voices.

He recognized them somehow, somewhere deep in his consciousness, though he had never lain eyes on them before.

"Go back, Marco. She needs you . . . our little girl needs you . . ."

Lia's parents.

And they were shaking their heads, motioning him back.

"She's alone, Marco . . . without you she's alone . . . go to her. She needs you. It's not your time."

Their voices joined the conflicting pleas of Carla and his parents, all of them growing louder, more persistent.

And Marco, torn, hovered on the brink of life . . .

And death.

Chapter Fifteen

The Miami sunrise was dazzling; a glittering extravaganza of golden rays bursting over the horizon, transforming the placid bay into a translucent rainbow of rosy pinks and pale blues and soft greens.

Lia saw it through the sixth-floor window of Saint Odilia's Hospital, where she had been pacing the Intensive Care waiting room for hours. An armed policeman stood sentry at the door, another sat silently on the Naugahyde couch, and a third was posted down the hall, outside the cubicle where Marco's battered body lay.

Every so often, one of the government officials gathered in the hallway would stick his head in to ask if Lia was all right, if she needed anything.

She always responded that yes, she was all right, and no, she didn't need anything.

Lies.

She *wasn't* all right, and she desperately *needed* Marco. She hadn't seen him since the paramedics had rushed him from the Caval mansion. His face had been ashen, his body still, his eyes closed. She had hurried alongside him, clutching his hand, telling him over and over to hang on, that he was going to be all right, that she'd be with him.

But then she wasn't allowed to go into the rescue truck with him. She screamed as they forced her to let go of his hand. She'd been clutching it from the moment she had rushed to his side, as though she could will strength back into him somehow through his limp, cold fingers.

She hadn't recognized the balding, middle-aged man who restrained her as the ambulance pulled away, sirens wailing. But he knew her. He had called her "Ms. Sutton," and had gently led her over to an official-looking black sedan parked just inside the compound gates.

There, in the plush backseat, he had told someone to bring her a cup of cold water, and he had kept a protective arm around her shoulders while the authorities interrogated her endlessly about what had happened.

"Where's Enrique?" she kept asking in between their questions, searching the bustling crowd in the courtyard outside the mansion for the bodyguard who had saved her life.

No one would tell her. She assumed he had been arrested like the others who had been led away in handcuffs when the house was raided. It seemed like it had been moments after the shooting, but that would have been impossible. Anyway, time was a blur to her; she hadn't realized the hellish night was over until she'd noticed the sun coming up.

It should be a sign of hope, she told herself vaguely as she gazed out the window. But—

"Ms. Sutton?"

She glanced away from the sunrise and saw Gordon

Trask standing behind her. It wasn't until they had arrived at the hospital that she had found out that he was the agent who had been so protective of her back at the compound.

She cleared her throat, trying to read the expression on his face. "Yes?"

"He's asking for you. You'd better go in."

"Is he . . . " She couldn't phrase the question, couldn't face the possibility that she might be losing Marco now, so soon after she had found him.

"I don't know," Trask answered quietly. "Do you want to see him?"

She nodded.

He escorted her past the security guard at the door, down the hall, and past the second guard outside Marco's room.

She froze just inside the doorway, suddenly unsure whether she was strong enough to get through what lay ahead.

Trask's hand fell reassuringly on her wrist, and she looked up at him. His gray eyes were somber. "Do you want me to come with you?"

She shook her head and walked slowly forward.

A nurse was standing by the bed, shielding Marco's face from Lia's view as she wrote something on a chart. Then she stepped away, and a sob choked Lia's throat.

How could that pale ghost of a man be Marco? Mighty, vital Marco, who perpetually radiated power and strength.

She had never before seen him helpless and feeble. Never.

Denial surged through Lia as she took another step closer. It didn't seem possible that this was him, lying still beneath the sheet, his once-robust body hooked up to a tangle of wires and monitors.

Yet she couldn't mistake the prominent nose, the

golden hair on the pillow, the blue eyes that met hers when she stood over him. His gaze was startlingly direct.

You really are in there, she thought with a nebulous twinge of relief. *You've got to hang on, Marco . . .*

But his eyes were sending her a message, one she didn't want to see. His expression was knowing . . .

Desolate.

He opened his mouth as if to speak, and she shook her head. "No," she managed to whisper around the ache in her throat. "Just rest, Marco. You need to get your strength back. You're going to be fine."

He moved his head slightly, as if to protest, and she felt herself beginning to tremble.

She looked at the nurse, hoping she might be able to offer some reassurance, but she stood by impassively, refusing to meet Lia's gaze.

"Marco," Lia said, turning back to him, almost desperately, "there's something you need to know. I have to tell you, not because—"

She broke off, unable to voice the terrible thought that had taken hold in her mind.

"Just because you need to know," she said softly, reaching out to stroke the blond hair matted above his forehead. "I need to tell you that I love you."

She saw something flicker in his eyes, and then they drifted closed and horror gripped her.

"Nurse!" she yelled, alarmed, and the woman immediately scurried forward.

But then Marco's eyes were opening again, and Lia, overcome with relief, saw tears glistening in them.

The nurse discreetly moved away again.

Lia stroked Marco's head and murmured, "I really do love you. I knew it before, but I couldn't say it. I trust you, and I'm not afraid anymore . . ."

And yet she was.

The same old fear, yet it had taken on new intensity.

She was terrified, still, of losing Marco. More terrified than she had ever been of anything in her life.

He opened his mouth, and though she shook her head and laid a gentle finger against his lips to quiet him, he struggled to speak.

His voice, when it emerged, was a guttural croak, but she understood the single word he was able to utter.

Love.

And she knew what he was trying to say.

That he loved her in return.

She wept, and stroked his hair, and told him that she understood.

And then, like a cued actor in some macabre drama, a somber-faced doctor in maroon scrubs was briskly entering the room, and the nurse swiftly stepped forward.

"I'm sorry, you'll have to leave," she told Lia.

"No, I can't," Lia protested, shaken. "I have to be with him. He needs me. We—"

"I'm sorry," the nurse repeated, and took her arm firmly, steering her away from the bed.

"I'll take her out," Gordon said from the doorway, and he quickly stepped forward to put an arm around Lia's shoulders.

She was shaking her head, tears streaming down her cheeks, as Gordon ushered her back into the hall. She couldn't glance back at Marco; she was afraid to. If she did, it would be for one last look . . .

And this couldn't be the last time she would see him.

It couldn't . . .

Oh, God.

"He's going to die, isn't he?" she asked Gordon, struggling to regain her composure as a murky shroud of dread swept over her.

"It's pretty bad," Gordon told her. "But he might

pull through. If anyone can make it, it's Marco. He's as tough as they come."

Lia was silent.

They returned to the lounge.

Again she took up her post, staring out the window at the distant sea.

We were going to sail away, she thought incredulously. *Just the two of us.*

To paradise.

Lia's legs had long since given out on her.

Exhausted, yet beyond able to sleep, she was vaguely aware that it was well after midnight. She sat in a straight-backed chair staring unseeingly at the late-night talk show on the small television. It seemed ludicrous that somewhere out there, the world was still going round as usual. People were laughing at the talk-show host's monologue, and people were dancing in the glitzy South Beach clubs, and people were sleeping and eating and making love . . .

The hospital's vast corridors were vacant and silent, except for the occasional echo of footsteps or a distant burst of chatter from the nurses' station.

Lia was the sole occupant of the lounge, and a new guard was stationed at the door. She knew that Trask and the others were somewhere in the hospital. Earlier, a short time after someone had brought her a sandwich she hadn't touched, she had heard them holding an urgent, whispered conference in the hallway. Then they had disappeared, leaving Lia gratefully alone, to hope and pray.

And remember.

In those endless, melancholy hours, she had gone over everything she and Marco had done in the fleeting summer months when they were together in Miami. She had smiled, remembering the steamy night when she had tried to teach him to do the Macarena; she had wept thinking of the intense betrayal she had felt in the instant she saw him in the shadows the night she had fled.

And she had wondered what either of them could have done differently along the way, to change the tragic course their relationship had taken.

She could think of nothing.

Yet she had learned so much in the past few days with him. She was ready to tear down the barriers she had erected, ready to start over, to make it work this time. To forget, to forgive . . .

If only they got the chance.

It seemed implausible that they could have come this far, could have realized what they meant to each other, only to face the possibility of being wrenched from each other's arms once again.

This time, forever.

Two days ago, when she and Marco had found themselves in Victor's deadly grasp, Lia had held out for a miracle.

A miracle had occurred.

They were still alive.

Was another miracle too much to hope for?

"Ms. Sutton?"

Startled, she glanced up and saw Gordon Trask standing in the doorway once again.

And in that instant, as her expectant gaze met his sober one, she knew.

"No . . . " She gasped, pressed her hands against her quivering mouth. "Oh, God, no . . . "

But he was nodding somberly.

She wailed, a high-pitched, keening sound.

She rocked back and forth on the couch, huddled with her knees against her chest, sobbing. She brushed

Trask away when he tried to touch her, needing to be isolated in her intense grief.

Marco was gone.

Oh, dear God.

No . . .

The room whirled; her thoughts swirled madly.

How could this have happened? Just when they had truly found each other . . .

Marco was gone.

There would be no miracles, no second chances . . .

Marco was gone.

And Lia would be alone forever.

There was no funeral.

Who would have made the arrangements?

Lia wasn't his wife; they hadn't even been together the last year of his life. The few fleeting hours they'd spent together until the end counted for nothing, legally.

And of course, Marco's parents were long dead; his brother, Chico, couldn't be found.

Only his sister, Jacinta, had been contacted; the woman was indifferent. According to Gordon Trask, the only thing she had said when she'd been contacted with the news was, "Did my brother leave a will?"

If he had, Gordon didn't mention it, and Lia didn't ask. She wanted nothing . . .

Nothing but her memories.

Marco's body had been cremated, according to Gordon. But his DEA friends and acquaintances wanted to have a memorial service for him.

And so, a month to the day after he died, on a sunny November morning, Lia found herself sliding into the front row of seats at a breezy bayside park. She was flanked by the two police bodyguards who had followed her everywhere, and would, according to the DEA, stay with her until she had testified at the upcoming trial against Ramon, Hondo, and the rest of the cartel.

Victor may have been gone, but Lia knew she wasn't out of danger by any stretch. The posse was ruthless, and if several of its members went to prison, Lia would be at the top of its hit list.

Her security team had fought against the notion of her attending the memorial service. They had said she would be a sitting duck, and they were probably right.

But Lia knew she had to be there, for Marco . . .

And for herself. She couldn't spend another moment holed up in the sterile hotel where they were keeping her.

Maybe, on some level, she *wanted* to take the risk.

Maybe she had finally realized there was nothing left to live for.

Or maybe she was no longer sure she deserved to keep on living.

She couldn't stop thinking of those final, fateful moments in the secret room, when she had seen Enrique pointing his gun as Marco struggled with Victor on the floor.

The more she mulled it over, the more certain she had become that he had intended to shoot Victor.

If she hadn't intervened, he would have.

And Marco would be alive.

As she took her seat on a drab gray folding chair, she swallowed hard, fighting back the nausea she'd been battling all morning. For the past few days, really. The stress had finally gotten to her; she was a physical wreck. Besides an upset stomach, she felt utterly exhausted, and she'd been having dizzy spells. Several times in the past few days, her security guards had caught her swaying on wobbly knees.

Maybe it wasn't so much stress, as fear.

Lia turned her head slightly, her eyes shifting nervously over the small crowd gathered beneath the gently
swaying royal palms. The park was bordered by the highway on one side, and on the other by a bike path that
ran along the water. Both were teeming with traffic.

She watched the Rollerbladers and bikers passing
along the bike path, and at the cars and trucks that
whizzed by on the road, and wondered if someone
lurked, somewhere just beyond her view, waiting to take
a shot at her.

She felt sick at the thought; yet she was powerless to
get up and leave.

She wanted, *needed,* to tempt fate.

"Lia."

She turned at the sound of her name, and saw Gordon
sliding into the row behind her. He wore a well-cut dark
suit.

With him was a similarly dressed young boy whose
face she instantly recognized, though she hadn't seen
it in a year.

"This is my son, Tyler," Gordon said quietly. "He
wanted to come today."

"You're the one who tried to save me and my mom,"
the boy told her solemnly.

She nodded, overcome by emotion.

"I wanted to say thanks, and . . . Uh, this is for you."
Tyler reached out and handed her something.

She looked down and saw that it was a small velvet
box.

"I think my mom would have wanted you to have it,"
the boy was saying. "Dad thinks so, too. She used to
wear it all the time."

Unable to speak, Lia snapped open the curved lid.
Inside the box, in a nest of satin, lay a delicate cameo
pin. Against a pale blue background was the carved

silhouette of a woman cradling a baby. Mother and child.

"It's beautiful," Lia managed to tell him at last, her voice choked. She ran her fingertips over the cameo. "I don't know what to say . . . "

"It's okay," Tyler told her with a shrug. "A lot of times, I don't know what to say, either."

She smiled tearfully, then turned to face forward as the service began.

A harpist played classical music. Several of Marco's colleagues got up to speak, sharing memories of his courage and loyalty. Lia was stunned that so many people had recognized him as a hero long before his final act of bravery.

"Does anybody else wish to come forward and say a few words?" the minister finally asked.

Lia wanted to walk up to the podium, to honor him with well-chosen words. But she knew that even if she could keep her composure . . .

Even if she could trust her legs to transport her to the front of the crowd and hold her up once she got there . . .

She would never be able to voice what she felt for Marco. Not publicly.

And anyway, she had been carrying on a perpetual private, silent eulogy for weeks.

So she let the moment pass.

Then there was more music, and, at the end, a large box was opened. Dozens of butterflies flew out, their wings carrying them into the dazzling blue sky until they disappeared.

Lia sighed softly, watching the horizon.

She heard the crowd stirring, talking quietly around her, and she started to get to her feet.

Bile rushed to her throat and the world began to sway.

Then she was falling dizzily to the ground, where darkness swooped in to carry her away.

"Well? How are you feeling?" Frank, her favorite bodyguard, asked as they stepped onto the hotel elevator and the doors closed behind them. He punched the button for the sixth floor.

"Relieved it's all over," Lia told him.

And that was the truth.

She had just finished giving her testimony before a federal grand jury. After months of anticipation, the actual moments on the witness stand had seemed lowkey. The defendants weren't present, so she didn't have to face them as she answered the questions in a loud, clear voice. The testimony seemed to take forever, but when she finished she was surprised to see that not even an hour had passed.

She had been told that the jurors would have the opportunity to submit written questions at the conclusion of her testimony, and had been prepared to be detained to answer them. But there were no questions.

Now here she was, back at the familiar hotel that had been home to her—but not really—since October.

The doors slid silently open on the sixth floor, and Lia, Frank, and Pete, her other bodyguard, moved swiftly along the carpeted hallway. They reached her door, and she waited in the corridor with Frank while Pete went in to make a security sweep of the room.

Funny how this whole routine was second nature to her now.

When the day came that she had her life back . . .

If the day came . . .

She might miss the constant companionship.

And protection.

Gordon had begun to discuss with Lia the various

options for her future. The witness protection program had been mentioned several times.

Lia knew she wouldn't have much choice about that. Not if she wanted to stay alive.

If it was only her own life that would be at stake, she might have considered taking her chances, but . . .

"All clear," Pete said with a brisk nod, emerging from her room.

"Thanks. I'm going to lie down for a little while," Lia told them, and closed the door behind her.

The first thing she did was rush to the bathroom. Her bladder was bursting.

The next thing was to kick off her low-heeled dress pumps and shed the panty hose that felt like a tourniquet around her swollen middle.

Then she padded over to the kitchenette, opened the freezer, and removed a half-gallon container of chocolate chip cookie dough ice cream. She considered heaping some in a bowl, then shrugged, grabbed a spoon, and returned to the other room with the container in hand. She sat in the straight-backed desk chair, propping her aching feet on the queen-sized bed across from her.

As she shoveled the ice cream into her mouth with her right hand, she rubbed her belly with her left.

As she ate, she spoke softly to the child growing in her womb, telling it not to worry, that soon they would put all this behind them, and they would both be all right.

The book she had bought claimed a fetus couldn't hear until well into the second trimester, but Lia had been talking to her child from the day she had discovered it existed. It made her feel less alone.

Soon, she knew, she would have to share the news of her pregnancy. She needed to see a doctor, not to confirm what the home test had told her so long ago—the day of Marco's funeral—but to see that her child got a healthy start in life. She should be taking vitamins, having tests, whatever women did when they were expecting babies.

Besides, it was no longer simple to hide the growing bulge at her waist. She knew her body would soon reveal her condition, whether or not she was ready to tell.

It was her secret that had kept her going these past few months. The knowledge that some part of Marco lived on—not only in her memories and in her heart, but in the child she carried—had sustained her through the dark, lonely days and nights.

Now, wondering what lay ahead for her and the baby, she could only hope she would continue to be strong.

She supposed the DEA would arrange for her to be brought to some distant, small town, perhaps in the Midwest, where she would take on a new identity. The baby would never know who it really was, at least not for years. You couldn't entrust a child with a secret that could be deadly if it ever got out.

And maybe they could have a normal life, at least in some ways, Lia thought optimistically. Her child could go to school, and have friends . . .

But no father.

No family.

She frowned faintly as a disconcerting thought drifted into her mind.

It wasn't the first time she had considered it in the months since she'd lost Marco. The idea had nagged repeatedly at her, though she told herself to forget it.

It would only hurt to get her hopes up.

Still . . .

She kept hearing Marco's words echoing in her mind.

I found Javier and Rosalita Santiago.

Her mother's family.

Were they really out there somewhere?

Or had he lied about it, as he had lied about so many other things to protect his cover?

She wanted to believe that it had been the truth, that her family was out there somewhere, that she might actually find them someday.

That her child might have a family.

"Don't you worry about a thing, little one," she said softly, pushing the empty ice cream container aside and closing her eyes. "Your mommy will always take care of you. And so will your daddy. I know he's watching over us from wherever he is."

She fell silent; then she felt it.

It was only the merest fluttering sensation deep in her womb, but she knew it was Marco's baby, stirring at the sound of her voice.

She smiled in wonder, and joy surged through her as she realized—not for the first time—that she had been right to believe in miracles.

Chapter Sixteen

"I'm not dead after all, Lia."

"Oh, Marco . . . "

She hurtled herself into her arms, and he held her close, and she sobbed with elation, and she cried, "I knew you couldn't really be gone. I knew you would come back to me."

"I love you, Lia."

"I love you, Marco. And I have a surprise for you . . ."

And then she woke up.

The glowing digital clock on the bedside table read two thirteen.

Lia turned over restlessly and bunched one of the flat hotel pillows beneath her head.

Her heart was pounding.

The dream had seemed so real . . .

Waking to discover that it wasn't had left her numb with renewed grief and loneliness.

She placed a hand against her rounded belly, needing

to feel some movement from the child within her, some reassurance that she wasn't alone.

But the baby hadn't stirred since yesterday afternoon, when she had first felt its movements.

How she longed to share that gratifying sense of awe with Marco, to rest his hand against her bare belly and see his blue eyes widen when he felt the ripples beneath her skin.

That would never happen.

Her child would never know its father.

She sighed, staring bleakly into the dark, empty room.

And then . . .

She thought she saw something move, over by the window.

Had it been her imagination?

She lay still, frowning, watching, listening for some sound that would prove she wasn't alone.

There was nothing.

She closed her eyes, willing herself to calm down, to go back to sleep. Her heart was pounding, and she felt the baby flutter slightly, probably in response to her surge of adrenaline.

"It's all right, little one," she murmured aloud, patting her stomach. "Your mother's just jittery. She's seeing things in the dark."

Then she heard the footsteps moving swiftly across the carpeted floor, approaching her bed.

"Don't be afraid," Enrique told her, glancing back at Lia as he had countless times. "You have to trust me."

His voice carried over the rush of wind and waves to where she was huddled on the seat behind him.

How could she not be afraid?

How could she trust him?

He had crept into her room as she slept, had told her urgently that she had to come with him. He'd had a firm grasp on her arm as he escorted her down the service elevator and out to a van parked behind the hotel.

How had he found her?

Where were her security guards?

Where was he taking her?

It had to be Jamaica, where the posse would take over.

Enrique hadn't flashed a gun at her, or even said much, but Lia knew better than to assume he didn't mean to harm her. He may have saved her life that night at the compound, but he was one of Victor's men. His own life might depend on his carrying out the orders of the posse.

Deep in her gut, she knew she was in grave danger.

After they had left the hotel, they had driven for a long time on back roads before they'd reached the yacht moored at a private, secluded dock somewhere south of Miami.

And now they had been out on the water for hours. It was late in the afternoon. The winter sun dipped low on the horizon, and Lia knew from its position that they were heading south.

The sea was calm, but her stomach was queasy from the boat's motion and from hunger.

Enrique had offered her bottled water and sandwiches, but she had refused it, thinking it might be poisoned. Though he seemed sincere, she refused to trust him. She could only pray that somehow, she would survive this final challenge, whatever lay ahead.

She desperately longed to live, to have her baby—hers and Marco's. She wanted so much to start a new life for the two of them—a life where she wouldn't always have to be looking over her shoulder.

As she stared bleakly at the horizon, a scrap of land came into view.

Frowning, Lia looked at the distant, tree-dotted coast, then at Enrique.

He seemed to be steering the boat right for it.

Jamaica?

She shifted uneasily on the seat.

It *was* an island, she realized as they drew closer. But just a tiny island, seemingly all alone in the middle of the sea.

The yacht was powerful and Enrique was a skillful sailor. It wasn't long before Lia could clearly see the white sand and palm trees on the distant shore.

And people.

They came into view gradually, as though they had spotted the boat and were spreading the word, summoning others to the edge of land to watch its approach.

Bewildered and frightened, Lia could only stare, wondering who they were.

Enrique glanced at her. His eyes were hidden behind dark sunglasses, but there was an aura about him . . .

And there was something about the figures silhouetted on the beach . . .

For the first time since he had abducted her from her hotel room, Lia allowed herself to believe that maybe she wasn't in danger after all.

Nothing made sense.

Unless . . .

But that was impossible.

Wasn't it?

Lia stared at the island.

Enrique cut the boat's engines. They continued to drift toward shore, with Enrique leaning over into the water, guiding them with an oar.

Lia could see the people more clearly now, see them clustering on the sand, pointing at the yacht . . .

Almost as though they had awaited its arrival.

Eagerly.

All of them had dark coloring; not the deep, black complexions of Jamaican natives, but the honey-bronzed shade that signified Latino heritage.

And there were women among the men on the beach . . .

And children.

Roughly two dozen people in all, she realized. Their faces were still too distant to make out clearly, but snatches of excited Spanish began to travel out over the gently lapping water to reach her startled ears.

She had been right.

They *were* Hispanic.

The bizarre thought she had earlier tried to banish had returned to take root in her mind . . .

An idea so illogical she had to be insane.

And yet she stared at the people on shore, and then back at Enrique, and she wondered if somehow he had . . .

No. How could that be?

As the boat drifted closer, several men broke away and splashed out toward it.

Lia's hands clung to the edge of the seat, and she could only watch them mutely.

And listen.

She understood the language, and she realized it was spoken in a dialect that was hauntingly familiar.

A Cuban dialect.

It's her!

She's here!

She translated automatically, first just the words, and then the actual meaning of what they were saying.

But it couldn't be . . .

And then she heard her own name uttered, the name her mother had given her at birth . . .

Aurelia.

A sob broke from her throat as she stood and stared at the faces that beamed up at her from the water.

"Bienvenida," said a young man who couldn't have been more than seventeen.

Welcome.

He was a stranger . . .

Yet his almond-shaped, rich brown eyes were familiar.

And Lia knew, without a shred of doubt, exactly where she had seen them before.

In her mother's face.

Aurelia Santiago Sutton.

Her mother, who had left her family behind so long ago in Cuba, who had died without ever seeing them again.

"I am your cousin," the boy said in Spanish. "My name is Tomas. My mama and your mama, they were sisters. Mama is waiting on the beach. She says she wants to hug you."

A tremor shook Lia so that she couldn't speak, could only look up incredulously at Enrique, who smiled and nodded, and then at the people in the water and on the sand.

Her *family.*

At last.

Trembling with joy, she allowed herself to be helped down the ladder at the back of the boat. The moment her feet reached the shallow water, she was swept into one pair of arms after another, as her mother's brothers and brothers-in-law and nephews took turns welcoming her, telling her how happy they were that she was finally with them, where she belonged.

Then Tomas swept her up into his arms and splashed with her toward shore, shouting, "Mama! Come hug your sister's child—your niece, Aurelia!"

The women and children swarmed around her, laughing and crying and smothering her with kisses. She was led to her elderly grandparents, clutched by one and then the other, and told that she looked so very much like their dear, lost child, Aurelia.

Lia wept with joy; she was living a dream.

And this time, she knew she wouldn't wake to discover it hadn't been real; her heart was swelling with the peace and fulfillment that could only come from being home at last, after so many years of searching.

She wiped at the tears blurring her eyes, and she looked around for Enrique, to thank him.

She spotted him a few feet away on the sand.

He hung back from the reunion, his arm draped around the broad shoulders of a man . . .

Lia froze.

A man who looked like . . .

She gasped and blinked to clear her vision, knowing it couldn't be . . .

"Marco!" She shrieked his name and ran toward him, hurling herself into his waiting, welcoming arms.

"Oh, Lia," he murmured, holding her fast against his solid chest. "I've been waiting for so long . . . "

Behind them, she could hear the happy, excited chatter of her family.

"You're real," she breathed, looking up into his face, running her hands over his familiar features. "How can this be happening? Am I dreaming?" Dismayed, she realized what had happened again. "God, I must be dreaming . . ."

"You're not dreaming, Lia."

"But how—what—"

"It's actually simple. The government faked my death to protect me from the posse."

"But I saw Victor shoot you. It was real! I saw you in the hospital—"

"It *was* real. I almost didn't make it," he said somberly. "But when they realized I would pull through, they arranged for a cover-up. And I knew where I wanted to go. I knew your family would welcome me when I told them who I was, that they would want you to join them here."

"But ... Enrique ... ?" She glanced at the man who had delivered her.

"I'm with the DEA, too, Lia," he said, stepping forward with a grin. "I was undercover at the compound, like Marco was. I was going to help him get you down here from Canada, but Victor's men got to you before I could."

"You saved my life," Lia murmured gratefully, then blurted, "But I made a mess of everything. When Marco attacked Victor, I got in the way before you could—"

"You couldn't have known I was aiming at Victor and not Marco," Enrique told her, and Marco nodded.

"What you did was incredibly brave, Lia," Marco said, and she could hear the pride beaming from his voice. "You risked your life to save me."

"I almost got you killed."

"But you didn't, Lia. I'm alive." Marco's arms tightened around her shoulders. "And you and I are going to live happily ever after, after all. I love you so much."

"I love you, too." She leaned her head on his shoulder and smiled a dreamy, contented smile.

Then she felt a sudden flutter in her belly. She gasped.

"Oh, my God, Marco ... I almost forgot!"

"What?"

She lifted her head to look up into his blue eyes. "You're going to be a daddy," she said softly.

For a moment, he only stared at her. Then his gaze dropped to her waist and he reached out with a tentative hand. She felt his fingers graze her swollen stomach, then he rested his palm over it.

"You're going to have a baby?" he said in awe.

"We're going to have a baby."

He dropped to his knees in front of her, resting his cheek against the slightly rounded curve that concealed his child, and she felt him shuddering.

She looked down and saw that he was sobbing.

"Marco?"

"We found it," he said, smiling through his tears. "I told you a long time ago that we'd find it."

And Lia knew what he meant.

She looked around her, at the happy faces of her family and Enrique, and at the sparkling open sea and clean white sand, and at the man she loved.

They really had found it at last.

Paradise.

Epilogue

Marco paused on the sandy path several yards from the door of the small cottage, his senses capturing every essence of home.

Over the distant outdoor sounds of crashing waves and chirping birds, he heard faint, familiar voices; children's laughter. And, along with those comforting human noises, the clatter of plates and utensils and the sweet strains of music that floated to his ears; an old love song on the radio.

He inhaled the heady scent of brilliant, exotic blooms that spilled from the flower boxes beneath the shuttered front windows; a fragrant riot of reds and purples and yellows. Mixed in was the ever-present salty tang of sea air and the unmistakable aroma of supper—something Spanish and spicy, no doubt.

The cottage's whitewashed stucco facade and red tile roof sparkled in the late afternoon sunlight. Palm trees towered overhead, swaying slightly in the island breeze, their fronds rustling like lovers' gentle whispers.

He began to move forward, impatiently.

It had been only hours since he had left for a day's fishing in the deep water just off the coast, yet every moment he was away seemed to drag.

On the path lay a battered red bike, casually tossed on its side as though the young rider had abruptly discovered something more interesting to do. Just beyond were two small tricycles, and on the doorstep, tiny race cars and dump trucks and a familiar rag doll in a pink dress.

He picked up the doll and tucked her under his arm, then turned the knob and stepped over the threshold.

Instantly, he was tackled by a small figure that leapt on him from the deep windowsill beside the door.

"You were watching for me again, you rascal?" he asked, swinging his youngest son onto his shoulders.

"I always watch for you, Daddy. Did you catch anything today?"

He nodded. "I *always* catch something."

He had to. It was his livelihood; fishing. That, and the woodcarvings he fashioned from driftwood and sold at tourist resorts on nearby islands.

He didn't make much money, that was for sure.

But then, he didn't need much money.

He didn't need much of anything these days . . .

Except, of course, for his family.

"Where's Mommy?" he asked, though he already knew the answer.

"She's busy."

He carried his son jauntily through the cluttered living room to the kitchen at the back of the cottage.

There, he saw that the table was crowded with pint-sized diners, all of whom jumped up, rushed toward him, and started chattering about their day.

"Here, peanut," he said, reaching down to hand the rag doll to his only daughter, Auria, whose sun-streaked hair tumbled below her shoulders. She looked so like her mother, right down to the spirited gleam in her big brown eyes.

"Thank you, Daddy," she chirped, cuddling the doll. "What are you all eating?"

"Paella," they answered, practically in unison.

"Where's Mommy?"

Paraiso, his oldest son, whose name meant *paradise* in Spanish, said, "Outside, taking the laundry off the line."

Laundry . . . there was so much of it, and it took hours of her time, thanks to five children and a lack of modern appliances.

"I'll be right back," Marco said, setting his youngest child on his feet and extracting himself from the bustling brood.

He slipped out the kitchen door and stopped, watching the woman who stood several yards away, bending over a heaping laundry basket she had woven herself.

Even after all these years together, the sight of her still managed to catch him off guard from time to time. He still found it hard to believe that she was his, that all of this—the children, the home, the rosy existence—belonged to him.

She straightened, and the late afternoon sunlight fell on her golden hair and illuminated her beautiful face. She was barefoot, as always, clad only in a long, sleeveless cotton dress that fluttered around her ankles in the warm sea breeze.

She glanced up, though he hadn't made a sound, as though she sensed his presence.

And she smiled and called, "Get over here and help your wife lift this heavy load."

"You bet." He crossed the sandy, grassy yard and took her into his arms, holding her close.

"I missed you, Lia," he said, planting a soft kiss on her lips.

"I missed you, too."

"How are you feeling?"

"Exhausted. Achy. Impatient."

"You always get this way at the end," he said, reaching out to pat her round, protruding belly beneath the dress.

"Yeah, but this time it's worse than before."

He grinned. "You always say that. And then, as soon as you have a brand new little baby in your arms, you insist that the whole pregnancy was a breeze."

"Not this time."

"You always say—"

"Nope. This is the last one, Marco Estevez," she said, grinning and reaching up to ruffle his hair. "Six children is enough for anyone. Even for you. Besides, I don't even know where we're going to put this new little guy. Every inch of the house is filled."

"We'll find a way to make it work," he promised her, smiling into her eyes.

"We will," she agreed, squeezing his hands in her own. "We always have."

"Mommy!" called a voice from inside. "I need you."

"Dad?" clamored another. "Can you come here?"

They sighed.

He picked up the laundry basket, balanced it on one arm, and draped the other around his wife's shoulders.

And together, Marco and Lia walked back into their home.

Back into their paradise.

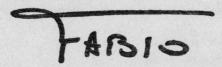

ROMANCE FROM JO BEVERLY

DANGEROUS JOY   (0-8217-5129-8, $5.99)

FORBIDDEN   (0-8217-4488-7, $4.99)

THE SHATTERED ROSE   (0-8217-5310-X, $5.99)

TEMPTING FORTUNE   (0-8217-4858-0, $4.99)

DANGEROUS GAMES   (0-7860-0270-0, $4.99)
by Amanda Scott

When Nicholas Barrington, eldest son of the Earl of Ulcombe, first met Melissa Seacort, the desperation he sensed beneath her well-bred beauty haunted him. He didn't realize how desperate Melissa really was . . . until he found her again at a Newmarket gambling club—being auctioned off by her father to the highest bidder. So, Nick bought himself a wife. With a villain hot on their heels, and a fortune and their lives at stake, they would gamble everything on the most dangerous game of all: love.

A TOUCH OF PARADISE   (0-7860-0271-9, $4.99)
by Alexa Smart

As a confidence man and scam runner in 1880s America, Malcolm Northrup has amassed a fortune. Now, posing as the eminent Sir John Abbot—scholar, and possible discoverer of the lost continent of Atlantis—he's taking his act on the road with a lecture tour, seeking funds for a scientific experiment he has no intention of making. But scholar Halia Davenport is determined to accompany Malcolm on his "expedition" . . . even if she must kidnap him!